"I cannot stay here," she said.

"Why not? You're so useful in Ward A, according to everyone. What will happen if you go home?" Jamie asked.

"Mama will weep and sigh, and Papa will deliver a lengthy sermon about the sins of deception and ingratitude."

His arm went around her and she leaned in. "Jerusha, do you really want to leave?"

The question hung in the air, delivered in total seriousness. Something sweet and certain told her he was really asking *Do you want to leave me?*

Did she want to leave him? Never.

Jerusha Langley took a deep breath and changed the course of her life. She held his hand to her cheek and kissed it. "No, I do not," she said firmly, the right answer.

He tightened his grip on her shoulder, which more than suggested that for the rest of their lives, this man would protect her, and if she was lucky, love her...

Author Note

I've worked in hospital and hospice public relations through portions of my writing life. I'm a historian by training and practice. Writing was always part of this, thanks to an excellent beginning in, yes, high school journalism. Had I continued beyond my master's degree in history, I know that a doctoral dissertation would have focused on US Civil War medicine.

All this research has taught me a fact of which I have no doubt. Pre-twenty-first-century medicine makes some shake their heads over "primitive" practices and beliefs of the eighteenth and nineteenth centuries, as in "My word, didn't they know better?"

Not me. All my historical research in medicine has given me nothing but respect for those men—they were all men then—*who practiced to the extent of their knowledge*. That's the key. I don't doubt they wished they knew more; their writings sometimes expressed this frustration. Even in our age of amazing medical procedures, I also have no doubt that current practitioners of the healing arts wish they knew more.

Think of it: knowing more. Isn't this something we all wish? I hope my fiction conveys this deep admiration I have for surgeons and physicians of earlier ages.

A NAVAL SURGEON TO FIGHT FOR

CARLA KELLY

HISTORICAL

H Harlequin°
HISTORICAL

ISBN-13: 978-1-335-53968-7

A Naval Surgeon to Fight For

Copyright © 2024 by Carla Kelly

Recycling programs for this product may not exist in your area.

Harlequin Enterprises ULC
22 Adelaide St. West, 41st Floor
Toronto, Ontario M5H 4E3, Canada
www.Harlequin.com

Printed in U.S.A.

Carla Kelly started writing Regency romances because of her interest in the Napoleonic Wars, and she enjoys writing about warfare at sea and the ordinary people of the British Isles rather than lords and ladies. In her spare time, she reads British crime and history. Carla lives in Idaho and is a former seasonal park ranger and double RITA® Award and Spur Award winner. She has five children and five grandchildren.

Books by Carla Kelly

Harlequin Historical

Her Hesitant Heart
"Christmas Eve Proposal"
in *It Happened One Christmas*
"A Father for Christmas"
in *A Victorian Family Christmas*

Lord Ratliffe's Daughters

Marrying the Captain
The Surgeon's Lady
Marrying the Royal Marine

The Channel Fleet

The Admiral's Penniless Bride
Marriage of Mercy
The Wedding Ring Quest
"Captain Grey's Christmas Proposal"
in *Regency Christmas Wishes*
"The Captain's Christmas Journey"
in *Convenient Christmas Brides*
A Naval Surgeon to Fight For

Visit the Author Profile page
at Harlequin.com.

In memory of all the men who fought so gallantly at Trafalgar, and the never-mentioned wives there, too.

Also in memory of my dear writing buddy.

Prologue

At the age of nine, Jerusha Langley was no shrinking violet, no meek female, in an age when meek females were highly prized. Children were to be seen and not heard, and females—no matter what age—were never to call attention to themselves.

Jerusha had long been curious about the duck-pond on her father's modest property, or rather, the parish's modest vicarage near Bolling, where the Langley family resided, thanks to a living furnished by Jerusha's aunt, Lady Oakshott, who had the good fortune to marry a baronet. The vicarage in Bolling was small, but ideal for an equally modest clergyman.

For a few weeks, Jerusha had observed tadpoles turning into frogs on the pond's fringe. Mama threw up her hands in exasperation when Jerusha trooped into the house bearing three little frogs. Papa gently reminded her that frogs belonged in ponds, and would she please return them?

She did so with no good grace, because she would have preferred to keep the frogs. Muttering to herself, she carried the frogs back to the pond, leaned over, and released them. In the process, she dumped herself in.

It was early spring, so her coat dragged her down. She sputtered and thrashed into the middle of the pond, which took on the proportions of the ocean so vividly described by her father's discourse upon Noah and his ark. She thought she might make sufficient headway if she flailed about enough, but that coat was heavy and now waterlogged. She began to sink.

When matters reached their worst, a boy appeared at the pond's edge, older and taller than she was. He hesitated not a moment but plunged in, swimming to her. He grabbed the back of her coat and hauled her to shore.

'You're all right, now then?' he asked finally, in that Scottish lilt of his.

She recognised him. His father was secretary to the solicitor who lived next door. Jerusha didn't know his name—he was a twin and either Douglas or Jamie—but she thanked him for saving her life.

'You should learn to swim,' was his reply.

He walked her home, all sodden and squelching. Mama shrieked and accused him of pushing her in the water. Jerusha protested. The boy calmly assured her mother that he was merely walking by and rescued her. Mrs Langley whisked her inside and slammed the door in his startled face.

And that was that, even though Jerusha protested as Mama dried her off, and stated that the boy had saved her life.

'I've heard complaints aplenty about the secretary's twins,' her mother said, when Jerusha was dry and sent to bed—over further protest—mainly because Mrs Langley had personal tendencies towards hypochondria. 'I know for a fact that one of them stole a pig. That's the rumour, but it came from a good source.'

Jerusha's 'But Mama...' fell on deaf ears.

Mrs Langley carried the news of Jerusha's near death to Vicar Langley, who carried the tale to the solicitor, who grilled his secretary, Daniel Wilson, and then sacked the man over his protests that Douglas, his more obstreperous son, would never push someone in the water just to turn around and appear a hero, and Jamie, his twin, wouldn't, either.

The solicitor told the vicar later that he was happy enough

to see the backs of the whole Wilson clan, because his secretary had a disturbing tendency to correct his grammar and spelling on legal documents, damn the man.

'Douglas or Jamie, those twins will never trouble the district again,' Jerusha's mother announced to her in triumph a few days after the Wilsons were sent packing.

'Mama, one of them saved my life,' Jerusha said.

'Oh, pish posh,' Mama said. 'It is a shallow pond. You could have just put your feet down and waded ashore, I am certain. They're gone and the district is the better for it, I am certain.'

At the age of nine, Jerusha learned three valuable lessons: Life isn't fair, Augusta Langley had a curious grudge against Scots, and she wasn't much of a Christian. When Jerusha attempted a mild protest—'Mama, you should have thanked him.'—Mama gave her a good shake.

A conscientious child, Jerusha nursed her own anguish, mortified to have been the reason a secretary was unjustly sacked. Her only consolation was the Langley's cook, a kindly woman. Jerusha moped in the kitchen until Mrs Pingree allowed her to pour out her misery at the whole wretched business.

'Lovey, the Wilsons will be fine,' Mrs Pingree soothed, wiping away Jerusha's tears and handing her two lumps of sugar. 'I hear that Scots are a tough lot.'

Jerusha did one thing of consequence that she never told her parents: She learned to swim. The whole thing was clandestine, but she had discovered a tendency to go her own way when she was certain she was right. The matter involved watching behind trees in high summer as boys gathered at a deeper pond for merriment.

Her education increased because they swam naked, but never mind that. From her secret spot she watched them push up from the bottom and lie on their backs. It looked simple and she tried it during late-night visits to the pond when the house was dark. Push up, lie flat, arms out. Easy.

She watched again at actual swimming, and at night repeated that flailing about with a purpose this time, arms moving in rhythm across the pond. She sank a few times, but figured it out.

Swimming was her little secret.

Through twelve years and more, Mrs Pingree kept up occasional correspondence with Mrs Wilson. Jerusha learned that Mr Wilson acquired better employment in the Highlands. As for the twins later on, Douglas took Orders in the Church of Scotland—so much for stealing pigs—and Jamie attached himself to the Royal Navy at age thirteen, not so long after the drowning incident.

'Last I heard,' Mrs Pingree told Jerusha when Jerusha was twenty-one, 'is that Douglas has a fine church in Spring Hill and a wife, and Jamie is a surgeon's mate in the navy.' Mrs Pingree handed Jerusha two more lumps of sugar and they both laughed. 'You needn't trouble yourself about Jamie Wilson.'

Then why couldn't she forget him?

Chapter One

Jerusha's twenty-first birthday had slid by unnoticed three years ago, in the Year of Our Lord 1802, but there was something intimidating about birthdays twenty-two, twenty-three, and twenty-four, mainly because nothing much had happened since 1802. It was more than that. As she sat up in bed on a drizzly morning in February of 1805, now twenty-four for heaven's sake, she knew that life had blown a kiss in her general vicinity and passed her by.

Jerusha's first inclination had been drummed into her since she was old enough to be accountable: Ignore it and find some useful Good Work to do. Typically, that sufficed, but not this time. Looking around Papa's parish, Jerusha saw women her age enjoying life. Liddy, the daughter of a joiner, had recently married an up-and-coming tenant farmer. Maude, widowed young and with a daughter, had contracted an enviable alliance with Bolling's butcher. Sally Brown, she with a large birthmark on her cheek, was anticipating another child with her husband the constable, and positively glowing.

Here I am, Jerusha thought, *with nothing and no one.*

She knew her parents would never countenance self-pity, so she said nothing. In that well-mannered but pragmatic way of hers, she entertained the notion that she deserved a turn of events in her favour.

It would never do to admit something so self-serving to her

parents. Vicar Langley knew he had married a little above his station. He was not an ambitious man, so his parish living sufficed. Augusta Langley, on the other hand, felt worldly things more keenly. In years past, that generally meant a querulous letter to her sister Hortensia, who had done the opposite and married up, no matter that Sir Harvey Oakshott was a squinty-eyed fellow, twenty years older than she. Such a letter to her older sister usually meant a week at the seaside for Augusta with her two children, and childless Lady Oakshott. Jerusha did like the ocean.

That Sir Harvey Oakshott, at his wife's instigation, had provided that living, Mama seemed to consider her due. After all, the Oakshotts did have lovely Oaklands, an estate near Plymouth. What did they know of genteel poverty? Or so Mama reasoned.

Lately, even though Mama still sent querulous letters, nothing came of it. 'The Oakshotts have forgotten me,' Mama announced dramatically over breakfast.

All that earned her from the vicar was raised eyebrows and a return to his perusal of the newspaper, the same paper Jerusha was hoping to pounce upon when both parents left the breakfast room. If she hurried, she could generally snatch it before the housekeeper used it to wrap wet rubbish.

All Jerusha wanted was a glimpse of the wider world beyond the parish. Taking her usual careful inventory of her felonies and misdemeanours, she knew she shouldn't chafe so about that wider world. No ladies of her acquaintance did. The matter came home to roost on her heart when coffins bearing young men were buried in Bolling Parish because of the war against Napoleon.

'I want to know what's going on,' Jerusha had told her mother only last week, when caught with the newspaper. Mama must have tattled to Papa, who must have directed the housekeeper to keep it from his daughter. Jerusha reminded herself that Papa meant well.

Lately, though, his kindness wore on her nerves. When he ventured some admonition, some reflection on her character, he used the same tone he used to speak to children. It grated. 'I am twenty-five,' she wanted to tell him. 'I am not six and recalcitrant. Papa, treat me as an equal.'

Such would never be the case, not in this household from which there was no escape. She remained single and no one's equal.

Then came the moment when she knew what lay ahead as clearly as if it were already written in her book of life. Her younger brother Gerald, a no-hoper currently studying at Cambridge, came home for a repairing rustication after performing miserably in the entire term. As it turned out, he must have learned persuasive argument.

Before she left to deliver soup to one of the least fortunate of her father's parishioners, she saw Gerald standing outside Papa's study, looking less than sanguine. *I would give ten years of my life to have a chance at Cambridge*, she thought, as she passed him in the hall. *What now, you ignorant twit?*

The result of Gerald's supposed dressing-down ended any of Jerusha's possible dreams. By the end of an evening in Papa's study, Gerald came out triumphant. He grabbed Jerusha and swung her around. When she asked what the fuss was about, he gave a modest smile.

'You are looking—or soon to be looking at—the British Army's newest cornet. And all it will cost is five hundred pounds!'

And how is that sum to be obtained? was Jerusha's first thought, followed by a faint, 'My goodness.'

'Papa scolded, but he assured me that he could borrow against our little legacy,' Gerald confided. 'He knew you would not mind.'

Little legacy. Wasn't that what Mama had assured her and Gerald would be evenly divided some distant day? Both of her parents must have been deficient in simple arithmetic. 'Four hundred for Gerald and one hundred for you,' Mama stated firmly, except all of it went to Gerald. Within a month he was outfitted, commissioned, and on his way to a regiment in distant Canada, with Cambridge a thing of the past, along with any stipend for her to please a possible suitor.

Her anguish increased the night she overhead Mama and Papa quietly arguing in his study. She only heard random bits—'My love, I did not know Hortensia would cut up so stiff about borrowing that money for Gerald.' This from Mama.

This next rejoinder came from Papa after a gasp. 'Augusta, do you mean you borrowed five hundred pounds from your sister? I thought you had kept that money safe all these years as our children's legacy. Did you…had you spent it on furbelows for yourself?'

This was followed by a long silence and then sobs. And this: 'Dear husband, Hortensia will not help me. There is nothing for Jerusha. With any luck, Hortensia will not press me for repayment. After all, we had to help Gerald.'

It was probably no coincidence that Papa's sermon the following Sunday was taken from I Timothy, Chapter Six: In a surprisingly loud voice, Papa thundered from the pulpit, 'For the love of money is the root of all evil!' Too startled to turn her head and stare at Mama, Jerusha's side glance took in tight lips and bright spots of colour in Mama's cheeks. Jerusha trod quietly around the parsonage that week and the next, until she was tired of both parents.

Whatever had been promised to her was gone with Gerald, the Cambridge dropout with empty space between his ears. The reality was that she saw her parents as they really were, vain and silly. The time had come for…something. She didn't know what, at least until a letter arrived from Aunt Hortensia, who preferred that everyone, even her niece, call her Lady Oakshott.

A letter from Mama's sister, Lady Oakshott, was a rare enough event. 'I wonder what Hortensia can want,' Mama announced to Papa at luncheon on a cold February morning. 'Oh, I hope it is not a demand for...' She lowered her voice. 'You know.'

Papa glared at her, after a glance in Jerusha's direction, as if trying to decide if she could hear their obvious conversation. Jerusha decided to ignore them both and leave the room. She could take luncheon in the kitchen with the cook and have more agreeable company.

Before Jerusha left, Mama opened the letter, read a few lines, and gasped, which only made Papa exclaim, 'Has she decided to demand our daughter as partial payment for...you know what? Has the bill come due already?' he asked, perhaps in jest or perhaps not.

Oddly enough for a vicar, Papa's strong suit was not forgiveness. He and Mama still addressed each other most formally, the matter of her borrowing money for Gerald's advancement at Jerusha's expense still a sore spot. Jerusha edged for the door, unwilling to hear another word.

Too late. 'Jerusha, sit down. This concerns you,' Mama said as she waved Lady Oakshott's letter about.

'Aha!' Papa declared. 'She is inviting Jerusha to Oaklands, where she will meet an elderly fellow who will marry her despite her lack of fortune.'

'Francis, that is quite enough,' Mama said, in tones frosty enough to make Jerusha wonder if Papa was sleeping on the cot in his dressing room.

'Here it is, daughter,' Mama said. Jerusha could almost feel her excitement. 'Lady Oakshott is planning to sell a Plymouth property of her late husband's estate. Apparently, she feels she should be there for some necessary repairs and would like your company.'

'She barely knows me, Mama,' Jerusha said. 'I wonder why she feels the need of my company.'

Mama was still reading. 'Here it is: Apparently my sister's lady's companion resigned, and she wants the comfort of relatives.'

Someone who insists her niece call her Lady Oakshott doesn't long for relatives, Jerusha thought.

'She wants someone to fetch and carry.'

Jerusha was not slow; there was a larger matter, the business of Mama's borrowing from her sister and using all that money for Gerald's commission. Perhaps this was Aunt Hortensia's recompense for her younger sister's profligate spending.

Mama's hesitation confirmed Jerusha's suspicion. 'It's not a bad thing, daughter. Perhaps there might be a future for *you* as a lady's companion.'

There it is, Jerusha thought. Still, it could get her out of the vicarage, which suddenly seemed like an excellent notion.

'I can entertain the offer,' she said, matching Mama's casual tone.

She'll tire of me soon enough, Jerusha left unsaid.

'You'll do more than entertain it,' Mama said. 'I shall return an acceptance this afternoon. No one needs you here.'

'True, Mama. No one needs me here.' Or anywhere, for that matter, Jerusha knew, but couldn't say.

No one needs me.

Chapter Two

Lady Oakshott paid Jerusha's passage to Plymouth on the mail coach; not for her a post-chaise as her mama made no effort to add enough Langley funds to make up the difference.

The mail coach it was, but not before The Lecture. Jerusha knew it was coming, even though she was twenty-five and beyond needing it. Her father warned her about the Royal Navy in general and sailors in particular.

It was a concerted parental effort, which relieved Jerusha's mind. At least Mama and Papa were speaking to each other again, even if she was the object of their interest. Mama added nothing to Papa's warnings, but she dabbed at her eyes and appeared concerned.

Finally, it was too much. Jerusha fixed a kindly eye on both of her parents. 'My dears, all I am going to do in Plymouth is see how I can assist Lady Oakshott. I have no designs on the Royal Navy and know it can have none on me.' She shouldn't have, but she added, 'I am still too poor to attract any officer, and probably too opinionated. Let me pack.'

Jerusha swept out of the room, pausing a moment, waiting for regret at her firm words. Nothing happened. In fact, she felt more cheerful than she had in ages. 'I am leaving the vicarage,' she whispered. 'Bravo for me.'

During her remaining days in the vicarage, she made a point to be extra polite to her mother, who moped about with some drama. She knew her father would find a way to work her plain speaking into a sermon, and she endured a scorcher on 'Children, obey your parents.'

The last night in the vicarage was a trying one, with Mama in tears through most of dinner and Papa opening and closing his mouth, ready with aphorisms, of which he had plenty, but reluctant to share them. She assured them in her quiet way that she would never do anything to embarrass them.

Mama tried once. 'Daughter, if you wear your nicest coat tomorrow and best bonnet, you won't be encroached upon in the mail coach,' she said. 'The other riders will see that you are Quality, and will leave you alone.'

And sit in superior silence? Jerusha thought in horror. No, never that.

'I'll be fine, Mama.'

Mama patted her hand and consigned her darling daughter to the mail coach, as though it was a fixture in Dante's rungs of hell. Perhaps her conscience bothered her. Jerusha almost told Mama that she knew her visit to Plymouth, however long, was a payback, destined to turn her into a lady's companion, since she could hope for nothing better. Her trunk was packed and already deposited at the Fox and Hound, where the mail coach stopped. It only remained for her to follow it in the morning.

When the house quieted, Jerusha tiptoed downstairs and into the servants' quarters, where she knew Mrs Pingree would be seeing to those last things that seemed to fall to a woman's lot.

'Will you miss us?' the cook asked.

'You know I will, Mrs Pingree. I have been welcome here.'

'You always will be,' Mrs Pingree assured her. She put down a half-dry pot. 'What is Lady Oakshott's game, do you think?'

Such a conversation opener would have stunned Mama, but then, Mama was a stickler on separation of upstairs and downstairs, while Jerusha was not. She knew Mrs Pingree well enough to assume she already suspected the deeper reason for Jerusha's visit to Plymouth. Why not put it to the test? 'I believe I have been summoned to Plymouth in at least partial payment for Mama's mishandling of a loan from Lady Oakshott that went entirely to Gerald. Apparently, I am to become a lady's companion.'

Ah, there it was: Mrs Pingree nodded. 'We have been suspecting that,' she said, then leaned closer in conspiracy. 'The upstairs maid noticed a letter to that effect when she was tidying up in the sitting room.'

Jerusha laughed inside at the euphonism of 'noticed.'

'Do you think I will make a successful lady's companion, Mrs P?'

'I supremely doubt it, Lovey,' the cook replied, using that endearment from Jerusha's childhood when she came below stairs for biscuits and sympathy when life upstairs was too tiresome. 'You're an opinionated lady, and you don't lack for good sense.'

She knew a high compliment when she heard one. 'My pretentious aunt will tire of me, and I will be home before the end of summer,' she predicted. 'Even the Royal Navy will fear me, and I have no fortune to tempt anyone.'

'I'll miss you until you return, but there's no rush,' Mrs Pingree said. She lowered her voice. 'And no fears about the Royal Navy. The men smell of brine and are always at sea.'

Jerusha could tease, too. 'Then I am safe from their machinations,' she joked. 'Gentlemen don't smell of seawater.'

'Here is a novel idea: Plymouth is probably full of ordinary men. Find one.' Mrs Pingree turned serious. 'Trust yourself, Lovey.'

Chapter Three

To Jerusha's surprise, she slept well. She was past feeling dismay at leaving the vicarage; she had resigned herself to being the Good Example. Her own brother had fled such responsibility. For all she knew, he was staring down large bears in Canada. At least he wasn't in Europe, with war on again.

No one will know me in Plymouth, she thought, as she sat on a bench outside the Fox and Hound, waiting for the mail coach, her bandbox beside her. *When I leave Bolling, I am on my own.*

Mama did not see her off. She was no early riser, and besides, enough shards and remnants of her more genteel life as a Pigott of Albemarle would have drawn back in horror at the very idea of waiting for a common conveyance.

Jerusha wore her plain brown wool coat, since early spring was a tease. Her bonnet was more tried and true than stylish, which suited her fine, because so was she.

She knew she still stood out, a youngish woman travelling alone, but obviously Quality. Heading north, the first mail coach that stopped, took away two hopeful riders. When the coach heading south arrived, she was the only boarder. The coachman flung up her trunk to waiting arms on top and opened the door for her when she handed him her fare.

'To Exeter?' he asked.

'Yes, sir. Then I take the local stage to Plymouth.' The idea that she was actually leaving Bolling for who knew how long struck her forcefully and she couldn't help smiling at him. Mama and Papa would probably have wondered if she had listened to a word of their admonitions. They weren't here, so she smiled.

'Got a sweet sailor boy in Plymouth?' he teased.

'Nothing that exciting,' she replied, knowing that Mama would be stunned at her daughter's easy camaraderie with one lower than she. 'I am going to stay with my aunt.' She wasn't about to mention Lady Oakshott's name and title.

He gave her a hand up, after leaning in first to address the riders. 'Make some room for the lady,' he said.

They did. On one side, she squeezed between a farm wife with a cage of three chickens, none of them happy, and a little boy on the other, with two more chickens. Across from them sat a middle-aged lady who looked up from her book, then glanced away.

None of the others made eye contact with her, confirming Mama's comments about the shield and protection of class. She sat back, preparing herself for silence, then reconsidered.

She, Jerusha Langley, had finally been allowed into the wider world, which obviously meant ignoring others, even though they sat cheek to jowl. If there was a more artificial situation, she couldn't imagine it.

She contemplated the lives of the others. Perhaps the lady only slightly older than she might be a governess en route to a house with people of quality inside it. Another look at the lady seated across from her suggested an old maid facing a change of employment and nothing more.

Perhaps this will be my life, Jerusha thought.

She decided to change the script. Where to begin? She looked at the lad with chickens in a small cage. Jerusha knew he would never speak first. It was her turn.

'Are these your very own chickens?' she asked, six simple words. If he replied, she knew she had changed her world.

As she thought he might, he looked first at his mother, who hesitated. To Jerusha's relief and triumph, the farm wife smiled at her boy and nodded, giving him permission to reply.

'Aye, ma'am, my birds,' he said, giving Jerusha a glance both shy and hopeful.

'Did you raise them from eggs?' Jerusha asked.

He nodded. She knew it could have ended there, but Mrs Farm Wife took her turn. 'One of our hens decided to hide a clutch.' Jerusha saw the pride in her eyes. 'Johnny, here, 'e found 'em.'

'I kept 'em warm and all three hatched,' he said proudly. 'Papa said they wouldn't make it, but Mama and me knew better.'

Jerusha watched with delight as mother and son shared a private glance suggesting they knew more about poultry than Papa.

'Look how fine they are now,' Jerusha said and kept up the conversation.

When mother and son left the mail coach, Jerusha hurried inside the inn, nabbing only a meat sandwich. When she returned to the coach, the silent lady still sat there, feet together and hands folded primly in her lap.

Jerusha decided to take another chance. She handed one half of the sandwich to the lady. 'I almost didn't make it back,' Jerusha said. 'That lunch counter is not for the faint of heart. You were wise not to attempt it.'

If that was your reason, she thought, pleased when the lady took the half sandwich. She finished it, losing not a crumb.

The lady looked around, but it was still just the two of them. 'I have wanted to do what you did,' she said. 'It can get so lonely, at times, sitting in silence.'

That was all she said until it was her turn to get off the mail coach at the stop before Exeter. The lady nodded to Jerusha, then departed.

Never get yourself into such a position, Jerusha told herself. Johnny had his mum and the promise of more chickens. The quiet lady had nothing. Perhaps, just perhaps, being Quality put up barriers. *Let that be a lesson to me*, Jerusha thought.

Jerusha left the mail coach at Exeter, with no fears about boldly asking an older woman how to catch the coastal carrier from Exeter to Plymouth. 'Follow me, dearie,' the woman said, 'I'm going a little farther.'

They were joined by two men. Soon the new coachman snapped his whip and Jerusha settled back, ready for this journey to be over. They meandered over miles, but in sight of the sea now in the gathering dusk. The woman was a widow of some years and well-acquainted with the route. 'Visiting me daughter, I was,' she said. She waved her farewell at Torquay, a village on the bay, with Royal Navy ships at anchorage. 'They come and go and fight Boney at sea,' were her parting words. 'Lonely navy wives on this coast.'

Funny how silent travel can be so tedious. Jerusha wanted more conversation, but the men chatted quietly together. She told herself it wasn't nosiness but boredom that made her mentally dub them Old Traveller and One Leg, because his left leg ended in a wooden peg.

Darkness settled in by the next stop, when a youngish man climbed aboard. There was no place to sit except beside her, so she shifted farther into her corner. His overcoat had a briny odour. Old Traveller and One Leg continued their low-voiced conversation about what she thought was the blockade of the French coast. The young man hunkered down and chewed his nails.

To her embarrassment, Jerusha's stomach protested loud and long against its fading memory of a mere half sandwich.

To her surprise and her gratitude, Old Traveller handed her an apple. 'There miss, we can't have you chewing off your arm, now, can we?'

When One Leg gave her a shy grin, she relaxed. 'It's been a long day,' she admitted. 'Thank you.' She munched her apple dinner and decided to chance some conversation. It had gone well with Johnny, and his chickens, hadn't it?

She had noted from years of observation that men liked to explain things. 'Pardon me, sirs, but I heard you mention a blockade?'

'It's part of war, miss, the boring part,' One Leg said. 'T' Frogs want England, and they can't have it.' He tapped his wooden leg. 'I served, oh, I did, at the Nile.' He explained the blockade as Old Traveller nodded, then closed his eyes for a nap, conversation over.

A few hours brought them to Plymouth, that navy town on the River Plym. It was too dark to see anything, and time for her to wonder how to find number twenty-eight Finch Street.

When the carrier stopped in front of an inn with a creaking sign—the wind was up—the door flew open, and a uniformed man with a cudgel leaned inside the carriage, swore, and shoved the cudgel under the chin of the man who had never spoken.

Jerusha gasped as the uniformed man pulled back the rider's briny coat. 'A little birdie says sailors got on at Exeter,' Cudgel Man shouted, as though they were all hard of hearing. 'Forget goin' home. The king wants ye now!'

With that, he jerked the rider from the coach. Jerusha made herself small in the carriage as two more men in uniform—who were they?—hauled down two more protesting riders from the top of the carrier.

'It's a good haul, sir!' Cudgel Man yelled to a younger man in uniform. Another curse followed a crack on the head to her former seatmate, who dropped like a stone.

Old Traveller pulled the door shut. 'We'll wait here until they leave,' he told Jerusha. 'No good for you to be on the street.'

'I… I wouldn't want to,' she assured him. 'Wh-what has just happened?'

'Press gangs all over Devon and Cornwall are rounding up sailors who try to sneak away,' he said. 'Thank the Almighty *I'm* too old. It's war, miss, and they have no choice but to serve.'

Chapter Four

No one waited for her a few blocks on at the coastal carrier's terminus, which surprised her not at all. Jerusha knew Lady Oakshott well enough not to count on much. She remembered disappointing visits when she was much younger that Mama chose to gloss over, calling them the eccentricities of the wealthy. Jerusha knew selfishness when she saw it, despite Mama choosing to ignore the matter.

When she and the remaining riders finally left the coastal carrier, One Leg came under the press gang's scrutiny. He sent them on with a brusque, 'Carpenter's mate here. I gave all at the Nile, ye fiends of hell.'

'Mind your tongue, anyway,' snapped the young officer.

'Do they just grab anyone that suits their fancy?' Jerusha whispered to One Leg.

'They're not supposed to,' he replied more quietly as the press gang moved on. 'They'll grab sailors off returning merchant ships, claiming the necessity of national calamity.' He chuckled. 'And God help ye if you're on an American ship, minding your own business!'

'This doesn't seem fair,' she said, flinching as a screaming woman ran after the press gang, clutching an infant and raising her free hand, begging mercy where there was none. Jerusha turned away in shock.

'It's war,' One Leg said simply. 'Boney has thousands of men just across the Channel, waiting to invade.'

The three of them stood shoulder to shoulder until the press gang moved off to terrorise another public house. The woman with the baby ran after them, sobbing.

Old Traveller sighed and took out his timepiece. 'Is someone coming for you? It is nearly eleven of the clock.'

'I doubt it. My aunt is…' How to describe Lady Oakshott? 'Let me say that she is scatterbrained. I know her retainers are old.'

'Retainers?' One Leg asked. 'What sort of household is this?'

Better spill the budget, Jerusha decided. 'My aunt is Lady Oakshott of Oaklands, and I am a poor relation.' Blunt but true, and certainly no more shocking than the press gang, which, from the sound of things, was creating merry hell on the next street.

Old Traveller stopped a passing hackney. 'If you have an address, we will drop you off.'

'Thank you, sir,' Jerusha said. She took the address from her reticule. 'Here it is. I am in your debt.'

Twenty-eight Finch Street was not far from the old town. Old Traveller called it the Barbican. The jarvey pulled up sharp and handed down her trunk. She waved goodbye to her fellow travellers, took a deep breath, and knocked on the door of what looked like a dark house.

Nothing. She knocked again, but louder, then once more, and pressed her ear against the door. To her relief, she heard footsteps and stepped back when the door opened a crack.

'Yes?'

'It's Jerusha Langley,' she said through the crack. 'Lady Oakshott is expecting me.'

The door swung open on a man even more ancient than Old Traveller. He was thin and squinty-eyed, which suggested a need for spectacles. When he straightened up, she knew she was looking at a butler, albeit a superannuated one.

'Jerusha Langley,' she said again. 'Did...did Lady Oakshott mention me?'

'I forget,' the old fellow said. 'I am Napier, and I am seventy-five.'

A little old to be working, she thought, even though what he said amused her.

Or maybe she was tired. She looked into his eyes and even in the gloom saw kindness, something so far in short supply in Plymouth. She indicated her trunk leaning against the bottom step. 'If you help me, I believe we can get my trunk inside.'

They did, after some theatrical grunting on the butler's part. The trunk made it to the foot of the stairs, and the butler stopped. 'I'll get the maid of all work to help me in the morning, Miss Langley. Goodnight.'

With that, he wandered away, after blowing out the candle and leaving her in darkness. Jerusha sat on her trunk and laughed at the absurdity of her situation. In all their admonitions about sailors, her parents hadn't thought to warn her about antique butlers.

Jerusha tiptoed down the corridor, peering into rooms, until she found one with a promising sofa. A pillow from a wingback chair met her approval. With a sigh, she took off her shoes, removed her overcoat and bonnet and lay down. She was asleep in moments.

I would give my left testicle for a good night's sleep, James Wilson thought, as he stared at his dark house.

Sound asleep inside was his housekeeper, Margaret McDonald, widow of a bosun who had extracted a promise from his surgeon as he lay dying of an unidentified tropical fever. 'Take care of her, laddie,' his fellow Scot had demanded with his last breath.

True to his word, James found her in a rooming house in Plymouth, delivering both the news of her husband's death and his offer of employment as his housekeeper. She was as Scottish as he was. When she finished crying, she gave her shoulders a shake, packed her bags, and followed him to this little house.

Mags was a jewel and a wonder, and James had no regrets. Now, his sole aim was to get inside, upstairs, and in bed without waking the old lady. She was used to his weird hours, most of which he blamed on his profession. Only an idiot among the Stonehouse surgeons would ever have declared that he never got seasick, and sea duty suited him fine. His cheerful statement led to an epiphany among senior surgeons. As the most junior of surgeons currently working in the hospital, Jamie Wilson found himself sentenced to ship *and* shore duty, shuttling between the blockade and Stonehouse with medicine and patients.

He had to agree it was a good system before the Treaty of Amiens, which halted warfare and meant he had no sea duty. After the treaty broke in 1803, he resumed sailing with a messenger ship, going back and forth to the blockade to return any badly wounded back to Plymouth's naval hospital and deliver medicine.

Jamie would have been the first to admit that his was a thankless business, but better than letting the seriously wounded languish on the blockade. Because one badly wounded lieutenant required around-the-clock attention on the return trip, usually three to five days, depending, James couldn't remember when he had last put his head on a pillow.

He was tired beyond belief. After he found his bed, he lay awake only a few minutes, doing what he always did, because medicine was his calling. He thought back over a few thorny cases, analysed them, and wondered what he would do different.

The mattress felt good, but his mind refused to let him go.

Since he knew he would rise early, he let his mind wander to a small success, one that never failed to assure him that not all his patients died. He settled in to remember rescuing the vicar's daughter in Bolling, where his father had briefly clerked for a solicitor. He had rescued her from a duck-pond, pulling her out by her cloak and nearly strangling her in the process.

He set her on her feet, but not before extracting a promise that she would learn how to swim. He remembered her eyes, so big and blue, with a little mole beside the left one that acted like a directional sign pointing to those memorable eyes.

She nodded so solemnly, fixing those eyes on his with no hint of guile. 'I promise to learn,' she told him, then, 'Thank you for saving my life. You are my hero.'

James knew he was nobody's hero. That title belonged to the iron men of the blockade, who in all weather kept their wooden walls between Napoleon and invasion. It was a harmless memory that sent him into the arms of Morpheus more content with his lot.

And so he slept.

Chapter Five

'Lady Oakshott, I have only misplaced her temporarily. She is here somewhere.'

Through her sleepy fog, Jerusha recognised the voice. She squinted at the clock on the mantelpiece then opened her eyes wider. Half twelve? A glance out the window confirmed that she had managed a long slumber on a lumpy sofa.

She sat up and stretched, her bones protesting from a night spent…she looked around at shelves of books…in a library.

There are worse places, she thought, glad she had at least removed her bonnet, and happy there was likely no press gang roaming Finch Street, at least not in broad daylight.

She tried to smooth the wrinkles out of her travelling dress, and gave it up for a bad business, opening the door and peering out instead. 'Um, good morning, Lady Oakshott.'

When her aunt glared at her, Jerusha suspected it was not going to be a good visit. However, the glare modulated into something resembling a smile. 'Left to my own devices, Jerusha, I never go into the library.' She held out her hand to her niece, who didn't know whether to kiss it, shake it, or genuflect.

Jerusha attempted humour. 'You never would have found me then?'

Lady Oakshott cleared her throat in most impressive fashion. 'Not until a stench arose.'

Jerusha laughed, but her aunt frowned, opening the possibility that Lady Oakshott did not possess a sense of humour. Napier managed a butler smile, which gave nothing away. When neither of them made a move, Jerusha cleared her throat. 'Aunt,' she began, and was frozen in place by a glance. 'I mean, Lady Oakshott, if someone would show me to a room, I can unpack and perhaps be ready for luncheon.'

'Abbie!' Lady Oakshott called. 'Tiresome girl, where are you?'

Silence, then the sound of someone running. 'Just dusting, my lady,' the girl said, out of breath. Jerusha thought she didn't look a day over eleven.

What sort of place is this? she asked herself, surprised. She remembered a much earlier visit to Oaklands when Sir Harvey was alive, when there were servants enough to trip over. Obviously, things had changed.

'Abbie, take Miss Langley upstairs to the blue room.' Lady Oakshott dragged out a timepiece from somewhere in her bosom. 'In thirty minutes, luncheon will be served in the breakfast room.' She left the room, sweeping out grandly, Jerusha thought, for someone in a nightgown and shawl. What a strange household.

Jerusha followed Abbie to the next floor, while Napier thumped her trunk up behind them, wheezing as he followed. She picked up the other handle on the trunk. 'This will be easier,' she assured the old man. 'Better still, just rest a moment until you feel like it.'

Abbie waited impatiently at the top of the stairs, or was it impatience? Jerusha took a closer look. *She's afraid*, she thought. 'My dear, tell me which room, if you need to be elsewhere.'

Abbie's eyes softened.

No one has ever called you 'my dear,' have they? Jerusha thought, as her heart softened, too.

'The blue room,' she announced, and opened a door.

Perhaps the wallpaper had been blue at one time, but everything had faded. The room smelled unused and somehow sad. 'I don't suppose anyone has lived here for a long time,' she said.

Abbie shrugged. 'I've never been in here. 'Course, I was raised at Oaklands.' She went to the window and after a struggle, raised the sash. 'Let's get some air. Smells like a wet dog in here.' The maid leaned on the windowsill. 'And lookee, you can see the ships.'

Jerusha saw more ships in the distance. 'My goodness. Is everyone at war?'

They stood in silence at the window until Abbie turned away. 'I have to help the cook now. You'll be all right?'

'A basin of water would be nice.'

The frightened look returned to Abbie's eyes. 'I… I don't have time.'

'Then don't worry,' Jerusha replied. 'I can see to that later.'

Abbie darted for the door. 'One moment,' Jerusha said. 'How many of you does my aunt employ?'

'There's old Napier, and René the cook, 'cept we are to call him a chef, Lady Oakshott's maid, and me.'

We have more servants in the vicarage, Jerusha thought, startled.

'You are a busy girl. Hurry on. I'll manage quite well here.'

Abbie pelted downstairs, gathering speed for a run down the hall. Abbie sat beside Napier until he recovered, then helped him get her trunk up the few remaining steps. She thanked him and closed the door, wondering why her aunt had left everyone else behind at Oaklands.

She went to the window again, looking out until the alarm bells in her brain stopped. Or did they? She leaned out a little farther, hearing real bells to the west, and wondered about them.

Her clothes quickly went on pegs in the dressing room that

needed a swipe with a duster. She knew a basin of water could wait. She shook out a simple muslin dress, tucked in her stray curls here and there, and took her own time down the stairs, observing dingy walls. The house was old and ill-used. Jerusha thought of Lady Oakshott's letter to Mama, something about improving the house to sell. Her aunt must have been here several months now, but nothing appeared to have happened.

The breakfast room was no grander than the blue room, with faded walls and the general sad air of a grand lady down on her luck. Still, no one could fault the menu of toast, shirred eggs, and bacon on the sideboard. She filled her plate and sat down, all under the watchful eye of Lady Oakshott, who sipped tea.

'You would have a trimmer figure if you didn't pile your plate so high,' her aunt commented, after another parsimonious sip.

'All I had yesterday was one apple.'

'One should always travel light.'

The eggs turned into boulders, Lady Oakshott eyeing every forkful. Jerusha thought better of that second strip of bacon and drank her tea instead, weak tea, as though the tea leaves had been used too many times.

I will starve here, she thought.

When she put her napkin beside the plate, Abbie whisked it away. When the door closed, only she and Lady Oakshott remained. Her aunt looked her over in silence. Jerusha felt her heart begin to fail her. Was conversation also rationed here? She cleared her throat, determined to maintain her equilibrium in the face of what looked like disapproval.

'Lady Oakshott, I'm delighted to be here,' she began, immediately recalling Papa's frequent sermons on the sin of prevarication. 'Your letter mentioned something about renovations here so you could sell this house?' Nothing. 'Wh-when are you planning to begin the work?'

'I have changed my mind,' her aunt said, then managed a laugh. 'Silly me, I have already let Oaklands for the summer to an enterprising man who smells of the shop, but who won't irritate my neighbours.'

'You've *rented out* Oaklands?' Jerusha asked in amazement. She met her aunt's gaze, prepared for a sharp reply. 'I mean… I suppose it is a big property to rattle around in, and this might be cosier, even if it is only Plymouth and…' She stopped, aware that she was babbling, but still, renting out an ancestral manor?

'Precisely,' Lady Oakshott said. 'I had intentions of doing as I said in the letter—by the way, your mother uses such poor stationery—but I am reconsidering.' She managed a laugh with no mirth in sight. 'Since I have let Oaklands, I will have to live here for the term of that lease. Such a bother, but there you are.'

'What…what am I to do for you here?' Jerusha asked, more curious than afraid. With its press gangs and general air of the commonplace, Plymouth did not seem to hold much attraction for a late baronet's widow. *Plymouth?*

'You strike me as the useful sort,' Lady Oakshott said. 'Biddable and quiet, so your mother describes you, and someone not unfamiliar with light housework.' She cleared her throat, as if to drive a point home. 'And you're not getting any younger.'

'That's true,' Jerusha said. 'I can polish silver with the best of them, even if I am an antique,' she joked, and regretted it.

Lady Oakshott merely raised her eyebrows at this feeble attempt at humour. 'We can include that in your duties, along with sweeping and tidying. The walls need washing in the entryway. Hopefully you can climb a ladder without getting dizzy. The walls should probably be attended to first. Did you bring along an apron or two?'

'No, Lady Oakshott, I did not,' Jerusha replied. She remembered overheard conversations about turning into a lady's companion for her aunt.

Am I to be a common servant, too? she thought.

'There should be aprons in the pantry.' She rose, and glared at Jerusha until she stood up. With a nod, Lady Oakshott made her stately exit, pausing in the doorway. 'It's nothing onerous, niece. I am preparing you for a life of service to others.'

Aren't I the lucky one? Jerusha thought, angry, but at whom?

She reminded herself that she was twenty-five, without a dowry or prospects. But in what universe was a lady's companion also a drudge?

Her cheery nature attempted a recovery with the thought, *We can laugh about this when summer's over and I am home.* Still…

She looked up from her contemplation of her hands at a scratching on the door. 'Yes?'

Abbie opened it, carrying an apron over her arm. 'Lady Oakshott says you are to begin with me right now in the sitting room.'

'Certainly,' Jerusha replied, amused at what had to be a little mistake on her aunt's part. Imagine what Mama would say to all this. 'I am puzzled about something.'

'Yes, miss?'

'Abbie, you told me there are four servants here—you, Napier, and René the chef, and Lady Oakshott's maid. When am I to meet *her*?'

It was Abbie's turn to stare at her. 'Lady Oakshott meant you.'

Chapter Six

Lady Oakshott most certainly did mean her, a matter made
amply clear, as March passed into April. Jerusha vacillated
between asking her aunt when she might learn about being a
lady's companion and whining to Mama. She knew she could
have whined, but something odd happened: Working for Lady
Oakshott came with a measure of freedom she hadn't reckoned on. She liked it.

Jerusha knew this was better than whining to Mama. Besides, she knew how to clean a room within an inch of its life.

She was ready to at least masquerade as a maid. A long
moment staring into the mirror in the shabby blue room made
her look deep into her own eyes and acknowledge that there
wouldn't ever be a husband, and certainly not a surprise in-
heritance from an unknown relative to allow her any independence. Whatever tiny pittance might have tempted a would-be
suitor was gone with the purchase of her brother's commission.

Jerusha reconciled herself to the prospect of eventually
turning herself into a lady's companion. She would have a
home, and it was a genteel occupation. She never had been one
to put herself forward, so blending into the background posed
no difficulties. Why, in no time at all, she would turn into
wallpaper. *That* thought made her look away from the mirror.

As she dusted and cleaned that first afternoon, she resolved
upon the truth, with variations as needed. Abbie was gullible
enough to believe a slightly manufactured tale of an impov-

erished relative of Lady O, even though Mama would never see herself in such a light.

'It's this way, Abbie,' she said, as they polished the fireplace attachments. 'Lady Oakshott will eventually find me a situation as a companion someday. In the meantime, it never hurts to make things tidy.'

'You don't really mind this sort of work?' Abbie asked, sounding dubious. 'I mean, a lady's companion would never have to do *this*.'

'I don't mind cleaning,' she replied, thinking of floors she had mopped, and corners dusted in homes of the deserving poor of Papa's parish. 'I've had plenty of practice…uh…working in a vicarage. It's our Christian duty to be of service.'

'Hmm,' was all Abbie contributed. 'If you say so.'

'I do,' Jerusha said, and it was no lie. Yes, she was under another's thumb, but she was free from the tyranny of a complacent parish with judgemental ladies who pitied their vicar's unmarried daughter. 'Things change. Just wait.' Maybe they would, maybe they wouldn't. There was no harm in hoping.

Her only hesitation came on that first supper below stairs. Heaven knows she had been below stairs in the vicarage, but never to actually eat with servants. Two deep breaths and down she went. There they were, waiting for her—Napier, the antique butler; René, the chef whom she had yet to meet; and Abbie. Obviously, Abbie's duties included the kitchen, as well as everything else. Napier nodded, René winked, and Abbie shyly passed her the potatoes.

Napier introduced René des Champs. 'He cooks very well and he hates Napoleon.'

René bowed from where he sat. 'Mademoiselle Langley, you are welcome to this household.'

René sounded no more French than she did. 'Thank you. Umm…'

René looked at Napier and shrugged, then both men chuckled. René leaned forward with a smile in his eyes. 'I am no more French than you are, but Lady Oakshott doesn't know that.' He smoothed his eyebrows. '*Mademoiselle*, I can put on zee accent as required, and *allons*, it got me a job.'

Jerusha laughed.

'I trust you will overlook our various eccentricities.'

'If you will overlook mine,' she replied, which made Napier nod and look heavenward.

What sort of place is this? she asked herself again.

They ate in silence, then Napier cleared his throat. 'Miss Langley, Lady Oakshott assured us that you are a useful sort.'

'All my life,' she said cheerfully.

'We haven't too many rules.' He held up one finger. 'First, the cardinal rule: There will be no noise of a housecleaning nature before twelve of the clock. Lady Oakshott rises at noon. She is adamant about this and there are no exceptions.'

Jerusha wanted to ask that if someone broke that rule, did it mean the rack or drawing and quartering, but she prudently didn't. Napier seemed entirely serious.

'Lady Oakshott specifically wants you to attend to her in the evenings in the sitting room.' When his lips twitched, Jerusha suddenly realised she might like her social descent into the bowels of number twenty-eight Finch Street, where people at least had a sense of humour, unlike upstairs. 'She likes to play Patience and she cheats.'

René rolled his eyes in most Gallic fashion, and Abbie laughed. 'Sir, perhaps this is part of training me to be a lady's companion someday,' Jerusha said calmly, wincing only a little at that social descent.

Napier continued his list of dos and don'ts. He gave her a kindly look, which seemed like permission to ask her own question. Why not? The worst that could happen would probably be a sorrowful headshake from Napier, who had obviously had years of experience as a butler, assuredly in grander homes than this.

'Why is Lady Oakshott so intent on maintaining the sitting room impeccably and the entryway, when other rooms need more attention?' Jerusha asked. 'I heard from…a source that she plans to sell this house. Shouldn't she be employing restorationists?'

'It is not our position to divine Lady Oakshott's intentions,' Napier replied. He said it kindly, which barely embarrassed her. My, but he had a knack.

René was another matter. Perhaps Lady Oakshott didn't pay him enough. He gave the butler a glance, and her, his attention. 'Shall we say, Lady Oakshott is working herself into the good graces of the local grand dames, such as there are in a navy town. She wants the sitting room to look up to the mark, and the foyer, certainly.' He looked around at what Jerusha suspected were already co-conspirators. 'We planted flowers in the front after dark a few weeks ago. Can't have the neighbours thinking she cannot afford a gardener.'

'Oh.' Jerusha could think of nothing more profound than that. 'Frugal zinnias?'

Everyone laughed, and Jerusha knew she was now a co-conspirator, too.

She reminded herself that her tenure here would likely be for the summer only, but then what? And if her aunt needed a lady's companion, or even a maid, Jerusha didn't have a better plan.

The thought stayed with her as she and Abbie cleaned and polished. By unspoken consent, it became her duty to deliver her aunt's breakfast to her promptly at noon and listen without comment to her various complaints. Jerusha delivered mail then, too. She noticed bills from tradesmen, but Aunt Hortensia usually brushed those aside and pounced on invitations to take tea.

She waved those at Jerusha in triumph, when they came. 'See there, I had feared that once Sir Harvey shuffled off his mortal coil I might be forgotten, because we did not spend much time in Plymouth—Lord, these people are common— but such is not the case.' If there were no invitations, she made herself comfortable in the sitting room, waiting for visitors to materialise, which they often did not.

It wasn't the sort of news she thought Mama would like in her weekly letter to the vicarage. She reasoned that Mama would also not care for what else she discovered she was enjoying: going to the market in the Barbican with René and Abbie.

She had not thought she would ever be in a market by the docks with a basket on her arm, haggling over the price of potatoes, but there she was, triumphant over five pounds of potatoes, with three leeks thrown in because she smiled at the vendor.

Her delight was overshadowed by the clanging of the bell she had noticed earlier. 'René, what is that?' she asked, after he paid the vendor.

'War against an evil man,' he said. He pointed west. 'Stonehouse is a few miles that way in Devonport, a hospital for Royal Navy and Marines. When ships make their way to Stonehouse Creek with their wounded, the bells summon the surgeons.'

'Ha…have you ever been there to see it?' she asked.

'Once.' He looked out to sea. 'It is a terrible sight.'

She looked around the market—the women bargained for chickens, teased the grocers, asked for samples—and wondered how easy it was, even in Plymouth, to see nothing of war, and only hear distant bells.

She thought of Jamie Wilson and wondered where he was, on what ocean he sailed. She stood still, her hand on an onion, and wondered if he even lived. 'René, do you think that someday there will be a way for people to know where friends and families are by…oh, it would take a magic potion.'

'You're missing someone?' he asked, taking the onion from her and adding two more to his basket.

'Not really,' she admitted. 'I owe someone an apology. That is all.'

'Hopefully he has long since forgotten and you needn't fret.'

'*I* didn't forget.'

Chapter Seven

Lady Oakshott could never be accused of patience. Mama had told Jerusha of times when her older sister would threaten to hold her breath until she exploded, if she did not get her way. Jerusha noticed how her servants tiptoed around her when she sat and stared with a certain steely-eyed calm they found unnerving.

Apparently, Lady Oakshott could not manage without attention. When day after day passed with no invitations, her aunt began to snap at Abbie over trivialities or glare at Jerusha and demand to know if she were hiding the mail.

It's only for a summer, Jerusha reminded herself, even as she wondered about that. Did Mama tell her she could come home in autumn, or was that merely something Jerusha hoped? Ah well. She could clean the house to a fare thee well, and ready it for the time when the mouldering old place actually went on sale, once the lease on Oaklands concluded.

She and Abbie had advanced beyond the sitting room to the dining room and the tedious task of polishing chairs that had not seen linseed oil in years. The long-neglected wood soaked it up like thirsty mariners abandoned in lifeboats to float for months at sea.

She had come to appreciate Abbie's nearly constant good cheer, and even more, her tenacity. As they scrubbed and polished, the little maid told Jerusha about running away from a workhouse at age eight, wandering the streets in Plymouth, then curling up on the doorstep at number twenty-eight Finch Street because she was tired.

'Mr Napier found me, and I stayed,' she said simply. 'Pass the linseed oil.'

God forgive me when I whine, Jerusha thought.

'Here you go.'

When the post delivered the mail this morning, Jerusha set it beside the breakfast tray after a glance. There were the usual bills, which would likely join the pile of bills beside Lady O's bed, ignored, and two cream-coloured envelopes that looked like invitations. That should sweeten up the old rip.

She carried breakfast and letters upstairs at precisely noon, let herself into the darkened room, and pulled back the draperies on a lovely Plymouth morning. She knew better than to speak. Everyone knew to tread lightly before that first cup of tea.

Such a tyrant, Jerusha thought, as she closed the door. *If I am ever an actual lady's companion, I pray it will not be for someone like my aunt.*

She was down the stairs, heading for linseed oil and dining room chairs when she heard a mighty shriek, loud enough to stir Napier from tidying the already immaculate, if shabby, foyer, ready for visitors who seldom materialised.

Fearful, Jerusha took the stairs two at a time. To her enormous relief, she opened the door on Aunt Hortensia with a huge smile, fanning herself with one of those cream-coloured envelopes. To her further astonishment, her aunt patted the bed in an invitation for her to sit, a liberty Jerusha couldn't imagine.

'What on earth, Lady Oakshott,' she managed. 'You frightened me, but you look…'

'…over the moon,' her aunt supplied. She clutched the letter to her breast and looked heavenward for a moment. 'I have arrived, Jerusha. Finally.' She patted the bed. 'Sit. Who knew that war could lead to something so good for me?'

Horrors, Jerusha thought. Was war something to send anyone into ecstasies of delight?

'Admiral Stoppard's wife is organising us to take comfort baskets of food and special treats to wounded officers at Stonehouse,' Aunt Hortensia said, barely able to contain her glee. 'I am numbered among them!'

'Such an honour,' Jerusha murmured. 'But don't the officers already receive the best of everything? What about the ordinary seamen?'

Aunt Hortensia fixed her with a steely-eyed glare that Abbie said made her want to void. Jerusha tried to maintain the neutral face she had been nurturing in the past few weeks under her aunt's thumb. She must not have succeeded.

'You are an idiot,' her aunt said. 'It is the *officers* who matter to an admiral's wife.' She shoved the letter towards Jerusha. 'Here is a list of items for a basket. Assemble it and take it to Stonehouse.'

'Me?' Jerusha asked, surprised. 'The honour is yours, Lady Oakshott.'

'The credit is mine, my dear slow-top, the credit,' her aunt said. 'Mrs Admiral Stoppard writes here that servants are to deliver the baskets.' She jabbed her finger at the beautiful script. 'She wrote this: "I won't have you frighten yourself, dear Lady Oakshott, so do appoint a servant."' She turned kindly eyes on Jerusha now, the look someone would give the mentally deficient. 'You will take it. Here is the list. There must be a basket around here somewhere.'

There was, a dusty one in the pantry that smelled of smoked oysters, which Napier set Abbie to cleaning. René took the list with a straight face. 'Calf's foot jelly, a bottle of spirits, tea, slippers, cod liver oil'—the chef made a face—'sweets, an improving work by a distinguished author, comb and brush. Useless.'

'I brought along Shakespeare's sonnets,' Jerusha said.

Napier found an even dustier bottle of smuggler's sherry in the nearly depleted wine cellar and sent Jerusha with a pound note to the apothecary for cod's liver oil and calf's foot jelly. René shook his head over the whole thing and said he would bake macarons. 'Men who are wounded surely deserve something better than what is on this list,' he told Jerusha as she left. 'They will be boxed and ready tomorrow morning, or my name isn't René.' He laughed. 'Which it isn't!'

She stood a long moment on the front step, aware, even if the others weren't, that this was her first unaccompanied trip to the markets. She savoured the moment, choosing not to dread it. She didn't feel the same disquiet that followed her below stairs with the servants for that first meal, or the mop and bucket in the sitting room, or linseed oil to tackle the dining room chairs.

This was different. In her heart, this was no descent. She was walking independently somewhere by herself, something thousands did every day. She could dawdle if she chose, even flirt with the tradesmen or sit in the sun with nothing more in mind than enjoying the day. If there was a penny or two to spare, she could buy a sweet or hand the penny to a beggar. No one would scold her or give her that patient look destined to keep her biddable and obedient. Those days were done, and she seized the moment for what it was: liberation.

As she came closer to the Barbican, that warren of narrow, crooked streets familiar to many a mariner since Alfred the Great, for all she knew, Jerusha realised she had no plans to do other than what she was here for.

You are a dull dog indeed, she scolded herself as she opened the door to the apothecary and the bell tinkled.

The thought had made her smile, which meant the apothecary had a smile for her, too. She placed her little order, and he delivered it. Only a few months ago, that would have been that. Things were different now. She told him what it was for, which made him nod and add another jar of calf's foot jelly, think a moment, then stick in a package of throat lozenges.

'On the house,' he said with a grand gesture, which made Jerusha laugh.

'Thank you, sir. Lady Oakshott says it is for officers at Stonehouse.'

The apothecary shook his head. 'Lass, they're fawned over enough by the uppity ups. Take it to Block Three or Four, where the ordinary seamen are.'

'I'd like to, but I have my orders,' Jerusha told him.

He winked at her. 'Lady Oakshit…'

'Oakshott,' she corrected, determined not to go into whoops over that.

'Oakshit… Oakshott… She'll never know.'

He looked out the shop window, seeing something far distant, which made Jerusha wonder if he had served his own rough apprenticeship at sea in some long-ago war. 'Aye, miss, now that the treaty's broke, we'll be hearing that bell day and night.'

'Ships fighting in the Channel?' she asked.

'Everywhere. The sea can be cruel, and not as forgiving as land battles.'

She took that thought home and below stairs, where René was already working his magic with macarons, explaining to Abbie—standing by his elbow, her concentration fierce—how critical the right temperature was in the oven. Jerusha breathed in the fragrance, thinking of all the years when she had no idea just how divine a kitchen could smell.

The macarons were boxed and ready to go in the morning, long before Lady Oakshott was up. Napier appointed himself her escort. 'You've never been to Devonport, and there are all those sailors,' he said firmly, as if he saw a scoundrel behind every coil of rope.

The hackney took them past rows of houses, then warehouses, and a long building the butler identified as a rope-walk, then dry docks and ships half built. The area buzzed with the commerce of war. Jerusha looked down at the basket, wondering how something as silly as calf's foot jelly and throat lozenges would appear to the surgeons and physicians at Stonehouse.

'This is a fool's errand, isn't it?' she asked.

'Lady Oakshott and her friends don't see it that way,' he replied. 'There is no harm in wanting to do something.'

She nodded, unsatisfied with his answer. She thought of her useful years in Papa's parish, and wondered at the baskets she had delivered there. 'I would like to do more,' she said, but softly, not certain Napier would understand.

The jarvey let them out in front of a massive series of buildings, individual blocks forming a courtyard around a park with trees and benches. Her heart sank with the realisation that such a hospital was needed, as Napoleon continued to rage on the continent and the waters around their island.

'I wish I knew where to go,' she whispered to Napier.

As she stared, she noticed a middle building at the top of the courtyard with a more elaborate entrance. 'Let us start there,' she said.

Between them, they carried the heavy basket towards what she hoped was the administration building. Napier began to flag, so they stopped several times. Finally, he gave up and sat down on one of the benches for convalescents, some of whom sat here and there on other benches.

She left him with the basket. 'I'll find someone to take this…this thing,' she said, happy to abandon the basket that seemed to grow larger and heavier and more ridiculous by the moment.

She wasted no time hurrying up the steps and opening the door to stand in a hall with many doors. *Now what?* she asked herself. Maybe she could leave the basket on the lawn like an old, abandoned dog. She could stow away on a ship and move to America.

'Jerusha Langley, you are an idiot,' she whispered under her breath. 'This is not the wicked stage, and you are not emoting in a melodrama.' She stood there and took another deep breath.

Or I can knock on a door until I find someone willing to help me.

She walked down the hall, peering in open doors at men in uniform writing or talking to other men. No one looked up when she passed. Everyone was busy. She reminded herself there was a war on.

She passed another door and paused a moment. Two men in uniform stood with their backs to her. She heard a Scottish accent and smiled, remembering another accent like that years ago. One of the men turned part-way around and she hurried on.

When she was halfway through the width of the building, she saw a man sitting behind a higher desk. Perhaps he was an information clerk. She couldn't be the only one who ever got lost in a place this huge.

He looked up when she came closer, but seemed to be looking beyond her. In another moment she heard behind her, 'Miss Langley, did you ever learn to swim?'

Chapter Eight

It was only the briefest of glimpses, a woman in a dark dress and plain bonnet, but there was something about her. James Wilson couldn't have explained to a jury why that glimpse captured him, especially since he was wrangling with the purser over how much calomel and catgut a surgeon needed. The man had no imagination and he had never been to sea.

Still, the rustle of skirts caught his ear and he turned instinctively. He quickly turned back to the business at hand, which he knew he was losing. Too bad that a surgeon was not allowed to be a purser. There would be no question about what drugs and splints and bandages a surgeon needed when he shipped out on a water hoy or Fast Dispatch Vessel to take water or messages from ship to ship on the blockade, plus a surgeon was used to emergencies.

It was a strange duty, but he enjoyed it. He loved the sea and was never seasick. He liked patch-up surgery because he was a problem-solver from childhood. He also knew unerringly when a wounded man needed a hospital, and fast. So far, there was always a sloop carrying messages back to Portsmouth or Plymouth, which meant faster travel. There was also a satellite hospital at Gibraltar, if these were Mediterranean casualties. Most larger ships of the line had a surgeon, but sometimes needed more help.

Some of the wounded men died. Others survived with better care in a hospital and not a ship's sickbay. The odds were in no one's favour, but James trusted to chance and faith in a God who had no use for Napoleon, or so he reasoned, in his logical, Scots way.

'I'll be back, sir,' he told the purser, who gave him a gallows smile. 'Another matter calls me.'

But why this? He watched the woman walk towards the clerk at the end of the hall, who spent his days fielding questions about who was where in this enormous hospital dwarfed only by the larger one in Portsmouth.

He knew he was right as he watched her gait. She was quick of step, but some oddity at birth must have rendered her right leg slightly longer than her left leg, creating a barely noticeable limp. He was aware of it because years ago he dragged her out of a pond when she was much younger, and he noticed the hesitancy of her gait on land when he walked her home.

'What in the world are you doing here?' he asked under his breath. He followed her and stopped once. If he was wrong, he was going to make a complete fool of himself. In the greater scheme of things, that wasn't so awful and wouldn't be the first time. She'd likely tell him what she thought, and he would go back to the purser's office to fight a little more for supplies. The woman would never see James Wilson again, and she could go about her business wondering about cheeky Royal Navy men.

He paused behind her, searching for the best approach. Nothing witty or debonair came to mind, so he cleared his throat and took a chance.

'Miss Langley, did you ever learn to swim?'

He was right. She gasped and turned around, reminding him all over again why he remembered her: With those big blue eyes, she was even lovelier now than soaking wet, nine years old, and yanked out of a boggy pond.

What to say now? Make a joke. He staggered back and put his hand to his heart. 'I was right. Miss Langley, how are you?'

To his complete and total amazement, she started to cry. If he hadn't been a surgeon, he probably would have turned and run. After years of fraught events and people falling apart in front of him, he knew better. He gently took her by the shoulders. 'Miss Langley, I hope I didn't frighten you. Do you remember me?'

She nodded and her tears flowed. He whipped out his handkerchief and gave it to her. She held it to her face while he admired her dark hair.

He led her to a bench away from the clerk, who watched this whole exchange with rapt astonishment. A door had opened across the hall. When he frowned and shook his head, it closed.

He let her cry, because there wasn't anything else he could do. He knew she would dry up eventually. When she did, she blew her nose, tried to find a dry spot, and dabbed at her eyes. He took out another handkerchief. She smiled at that.

'Two?'

He reached inside his uniform coat for a third, and she managed another watery smile.

'It's a medical thing, Miss Langley. Why the tears? I didn't mean to frighten you.'

She took a few deep breaths, which meant he had to admire her bosom just a little. 'Jamie Wilson,' she said, and he heard all the wonder. 'I doubt anyone calls you Jamie now.'

'James,' he said. 'What are the odds I would ever see you again, and here in this place?'

'Miniscule, I am certain,' she said. 'For fifteen years at least, I have wanted to apologise to you.'

He heard all the uncertainty and shame. 'Why?'

'I know I was responsible… It was my fault your father was fired from that odious squire's employment.'

She said this in a low voice, her head down, as if she were remembering the whole event. He remembered the matter much differently.

'Nae, lass,' he said in his best Scots accent. 'Nae.'

'I told my father what you said about teaching me to swim, and he carried the tale to the squire.'

'Everyone should know how to swim,' he told her. 'I would give the same advice to you today.'

'Papa told me the squire got all indignant, called you a bad name, and swore to be rid of the Wilsons.'

Your father told you all that? James thought, startled. *How unkind to push the blame onto your shoulders.*

He remembered the squire's visit to their cottage. The man pointed his finger at James and declared, 'Your son is a menace!' Then the awful man had noticed Jamie's twin, Dougie, who did like a little mischief. '*Both* your wretched sons!'

The story *he* told was of a no-good youth leering at a young girl and telling her he could teach her to swim, but she'd have to take off her clothes. James shook his head at the memory. He tried to explain to the squire that he told Jerusha she would have to remove her coat for a swimming lesson. That was all.

As he looked at the pretty Miss Langley, who regarded him with shame in her eyes, he knew she wasn't someone he ever wanted to lie to, not then, not now, not ever. 'The squire accused me of wanting to take liberties with you and he sacked my father on the spot.'

'All you did was yank me out of a duck-pond and tell me I should learn to swim,' she said. 'I am so sorry it came to that. I truly am.'

'I hate to think that you fretted about the matter for fifteen years,' he said. 'Here's the irony: My father was heartily tired of the squire. He had been in correspondence with a laird in the Highlands, who offered him a position as steward. Da was composing a letter of resignation to the squire when he burst into our house.' He touched her cheek—couldn't help himself. 'We were gone in a week, and never looked back. You stewed about this for naught, dear lady.'

'Surgeon Wilson!'

James glanced towards the office he had left. 'Duty calls. Follow me?'

You either will or won't, he reasoned. *Please do.*

To his delight, she came with him. He wanted to ask her if she was looking for her husband. She was of an age to have one of those, and with such a lovely face, there must be someone in Stonehouse—damn the man—eager to see her. Perhaps an officer. But no, she had answered to Miss Langley. Not that it was his business, but here she was, hurrying to keep up with him. He slowed his steps, remembering that he was not due to sail for another week.

'Wait here, please,' he said, pointing to a bench outside the purser's office. 'I must do battle with the thief and rascal who controls the supplies.'

She smiled at that. 'Both of my parents warned me about the Royal Navy.'

'And here you are? You had better explain yourself, Miss Langley.'

He went into the office, ready to surrender and sign anything, if she would still be waiting on the bench when he finished. To his amazement, the purser declared, 'You win. Take the additional laudanum and silver nitrate. I'd rather lose my soul than argue another minute with a Scot.'

Pursers have no souls, James thought, but he did not say it.

He signed everywhere indicated and told the purser's mate to box the medicine and deliver it to Number Eight Quarters within the hour. His housekeeper, Mags McDonald, would stow it with the other supplies destined for the blockade when he sailed again. He had five days.

To do what? he asked himself.

He had no idea, really, beyond the pleasure of seeing a half-forgotten face in an unexpected place. He was far too busy to be lonely, wasn't he?

Well, wasn't he?

Chapter Nine

Jerusha knew it wasn't too late to hurry outside where Napier waited. She glanced inside the office, thinking for a moment that this was impossible. No, there Jamie stood, leaning over to sign some papers. She reminded herself that fifteen years had passed, and she didn't know a thing about *this* James Wilson.

She looked again. He was taller, certainly, and well built in that way of solid men. Capability came to mind, which was the one thing that she remembered from her childhood. He had just waded in and plucked her out of the duck-pond. He didn't waste a moment. No surprise to her that he was a surgeon.

I daren't waste his time, she thought. *I'll leave now.*

She couldn't. She waited, for what she couldn't say, but she couldn't leave. A few minutes would catch her up on his life. She could answer any questions he had, and that would be that.

'I'm glad you didn't run away,' Jamie said.

Startled, she looked up from an in-depth study of her hands. He had a satchel slung over one shoulder, which he pulled aside when he sat. She didn't move over to give him more room. She smiled to see freckles still on his nose, that brand of a Scot.

'I wasn't going to run away,' she told him. 'Do you remember Mrs Pingree? She was the vicarage cook.'

'Aye, she and me mum stayed in touch for a few years. Alas, Mum died four years ago. Is Mrs Pingree still there?'

'She is. Years ago, Mrs Pingree told me she thought you

were the twin who had joined the Royal Navy at thirteen years of age. She heard you were a surgeon's mate.'

'I passed my exams and orals four years ago, and I am a surgeon now.' He touched the caduceus outlined in green on his collar. 'How is it that you are here?'

She remembered Napier and stood up. 'It's a long story, but right now I need to rescue an old gentleman.'

'Did he fall into a duck-pond?'

She laughed and felt immeasurably better. 'No! He is a butler for Lady Oakshott, who is my mother's sister.'

He raised his eyebrows. 'I thought you were a vicar's daughter.'

'I am. My aunt married well.' She reconsidered and settled on the truth. 'I doubt *I* would have chosen an older man with bad breath and of staunch opinion, but she likes being called Lady Oakshott.'

He smiled at that. 'Let's find this butler. I'd like to know why *you* are here.'

Napier sat where she had left him. He was far enough away, giving her time to explain Plymouth. She didn't know why Jamie got a little tight about the mouth when she told him she was working as a maid for her aunt who insisted upon being addressed as Lady Oakshott.

He seemed equally unhappy that her mother considered her stay in Plymouth as good experience for a lady's companion, which was likely her fate, since no suitors ever came 'round. He opened his mouth to make a comment, then closed it, so she didn't have to explain her lack of dowry and embarrass them both.

She almost hated for the meander to end, but here was Napier. She introduced him and knew it was time to explain the basket. Since the whole business seemed faintly silly to her, she couldn't imagine how silly it must sound to someone who actually treated grievous wounds with items beyond cod's liver oil and throat lozenges.

'We are here to deliver a basket for poor, suffering officers. An admiral's wife engineered this scheme. My aunt is trying to work her way into Plymouth social circles before she sells the house where we are staying now.' Oh, dear, that was blunt.

'May I?'

She nodded. He lifted the cloth and chuckled. 'Looks harmless enough.'

'Will it do anyone any good?'

'My, but you go to the heart of a subject, don't you?'

She felt her face grow red. 'P'raps I am as opinionated as Lady Oakshott's late husband.'

'There's no harm in having an opinion. What this will do is cheer someone to know that his country cares about him. Would you consider taking it to one of the enlisted men's buildings? Mine, perhaps?'

'I would, but Lady Oakshott would not.'

Jerusha was certain her statement would create a sudden chasm between them, hers of gentle breeding and his, son of a steward. She decided to speak her mind. 'I would prefer that, too, but you of all people know that orders are orders.'

'Aye, miss.' He picked up the basket. 'On the condition that I drop it at Block One, then you come with me to Block Four, and see my bailiwick, at least when I am not at sea. Napier, would you care to join us?'

Please don't, Napier, Jerusha thought. *I want to walk with Jamie Wilson one more time when I'm not soaking wet and nine years old.*

Are prayers ever answered? As the child of a vicar, she hoped and was rewarded. 'I will enjoy remaining here, Jerusha,' Napier replied. 'There is a pleasant breeze and no one needs me.'

'I'll bring her back soon, Napier, and hail you a hackney,' Jamie promised.

They started across the quadrangle, Jerusha suddenly feeling too shy to do more than enjoy the lifting of fifteen years of guilt. It was a slow walk, one that included a stop where one convalescent with a leg *in absentia* sat in a wheeled chair, and another man with a bandaged eye was seated on a bench.

Jamie introduced her most properly. 'This is an acquaintance of mine from years gone by,' he told the men, then lifted the bandage on the partly absent leg. 'Looking good, Barlow. If we fit you with a peg leg, d'ye think ye might like to spend some time with the apothecary, learning a different trade?'

'Could I?' he asked. Jerusha heard the hope, and it touched her.

'Why not? You can fight Boney medicinally. I do.' Jamie glanced at Jerusha. 'It had to be medicine for me, Barlow. Firing your big guns would give me the shudders. That's why I cower on the orlop deck and take off legs.' His patient grinned.

'And me, sir?' the one-eyed patient asked. 'Is there something?'

'We'll find something,' Jamie assured him. 'I know you read, write, and cipher. If we put you with a purser, you can check *his* mathematics and keep him honest.'

The one-eyed man laughed. 'Really?'

'All it takes is one eye. You'd be rendering the Royal Navy a real favour. I'll do what I can.'

'I know you will.' The man looked at Jerusha, then back at Jamie. 'Is she your bonnie lassie?'

'Your imagination's runnin' away wi' ye,' Jamie said. He looked unperturbed, when all Jerusha could manage was to look away, her face flaming again. Did *nothing* disturb his goodwill? Then he compounded the felony. 'I dragged her out a duck-pond when she was a wee lass, and she's finally come to Plymouth to thank me.'

The one-legged patient threw back his head and laughed. 'Aye, miss, but the surgeon has a quip for everything.'

It was another one of those moments. Jerusha knew propriety suggested she return some wooden answer. She was a genteel lady, after all. She chose another path again. 'Between you and me, he lays it on a bit thick with his Scottish trowel, doesn't he?'

The patient gave her a little salute. 'Right so, miss, right so.'

They walked to a three-storey building with Block One over the entrance. 'Wait here,' he told her.

He returned minus the basket, good cheer still written all over his expressive face. 'Have you a moment for Block Four?'

'Certainly. I don't precisely understand what you do,' Jerusha said. 'You tell me you are at sea, and now we are going to Block Four.'

'I do both. As I mentioned, we are again blockading all ports in France. This means warships sailing back and forth just out of the reach of their shore batteries. The Frogs' ships are bottled up and they watch for a change of wind and our inattention to break free. It is tedious for us, and that makes it dangerous, because crews get careless.'

'These ships have surgeons, I assume,' Jerusha said. 'Then why…'

'It's a new idea, tried first at Haslar Hospital in Portsmouth. The smaller ships of war and some bomb kedges don't have surgeons. My sea duty is to travel with what is called an FDV, a Fast Dispatch Vessel, which takes messages from Admiralty to the fleet. I go along to deliver medicine and see to any emergencies.'

'Goodness.' She stopped. 'Does this sort of duty ever frighten you?'

'Always,' he said. 'I never know what to expect. Sometimes I can save a life, sometimes I can transport a grievously wounded man to a ship of the line with a surgeon, and sometimes I chance a return to England with a patient.'

How can you look so good-natured? she asked herself. 'How do you…?'

'Miss Langley, I love my profession and I love my country. Well, Scotland, and I suffer you English.'

She couldn't help her laughter. It ended when they walked up the steps into Block Four. She sniffed the odour of strong carbolic and washing soap, but it wasn't powerful enough to mask the rot underneath. She put her fingers to her nose and hesitated at the door. Jamie reached in his pocket and handed her a small jar.

'It's camphor. Dab a little under your nose. It helps.'

She did as he said, blinking at the equally strong disinfectant.

'Better?'

She nodded. She followed him up to the first floor. 'Jonathan Kidwell is chief surgeon in this block,' he said. 'I make it about one and a half when I am here. There are hospital stewards, one to a floor, plus a matron. Here we are.'

He opened the door on rows of iron bedsteads. All eyes turned towards them, even the bandaged ones. Jerusha pressed her lips tight to keep from bursting into tears.

Then an astonishing thing happened, something that made her take Jamie Wilson's hand like the commonest woman in Plymouth. They whistled at her. 'Three cheers!' someone shouted, and huzzahs rang out.

The surgeon squeezed her hand. 'You are an instant success, Miss Jerusha Langley,' he said quietly. 'Above and beyond throat lozenges for officers, will you come here and do some real good?' He leaned closer until his lips nearly brushed her ear. 'Um…perhaps this is how you pay me back for saving your life in that duck-pond.'

Chapter Ten

It was a quiet ride home in the hackney with Napier, until the butler's curiosity got the better of him. 'Miss Langley, kindly tell me what is going on.'

Oh, you mean when our heads were close together? she thought, wondering how an obedient, biddable young lady could for even one second consider James Wilson's suggestion.

'Nothing of consequence, Napier,' she lied, then regretted her lie immediately. As she saw the disappointment in his eyes, it occurred to her forcefully that servants, and she must remember to include herself, had so little to look forward to. Life with Lady Oakshott was nothing but dull.

There may have been a time when Sir Harvey Oakshott was still alive and there were parties, but those times were over. Lady Oakshott, always imperious, seemed oddly adrift. If she had an ally, it might be Napier.

Either trust him or don't, Jerusha told herself, and took a leap of faith.

'Napier, James Wilson asked if I would come to Block Four several times a week and write letters for his patients,' she said. 'Some are blind, some are illiterate, and others have missing hands. He…he said it would do them no end of good.'

'Lady Oakshott would never allow it.'

Jerusha knew that already. As she listened to the patient clop clopping of the horse, she asked herself how long it would take until she became like the horse, calmly plodding along the same roads until it died in harness.

Which is it to be, Jerusha? she asked herself. *You have only one life.*

That was her answer. 'Napier, I believe I will take the chance.'

She waited for him to object, but he did not. 'There was a time after I entered service for Sir Harvey Oakshott's that I thought I might take the King's Shilling,' he told her. 'There were wars in Germany, and I wanted excitement.'

'You, Napier?' she asked, then reminded herself that he wasn't always old.

'I was ready to run away from Oaklands.' He sighed, and she heard the regret. 'I lost my nerve, stayed, and here I am.'

Jerusha wanted to tell him that he probably made the prudent choice, and look, he was a butler, but she couldn't. 'This might not end well for me,' she said. 'I doubt Lady Oakshott will approve.'

The butler shrugged and turned his attention to the view. When the jarvey tugged back on the reins and spoke softly to his horse in front of number twenty-eight Finch Street, Napier helped her from the hackney and paid the man. They spoke for a few minutes and the butler indicated she come close.

'Jerusha, this is Jake O'Toole. He promised me that he will be here tomorrow morning at seven of the clock. He will also be at the head of the quadrangle at ten of the clock.' He noticed her hesitation. 'I will pay your fare until we at least decide if this is the course you wish to follow.'

'Oh, but…' she began.

He shook his head with a smile. 'If you don't take a chance, you will end up like me.'

Tears rose in her eyes. This kind man she barely knew was going to do something bold for her. The least she could do was match his kindness with courage. 'If I end up like you, Mr Napier, I will be a kind person.'

'You already are.' He stepped back. 'Mr O'Toole, stop at the corner tomorrow morning at seven.'

The jarvey touched his whip to his hat, then set his horse in motion, off to find another fare. 'Thank you, Napier,' she said simply. 'I don't have much money…'

'I have no family, Jerusha. Let me do this for you.'

'Why?' she asked simply.

'I have a good feeling about it.'

James Wilson watched the hackney leave Stonehouse and stood a moment in thought, hands in his pockets, wondering what Jerusha Langley would do tomorrow. He marvelled that his day had begun as all days did at Stonehouse, a quick breakfast, and a fast walk to Block Four, where he knew that once he stepped inside 'his' wards, there would be no peace or time to reflect upon anything except the duty before him.

The only change came when the bell clanged in the jetty to announce the arrival of the wounded, who were deposited in the quadrangle for a grim sorting. He went immediately to work, concentrating on the mayhem before him and doing everything in his puny power to alleviate suffering and keep Hippocrates content.

It was midnight when he walked back to his house, hands again shoved deep in his pockets. He guessed and second-guessed and told himself that Miss Langley was too smart to take him up on his generous offer to overwork her.

'You have some nerve, Jamie boy,' he muttered as he walked along. He wondered all over again how he had recognised her after so many years. It was only that slight limp, because he barely glimpsed her face. Why had he even remembered such a tiny detail? He smiled to himself, recalling a lecture at the medical school in Edinburgh where he had spent a spare six weeks, before heading to sea to be taught on the job by surgeons on the orlop deck.

The lecturer had spoken briefly of the brain, only enough to assure them that too much injury to the head warranted setting the poor sod aside in a quiet spot on a noisy, creaking ship with guns at play, to die, because die he would. 'Lads, we know nothing of the brain,' the instructor told them, then pointed at each student in turn. 'What goes on inside *your* brain will probably always be a mystery, especially during our oral tests.'

He smiled at the good-natured laughter that followed.

My brain is remembering something about Jerusha Langley, he settled on. *Thank you, brain.*

His was a short walk to the modest row of houses behind the administration building. There were two grand houses there for the physician in charge and a surgeon in residence. The four smaller quarters were for each block's chief surgeon, and two more for clerks. One of those last two had been allocated to him, since he had no family and required little space.

As small as it was, the house was his alone, an unheard-of luxury for a steward's son who went to sea and moved up the ranks because he had medical skills even he only dimly suspected, at first.

He had no hope that Mags, his housekeeper, would be awake when he returned, but somehow, she was, properly nightgowned and robed and her hair in neat braids, ready with a mug of steaming cocoa. With no fanfare, they sat down in the tiny dining room and he told her about his day. 'The name-less blind man still refuses to consider sending for his wife, there's a double amputee from York and too much diarrhoea.' He sipped his cocoa and felt himself relax.

'There's more,' she told him. 'I see it in your face.'

How did Mags do that? He drained the cocoa and told her about Jerusha Langley. 'She was a drowned rat and I yanked her out of a duck-pond,' he said. 'I doubt she was more than nine years of age, and there she was, in the Admin Building this afternoon.'

While Mags looked at him with lively eyes, he told her he had asked her to return to Block Four and write letters for the wounded men. 'I am an idiot,' he concluded.

'Do you think she will show up?' Mags asked. 'Thousands wouldn't.'

Would she? He felt his eyes growing heavy as the twelve-hour day took its toll. 'Would you?'

'That would depend.'

'On what, Mags?'

'On how I felt about you.'

He laughed. 'I have no idea what Jerusha Langley is thinking.'

'And what are *you* thinking, James Wilson?'

He had no answer, even as he felt heat move north and bloom on his face. Hopefully, it was too dark in the kitchen lit with only a branch of candles for Mags McDonald to see a surgeon blush.

Chapter Eleven

I am a thief in the night, Jerusha thought, as she dressed quietly.

The sun was already up and Finch Street looked as prosaic as usual. There weren't any squeaking steps to avoid. No suspicious persons lurked.

Napier met her in the foyer and opened the door on the beautiful day. He looked at his timepiece and nodded approvingly when Jake O'Toole pulled up at the end of the street.

Jerusha hesitated as the butler prepared to give her a hand up. 'Napier, this could backfire spectacularly.'

'Lady Oakshott is fixed in her habits,' he assured her, 'and we know that Abbie and René will never cause you grief. Go do some good.'

She doubted Plymouth and nearby Devonport ever slumbered during wartime. The dry docks already hummed with the sound of hammer and saw. As she watched, her mouth open, a gang of men stepped a mast in place. She held her breath as it quivered, then sank into its slot.

When the hackney stopped at the foot of the quadrangle, Jerusha lost her nerve.

What am I doing here, alternated with *Aunt Hortensia will never approve*.

She stared down at her hands as Mr O'Toole opened the door.

'Miss Langley?' he asked, when she didn't move.

'Mr O'Toole, I shouldn't be here,' she said, barely above a whisper.

'Miss Langley, listen now,' the jarvey said. 'My only child went to sea and died in a battle with the Frogs in the Mediterranean. He was buried at sea.' He took a deep breath. 'I think of him every day. Somewhere is a mother or father thinking about a lad here. They probably wish they could be where you are. Just give it a go this once, miss. Do it for Billy O'Toole.'

She let him help her down. 'For today. Then we shall see.'

He touched his whip to his hat. 'That's all I ask.'

She stood there, too afraid to move. 'This will never do,' she scolded herself, after looking around to make sure no one was listening. 'You are twenty-five. Move!' She moved, unaware that she was under observation on the first floor of Block Four, by Surgeons Wilson and Kidwell.

'Is that her?' Jonathan Kidwell asked.

'The very same, sir,' James assured his chief. 'I did not know if she would do this.'

'Encourage her.'

There she stood in the open door, which warmed his heart in ways unimaginable. 'I nearly turned around,' she admitted. 'I'm practising a great misdemeanour, being here.'

He motioned her closer, wanting to hurry her upstairs to his chaotic world. 'How so?'

'My parents made me promise to have nothing to do with the Royal Navy,' she told him, 'and Lady Oakshott said the same thing.'

'Wise of them,' he said, then couldn't help his laugh. 'Miss Langley…'

'Jerusha,' she said quickly, which warmed his heart another notch.

'Very well then, Jerusha.' He was so pleased he could have wriggled like a puppy, but he knew better. 'Let me assure you there isn't any patient in Block Four that you can't outrun.'

What she said next put him on notice. It was nothing he expected.

'Does that include you?' she asked, and gave him a clear-eyed look.

There was only one thing to do, because her plain speaking surprised him. He started to limp, which meant a hearty laugh from that person he saved years ago from a duck-pond. It was no simper, but the kind of belly laugh that made him laugh, too. Good God, she was perfect for Block Four.

He took his chances on the stairs, since she seemed determined now. 'There are between twenty and thirty patients per floor, Wards A and B. Some will recuperate and some won't. The ones who won't are on Ward B, and you needn't go there.'

'I might cry.'

'Then you'll join the rest of us,' he said without hesitation. 'Paper and pencil?'

'I brought some,' she said. 'Lady Oakshott will never miss it. I need a writing board.'

'I'll find one.'

As they approached Ward A, he thought to offer her more camphor from the jar in his pocket, but changed his mind. She needed to get used to hospital odours.

He opened the door and ushered her inside. Jon Kidwell turned from the window and executed an elegant bow, considering that he only had a leg and a peg. Jerusha dipped a curtsy and came to him, a nicety that made the older man nod his approval.

'Miss Langley, this is Chief Surgeon Kidwell,' James said. 'I believe he has forgotten more than I will ever know about medicine.'

Jon tapped his wooden leg. 'I earned this is an earlier war against the Dutch. The Powers That Be turned me out to pasture, but were happy enough to see me here at our sick bay that doesn't float, when our troubles began with Boney.' He gestured to James. 'This lad is faster on stairs than I am.'

'What *he* is, is superior to us all,' James said, in his Scots way, never comfortable with a compliment. 'Let me introduce you to our motley crew.'

He hadn't expected what followed, but there was Jerusha Langley, walking down the rows by herself. She stopped a moment by a one-armed Marine, who was trying to take a jar lid off with his teeth. She sat beside him and held out her hand. He handed it to her with a grin and she quickly removed it, then peered inside.

'You're the lucky one,' she declared. 'Cubes of sugar?'

'My wife sent them,' he said. 'She lives in Dover.' He popped a cube in his mouth, then held out the jar to her. James smiled inside when she popped a cube in her mouth, too, then rolled her eyes. 'Divine. She must really, really love you.'

The sergeant of Marines laughed. 'Aye, miss, she really, really does.' His face fell. 'Maybe. She…she knows about my arm, but I haven't written to her yet.'

Jerusha leaned closer to the man. James could only admire her animation. The Marine's arm, what remained of it, was bare and stitched with black sutures, but she did not falter. 'Are you right-handed?' she asked. 'I can write for you.'

'I'm left-handed, but th-that's not it. I'm just…' He looked away.

'Maybe a little nervous to write?' Jerusha asked, her voice gentle, but in no way condescending. 'It's probably a little hard to hold down a piece of paper and get properly situated, isn't it?'

He nodded, thought better of it, and shook his head. 'Maybe I'm a little afraid, too.'

'You tell me what to write and I'll do it for you this time,' Jerusha said. She removed her bonnet. 'You can write to her the next time.' She turned to James. 'Surgeon Wilson, could you find me that writing board?'

'I'll go.' Surgeon Kidwell limped away and returned with a tray. 'We were going to introduce you to these miscreants and malingerers, Miss Langley.'

'This comes first, sir,' she said. She returned her attention to the one-armed Marine lying in the iron cot, who, to James's amazement seemed to lie there a little straighter, and certainly more alert. Jerusha uncapped the ink, positioned the paper, and began.

The Marine opened his mouth, closed it, looked at his little secretary, and began to weep. Surgeon Kidwell leaned forward to take charge, but James put a hand on his arm.

'She has good instincts, sir,' he said. 'Let's step back.'

Praying he was right—how well did he really know her?— James watched as she put her hand on the Marine's remaining arm. When he stopped weeping, she took a handkerchief from her sleeve and wiped his eyes.

He gathered himself together, then must have remembered that he was a Marine. 'Miss... Miss...'

'Jerusha will do,' she said quietly.

James was suddenly aware that the entire ward had gone silent. No one was slapping down cards and there was no coarse laughter. Were they *all* listening? By God, they were.

'Jerusha, if my Marines ever find out what I just did...'

She laughed. 'It's our little secret, Sergeant.'

To James's delight, one of the sergeant's Marines called out, 'Three cheers for Sergeant Mulvaney!'

After the hip hips and huzzahs rang out, everyone returned to his bedbound business. The cards slapped down again and someone burped. The picture of serenity, Jerusha dipped her pen in the ink. 'What's her name, Sergeant Mulvaney?'

'Sylvie,' he said, his voice assured now. 'I met her in Montreal. We have three children.'

'Dear Sylvie?' Jerusha prompted.

'Dearest,' he replied, and began to dictate. 'My love, I know you already have the news…'

Surgeon Kidwell took James by the arm and led him to the matron's desk. 'She has a sure touch, James, my lad. How did you know?'

How indeed? he asked himself. His only association with Jerusha Langley had been a brief one at a duck-pond. A man of science and not of religion, he had no rational explanation.

'Dumb luck, sir.'

The letter took a lengthy time, with pauses where Jerusha simply sat there and held his hand while the battle-hardened Marine wept. When he finished, he looked at peace. In a few minutes, he slept. Jerusha carefully folded the many-page letter and handed it to James.

'He said you have Sylvie Mulvaney's direction,' she told him.

'I do. This will be posted today,' James told her. 'Let me walk you through the ward now. There will be time to meet the men tomorrow.'

'Wednesday,' she corrected. 'Three times a week. I daren't take more chances than that, and besides, Abbie and I are cleaning the downstairs rooms. I think Lady Oakshott is going to invite some guests for dinner. I have to help Abbie with the rooms.'

It seemed strange to James that Lady Oakshott was so short of domestics, but it wasn't his business to question Jerusha. Still, there was one pressing matter.

'I suppose your jarvey is waiting below,' he said. 'It's half ten of the clock.'

'Oh, my, yes,' she said, and put on her bonnet, which made the more alert patients practically sigh in unison. James put up his hand. 'Gentlemen, Jerusha has other commitments, but she will be here on Mondays, Wednesdays, and I think Fridays. Fridays, Miss Langley?'

'Aye,' she said. 'Always.'

Aye or nae? He paused at a cot with a long list of surgeons' notes, his among them. 'I doubt this man will make it to Wednesday. Please say hello to him. He's been watching you.'

'I can't imagine why.'

Have you no idea how lovely you are? he thought.

'Jerusha, you're so pretty. Don't blush; it's true.'

'Surgeon Wilson, you are a flirt and a danger to society,' she told him, which made him grin, something he never did at this particular bedside.

'Sit here a moment,' he whispered, before putting out a chair for her. 'Corporal Meade is another of Sergeant Mulvaney's men. They were mauled in a sharp fight before Brest, when their bomb kedge exploded. I doubt he had another day left in him.'

She sat without question. He knew then what it was he remembered about her, from the duck-pond. Her eyes met his and he saw all the determination in her. This was not a woman to be trifled with.

'Corporal Meade, Miss Jerusha Langley wanted to meet you,' he told the dying Marine. 'She's from near Bolling, which I believe isn't far from your home in Dalton.'

Corporal Meade managed a smile. 'Not far at all.'

'Perhaps you know my father,' Jerusha said, her hand on the corporal's arm. 'He is vicar of Bolling Parish.'

'Never went to church,' he said. 'Never had good clothes. Mam has a Bible, though.'

James saw a shadow cross her face, making him wonder if Vicar Langley was the sort of clergyman who differentiated between the poor and the deserving poor. He thought he knew the answer.

'I am certain she read it to you,' she told the corporal. 'Would you like me to read to you tomorrow?'

'But, Miss Langley, you told me you couldn't...' James began.

'I mixed up my days,' she said, silencing him. 'I will most certainly be here tomorrow. Until then, Corporal Meade.'

Chapter Twelve

'You're late,' Mr O'Toole told her when she ran to the hackney. She didn't think he was angry, but she burst into tears anyway.

He neither flinched nor faltered but clapped his arm around her shoulders. 'Hospitals are tough places, Miss Langley. D'ye want me to run Surgeon Wilson down in the street on some dark night and put you out of your misery?'

That brought a welcome chuckle. 'No, Mr O'Toole. I do need to be here tomorrow morning at seven of the clock. Someone needs me.'

'I hope you don't get in trouble with Lady Oakshott. I'm not supposed to pick you up again until Wednesday,' he reminded her, sounding remarkably like a parent.

'She is never an early riser. Tomorrow, please.'

She was back at number twenty-eight Finch Street before eleven, Napier watching for her at the open door. She didn't know him well enough to interpret his 'butler face,' but his 'No worries, Miss Langley,' set her at ease. She was soon dressed in what she thought of as her 'biddable dress,' a plain dark blue cotton with a modest lace collar, grand enough to greet mostly non-existent visitors, but with an added apron, good enough for helping Abbie with their latest task, washing windows inside the sitting room while René balanced precariously outside and did the same.

At precisely noon, she carried breakfast and the day's mail to her aunt's bedroom and opened the draperies on a day she was already quite familiar with.

What a lazy aunt you are, she thought.

As she plastered on a smile, she discovered that she didn't really care for subterfuge. It was not her first twinge of conscience about the matter, but she subdued it, considering all the good she might do at Stonehouse, whether Lady Oakshott liked it or not.

She spent this afternoon in trivialities. Her aunt had exclaimed over her excellent penmanship, so it became Jerusha's duty to answer all correspondence. This meant dictated letters to Admiral Mrs This or That, or a Lady Beecroft that Aunt Hortensia already informed her was a vulgar woman married to a wealthy merchant of marine goods whose title came from Prinny because he provided a loan that turned into a gift. Jerusha was wise enough not to comment that the late and mostly unlamented Harvey Oakshott had a similar background.

Wonder of wonders, there was even a visit from Admiral Mrs Stoppard, bubbling over with self-congratulation over the delivery of the baskets to Stonehouse officers' blocks. Jerusha listened from the desk by the window, where she attempted to translate her aunt's nearly illiterate scrawl unto lovely prose.

'Jerusha, how was your delivery received?' Aunt Hortensia asked.

'I took it to the front desk in Block One,' she said. 'I assume it was delivered appropriately.'

'You were supposed to speak to a physician and deliver the basket to an officer yourself,' her aunt reminded her.

'I apologise then,' Jerusha said. She tried to resist, but couldn't. 'Aun... Lady Oakshott, I wonder if any future baskets might be better appreciated among the ordinary seamen. Their families are not so likely to have the ability to travel to bedsides as easily as officers' families.'

Both ladies looked at her as if she was wanting, indeed. 'Rabble,' Mrs Admiral Stoppard said.

Rabble? Jerusha thought. *Your captains and admirals would never leave port without those rabble.*

She pasted on an apologetic smile, even more determined to hold that dying rabble's hand tomorrow, provided he survived the night.

'We deal *only* with officers and their families,' Aunt Hortensia reminded her. Mrs Admiral Stoppard nodded vigorously, which set the feathers on her bonnet expressing themselves, as well.

How will I survive a summer here? Jerusha asked herself below stairs that evening as they ate.

She told her below stairs companions of the Royal Marine sergeant who was so grateful she wrote a letter for him to his wife, and the others who flirted with their eyes, which meant that they would probably live to fight another day.

She dreaded another evening in the sitting room, knitting and listening to her aunt go on and on about life at Oaklands and wondering what crisis the Cit she had rented it to for the summer was causing among the neighbours and staff.

Jerusha looked up from her knitting. 'Why did you let it out in the first place?' she asked, and got a glare for her pains.

'Simple girl, I told you I am preparing to sell this place,' Lady Oakshott snapped. To Jerusha's relief, she turned her attention to her card table, where she played Patience and cheated. Eventually she flounced upstairs and Jerusha followed without the flounce. Another boring night at number twenty-eight Finch Street.

It was even easier to slip out of the house at half past six the next morning. No one was awake, not even the ever-watchful Napier.

'Mr O'Toole, am I crazy to do this?' she asked as Mr O'Toole nodded a greeting to her from his perch.

'You're entirely sane, in a world gone mad,' he assured her.

She thought about that as the jarvey made his way to Stonehouse. She leaned back, enjoying the momentary peace and thinking of all the times her mother had insisted, for form's sake, that even a visit to the local grocer's in Bolling included taking a maid along. To be by herself felt like liberation. True, the responsibility seemed to increase, but she welcomed it because she suspected she was a woman of good sense.

As they pulled up to the quadrangle and circled around to the ward blocks, Jerusha wondered if Jamie Wilson would understand what she was only beginning to learn about herself.

I could use a friend, she thought, as she thanked Mr O'Toole, and paid him for the journey this extra day.

As she watched Mr O'Toole drive away, she noticed bits of what looked like bloody bandages littering the courtyard's grassy expanse. She saw stretchers leaning against the buildings, and men slumped beside them. She sucked in her breath, thinking they were dead, until she heard snoring as she hurried to the entrance.

'I wonder...' she said out loud. The jetty bells must have rung last night.

There were more bloody stretchers inside, two of them with their occupants still in place, but shrouded now, their journey over.

You are right, Mr O'Toole, she thought. *This truly is a world gone mad.*

'Miss Langley, I didn't expect to see you today,' she heard over her shoulder, and looked around to see a bleary-eyed Jonathan Kidwell.

'What has happened here?' she asked, turning aside his question. 'Perhaps you should sit down, sir. Here's a chair.'

My, but I am commanding, Jerusha thought, as she pushed a chair forward.

The one-legged surgeon sat, and she saw the relief.

'The jetty bell rang at midnight,' he said, accepting a glass of water from her that she found on a nearby table. 'We have been sorting the wounded and stashing them here and there.' He set down the glass. 'Why are you here? Unless the ordeal was longer than I thought, it's not Wednesday yet.'

'It's for Corporal Meade,' she told him. 'I…held his hand yesterday, and I don't think I am done yet.'

He smiled at that, which threw off the years from his lined face. He nodded towards the stairs. 'He's behind a curtain now. James is with him.'

She hesitated on the stairs. 'No fears, Miss Langley. There's nothing as welcome as a kind touch.' He smiled and looked away. 'Be it for Corporal Meade or Surgeon Wilson, who doesn't like to surrender patients to death. None of us do.'

She lifted her skirts higher than she usually would on stairs, because these treads still were bloody in spots, waiting for the morning clean-up crew perhaps, or maybe for someone to have a moment to swab away.

The ward was silent. She passed the Royal Marine sergeant, asleep, who twitched as he slept, perhaps in the thrall of battle dreams. She hoped his letter to Sylvie would bring a prompt reply.

There was the curtain, navy blue with a fouled anchor in faded yellow. She drew the curtain aside and knew beyond question that she was needed. Corporal Meade looked at her, his eyes barely open. He managed a smile. He looked at her, then glanced to his left, not moving his head, to the sleeping surgeon who held his hand.

'I think he's had a night of it, Corporal Meade,' she whispered.

He nodded, then closed his eyes. She thought for one terrifying second that he was dead. In a panic, she watched his chest, then breathed out herself when it rose and fell again.

There was a basin half full of water, and a clean rag. Unsure but certain she could never hurt someone already so far gone, she wrung out the rag and wiped the corporal's face. He didn't open his eyes, but his sigh sounded contented, almost as if she was doing something useful and restorative, even though she knew that wasn't the case.

James's eyes opened. 'You came.'

Jerusha saw all the exhaustion in them and knew it had been an endless night. 'Said I would. Let me sit here a while beside Corporal Meade,' she whispered.

He stood up and she took his place, holding the dying man's hand. Corporal Meade opened his eyes and gave her a slight nod. 'Softer,' was all he said.

She stroked the man's hand as he breathed, forgot to breathe, then breathed again until the next time. For a few minutes she was Maudie, then pretty Maudie. As death pressed down, and as James Wilson watched from the chair next to hers, she turned into Mam, and then Mama, over and over.

'They always ask for their mothers when they are *in extremis*,' Jamie whispered. 'Even the lads who came to the navy from workhouses and probably never knew their mothers. I'll never understand it.'

They're only going back where they began, she told herself.

She held Corporal Meade's hand, then pressed it to her cheek, letting her tears water his fingers. She held her breath when he patted her cheek once, then again. Who comforted who? 'Sleep well, son,' she told him, and he died.

James dragged out his timepiece as if it weighed ten pounds and stared at it. 'I call it at zero eight one five,' he said, then reached for the chart, writing the time of death, and adding his initials. Without a word, he rose and pulled back the curtain, leaving her there alone.

Startled, she frowned at his coldness, then held her breath as his shoulders started to shake. 'Poor, poor man,' she whispered.

Imagine doing this day after week after year, Jerusha Langley, she scolded herself.

She had no idea of the usual protocol, but did it matter? She carefully straightened the collar on Corporal Meade's nightshirt and wiped his face again. Where she had seen pain, she saw only calm. 'Where are you now?' she asked him. 'I would write to Maudie, but I haven't an address.' She pulled the sheet over his face. Rabble, indeed.

Mrs Terwilliger, the matron, had watched the whole matter from her desk, her face impassive. Jerusha still had the washcloth in her hand. 'If you tell me where I can get more water, I can wash a few faces,' she said. She looked around at cots that were empty only yesterday. 'I'm not skilled for anything else.'

Mrs Terwilliger looked at James Wilson, who had walked to the end of the ward and stood there leaning his forehead against the wall. 'That one will be all right in a few minutes. I'll get you water.' She pointed to the new residents. 'These are the latest, courtesy of the jetty bells.'

Jerusha wiped away grime and dirt from drowsy men's faces. She shook her finger at one man who, livelier than most, patted her breast. The others were respectful and told her 'Thank 'ee,' as if she had done something miraculous. One sailor tugged at her skirt, and she sat beside him until he closed his eyes with something close to contentment and died.

James was nowhere in sight now. Surgeon Kidwell appeared to be setting a bone. Jerusha retrieved her bonnet and left the ward and then Block Four. She hadn't told Mr O'Toole when she might need him, so she walked back to Finch Street, arriving after eleven o'clock. She had moved along purposefully, so no one bothered her.

She didn't think the distance was much more than two miles. She passed men and women engaged in building, buying, haggling, and selling, as if this were an ordinary day, and not the day when she, Jerusha Langley, knew for certain there was work to be done that had nothing to do with Lady Oakshott.

Chapter Thirteen

'You weren't afraid to walk from Devonport?' Abbie asked, her eyes wide with worry. Watching from the window in the foyer, she opened the door before Jerusha could raise her hand to the knocker and dragged her inside.

'No pirates swooped down and carried me off,' Jerusha assured her, then couldn't resist. 'Someone must have told them I'm all of twenty-five with no dowry. What is the alarm? I know it is not noon yet.'

'I heard her moving around and muttering to herself,' Abbie whispered, as if Lady Oakshott stood in the next room.

In odd confirmation, the bell from that upstairs chamber jangled below stairs. 'You'd better hurry,' the young one said.

Jerusha looked down at her walking dress in dismay. 'I haven't time to change.'

'Just put on an apron. You'll think of something,' Abbie said. 'What can she want so early?'

Jerusha did as Abbie said. She hoped her aunt hadn't seen her from an upstairs window. As she climbed the stairs in some dread, Jerusha knew subterfuge did not sit well with her, even when the cause was most noble.

She opened the door to see her aunt sitting in bed, looking perturbed, out of sorts, and mostly spoiled. 'I cannot sleep in this wretched house,' she announced, then took a closer look at Jerusha. 'Where have *you* been?'

Tell the truth, Jerusha told herself, but could not. 'I went for a little walk,' she lied, hushing her conscience, for it was sort of true. 'It's a fine morning, Aunt Hortensia.'

'You are *not* to call me that.'

'Beg pardon, Lady Oakshott,' she said promptly, crossing her fingers that would be enough inquisition.

It was. Her aunt squinted at her bedside clock. 'Silly girl, why didn't you bring me the mail?' she asked. 'Add a biscuit to the chamomile tea. Go on now.'

She did as she was bid, grateful to escape without any more questions or scrutiny. 'I can't keep up this pretence,' she told René as he prepared two biscuits and Abbie poured tea.

The cook shrugged, a Gallic affectation he had mastered well. 'The old rip ain't much given to contemplation on any subject that does not involve her directly.'

But I know better, she wanted to tell him, then considered the source.

'René, I already know that you are not really French. Where are you from? What is your name?'

He snapped a towel at her. 'From Manchester. Me, work in the mill? Never. I ran away. I'm Robby Blair.' He bowed and she laughed. No, this wasn't a man to be concerned about anyone's false impression. Maybe she needn't give the matter another thought.

She did, though, all the way upstairs, and it weighed heavily on her, at least until she set down the tray and her aunt pounced on the cream-coloured letter with elegant calligraphy. She tore it open, read it, and clutched it to her bosom, her eyes gazing heavenward. 'I am saved!'

Jerusha stared at her. 'What…'

Aunt Hortensia held out the invitation to her. 'I have been invited to dinner at Sir William and Lady Beecrofts' house tomorrow night!' She pulled the invitation back as Jerusha reached for it. 'I suppose this means someone else turned her down at the last moment and she reckoned I would be doing nothing.'

'Still, Aunt... Lady Oakshott, this is an honour,' Jerusha said, happy to shove her lie somewhere in the back of her mind.

Her aunt held out the invitation again. 'She wants me to bring my lady's companion. That is you, of course.'

'Lady's companion?' Jerusha asked in surprise. 'Already?'

'Your mother knows. Do as I say, and you will end up working in one of England's great houses. How good that you are so biddable, niece! You'll give no one any trouble.'

There it is, Jerusha thought later, as Lady Oakshott busied herself in her closet, searching for the perfect dinner gown.

Her future stretched before her as this new development sank in. Lady's companion? She knew it was coming, but now, and so suddenly, when she had work to do in Block Four? She chafed silently at the unfairness of it.

She mulled over the matter that evening, counting the hours as Aunt Hortensia carried on about the treat awaiting them both tomorrow evening. 'If we play whist, remember that you are to lose, if a gentleman plays opposite you. Your mother has told me how you've beaten everyone in your small circle of acquaintances. It is no wonder that you are twenty-five and single.'

Jerusha lay in bed wondering if she should ask Mr O'Toole to direct her to the nearest mail coach stop. She could be home and better off, a declared spinster. Two things stopped her: She hadn't enough money for a return to Bolling, and James Wilson needed her.

She pounded her pillow, which seemed to hold equal parts rocks and lead bars. Before she closed her eyes resolutely, determined to sleep, the unwelcome thought struck her that perhaps *she* needed Jamie Wilson more. Thoroughly unhappy with all her lies, Jerusha, daughter of a vicar, knew she was still an honest soul—hopefully. She asked herself why *she* needed Jamie Wilson, a lad in her life fleetingly, gone so long and now a man.

'I am living in a world at war,' she decided on, which seemed more honest. Almost but not quite. 'I want to help.' That felt better, but still… 'I like him.' She said it softly, waiting for it to sound weird. It didn't.

Jerusha Langley must think I am a mutton-headed cry-baby, James told himself, as he ward-walked past sleeping men, his slatted lantern held high, looking for trouble before he sat down, because he knew he would fall asleep immediately.

Not this time. He sat beside Blind Man. His chart even said Blind Man, because he had been fished from the waters off Brest with the usual piecemeal uniform of a Royal Navy man long on the blockade. Some catastrophe had left him blind. He had no identifying papers on him and he refused to speak.

Trauma did that to some. It had been James's experience, though, that once a man was fished out, dried off, and fed, the mind began to right itself. Not in Blind Man's case, however. He spoke, and his accent was the slow drawl of the Cornishman, probably not so far from Plymouth. As the days passed, he sank into total silence.

They tried. The only thing in his pocket was a water-soaked miniature of a pretty woman and a baby. 'We know your wife is wondering where you are,' got them nowhere, except a tightening of Blind Man's lips. 'I wouldn't burden her with a blind man,' was all anyone could coax from him. That was it.

Surgeon Kidwell thought he was barmy. 'James, you have too much to do as it is.'

But James found himself sitting beside Blind Man when he had a free moment, and telling him about his day and the war, and the damned jetty bell. He discovered that Blind Man didn't approve of ribald commentary, oh, no. James had told him of one newly married surgeon in Block Two who came grumbling from his quarters as the bell rang, pulling on his trousers and grousing, 'I get my eager willy in me bride and that damned bell ends it. I'll never be a father.'

'Coarse humour is a curse,' Blind Man informed him, turned over and gave him the cold shoulder. The blind prude somehow knew who was who, and for too many days he had turned away when James sat down. Was it his accent? Just the fact that he sat down?

An apology from James ended the cold shoulder last week, so James sat now. But what to talk about, even if he talked to himself? 'I'm tired,' he said simply, which earned no response. Undaunted, he told Blind Man about Jerusha Langley sitting with the dying man that morning.

'She sang. I heard her,' Blind Man said to James's amazement. He heard something in his voice, a certain longing. Hopefully, he wasn't imagining it. Using a shred of wisdom—the kind that sometimes surfaced around midnight of an endless day—he stopped himself from leaping into what he knew by now was unwanted interrogation.

James groaned and stood up. 'I crack and pop when I get up. Goodnight.' He walked away, gratified by 'Goodnight,' from Blind Man, the first time he had said that.

He had one other stop before he lay down for one blissful hour, and the steward came to take over.

Sam Wycherly was a Welsh carpenter's mate, done in by the carelessness of another sailor, bored with the tedium of the blockade, who slammed down a maul on the mate's wrist when Sam held a wedge to shape a chair leg. When the mangled man arrived three weeks later at Stonehouse, amputation was the only recourse, even though Sam objected in two languages.

James discovered that Sam held no grudges. The matron wrote a letter Sam dictated, telling the man who mauled him not to dwell on the matter. James wasn't sure he could have been so forgiving, and admitted as much to Sam. All Sam did was ask James for some paper. 'I like to draw. I'm pretty good with either hand.'

Sam drew his first image of a patient across the aisle who had just drawn his last breath. He sketched quickly, but with a sure hand. 'It will bring comfort,' was all he said when he handed it to James. 'Give it to his wife, please.'

James sat a moment beside Sam, who reached for his latest work of art on the other side of his cot and held it out. 'If you know this lad's next of kin, send it on.'

James looked and looked again. It was Corporal Meade, with Jerusha Langley seated beside him, her hand in his. 'Hands are hard to draw,' Sam said. 'I can learn. Give me time.'

Time. Surgeon Kidwell had given him a memo, stating in two days he was to sail with a Fast Dispatch Vessel back to the blockade. This time, James Wilson had no urge to go, necessity be damned.

He glanced at the drawing again, absorbing some of the serenity emanating from the simple sketch of a lovely woman seated beside a wounded man, now dead, but ushered from mortality by the comfort of soft hands. The lovely woman was Jerusha, and that made all the difference.

He didn't want to go to sea, at least not so soon. He wanted to stay in Jerusha's peaceful orbit. It was a jolt of a thought: Didn't he tell her only yesterday that he loved his sea duty?

You are a drooling idiot, he told himself.

'Sir?'

James recalled himself and nodded to the artist who held out his hand. James returned the drawing with what he hoped was casual disinterest, nothing more. In this he failed. Maybe artists, even mangled carpenter's mates, heard beyond words and into the heart. James hoped he wasn't *that* obvious.

In this he failed, too. 'Sir, I'll dress it up a bit and you can send it to the corporal's widow.' He didn't stop there. James saw the Welsh shrewdness in Sam's eyes, or maybe it was understanding. 'I can draw you another picture of Miss Langley.'

There was no point in trying to bamboozle a Welshman. 'I would like that. She's a pretty lady.'

He looked up from the drawing when the door opened, and the steward stood there, looking bright and cheerful and ready for the night duty, generally peaceful enough because patients on the mend slept.

Still he waited, hoping Jerusha would somehow arrive a little early today—midnight now, if he wasn't mistaken. Lord, he *was* an idiot. She would be here in the morning! *I want to see her now*, he thought, reminding himself of a two-year-old.

'Sir?'

'Aye, steward?'

'Go to bed, sir. I'll watch them for you.'

James handed him the slatted lamp. Let the steward think he was only concerned about his patients, and not thinking of a child from his past who had come into his life again, grown up now and troubling the still waters of his bachelor complacency.

Baffled by his own foolishness, James walked the length of the ward, pausing as he always did by Blind Man, then letting himself out into the hall, down the stairs and into the cool of night. With any luck, the jetty bell would be silent and he could sleep. With even better luck, he would see Jerusha tomorrow, before he sailed for the damned blockade.

Chapter Fourteen

He overslept and woke up, his heart pounding, when Mags McDonald knocked on his door. 'Breakfast, sir.'

'You don't oversleep often,' Mrs McDonald observed, when she set porridge in front of him fifteen minutes later. She looked at him closer. 'Dab at your chin, James Wilson, for I see shaving soap.'

'What would I do without you, Mags?' he asked as he bolted his food.

'You'd be an untidy mess, unfit for a gentle companion,' she retorted, 'someday,' and made him blush, which made her laugh, a welcome sound. Maggie didn't laugh much. He knew she still missed her own companion, that red-faced, rough-hewn bosun.

James ate fast—a requirement for any surgeon or physician in wartime, he was certain—then sat back with a novel thought. No one better to ask than Mags, who knew him well.

'Margaret McDonald, do you see anything repellent about me?' he asked. 'My ears too large? Poor hygiene?'

Thank God she didn't laugh. She regarded him seriously, but he saw the lurking smile behind her eyes.

'Such a question, sir! Your ears are fine. I think you have all your teeth, and personally, I like to see a few freckles on a man's nose. Just enough, though. Some poor men have too many, in my opinion.'

He didn't tell her about the freckles on his shoulders and back, but Mags wasn't done. 'I don't recall that you have ever been drunk, in my presence, anyway. As for vices…' She plunged ahead, as any good Scotswoman would. 'At least you don't drink to excess, and you don't chase hoors.'

'No to that one! My mother warned me.'

He kissed her cheek and she cleared the table, her thoughts her own, until she sat down and laughed.

'What now, Mags?' he asked, enjoying this cheerful side of his housekeeper.

'Laddie, I was thinking of that patient of yours last year. The one wi' two wives.'

'Oh, aye,' he said, laughing, too, as he remembered Reggie Roundtree, he of the handsome visage and a leg broken in two places. It was a never-to-be-forgotten scene in Ward A, where two wives converged on his bed at the same time, took one look at each other, and fell to, shrieking and scratching at each other's eyes and rolling on the floor, affording amazed patients and surgeons alike bare-bottomed glimpses of which most women are more discreet about.

Once James separated them—getting a black eye and scratches for his pains—he gave them each a good shake and told them to sort it out or go to the brig. To his further amazement, they did as he asked, settling down, sniffling, and wiping noses on sleeves.

He should never have turned his back in them. Arriving at some mysterious comradeship, they took their understandable umbrage out on their 'husband,' who came out of *that* scrape with two black eyes and a broken nose, a wiser bigamist he.

'Reggie Roundtree! I never saw a sailor so eager to return to sea! Mags, he *was* a handsome man, and he had a way with women.'

It never failed, that tender moment when Maggie McDonald reminded him of his own dear mother, dead these four years, she with her own brand of good nature. 'Jamie, I have no idea how you are with the ladies, but I know you haven't much opportunity to find out because there is a war on.'

'Wish I did,' he said as he buttoned his uniform jacket and headed to the door.

She didn't stop there. 'You have someone in mind?'

Was he so obvious? 'I might,' he said. 'It's early days, though, Mags. Leave it at that.'

To his relief, she did, joking at him to mind his manners. He was still smiling about it when he entered Block Four and took the stairs two at a time, energised by good humour.

And there Jerusha Langley sat, giving her attention to the powder monkey who had followed her with his eyes yesterday as she moved among the patients, then sat with Corporal Meade until he died.

Her consolation now appeared as paper, pen, and ink, the very excuse he had used to enlist her help in the first place, since he admitted to himself now that he wanted to see her again and again. How else could he do it?

'I didn't know if you would come today,' he said.

'It's Wednesday, sir.'

'So it is,' he replied, professional again. He continued to his desk and the eagle eye of Mrs Terwilliger, who handed him the daily report. He looked over it—or overlooked it, because his mind and heart were both fastened on the pretty scribe at the powder monkey's bedside—until Jerusha finished, tucked the young boy's blanket higher to cover grievous wounds, and joined him at the desk.

'Who is young Michael writing to?' he asked. 'He's another product of the workhouse.'

She blushed. My God, what a lovely woman. 'I… I noticed him watching me yesterday.'

'A lot of men watch you.' James took a huge chance. 'I am not immune, either.'

Did he *say* that? She astounded him then, completely, utterly. 'Jamie, women look, too.' She smiled down at the floor. 'I happen to like freckles.' Then she hauled them both back to the business at hand. 'Mikey said he wanted to write to someone of my choosing, so he could tell his story.'

Professional again, he looked towards the powder monkey, knowing the extent of his injuries under that blanket. 'I doubt it is a cheerful story.'

She shook her head, and he saw all the sorrow of a caring person. 'It must take strong boys and girls to survive a workhouse. We both cried, and he was kind enough to hold *my* hand for a moment.' She looked at him out of lowered eyes, probably not aware of how attractive that was. 'I promised Michael Summer I would send his letter to Mr William Pitt, himself. That was who I chose. "I hope he reads it," was all Mikey said.'

'I will see that it gets to Downing Street, Miss Langley.'

'Better add a note of explanation,' Mrs Terwilliger said, from her desk. He saw she was visibly moved, and the matron was a woman who had seen everything.

'I will do that, too.' He glanced at the reports on her desk, the additions, the deletions, either because his patients were pronounced fit to serve again, or they had changed venues forever. He sighed at some of those names, wishing—as he always did—that medical knowledge was greater. With others, he felt relief that their pains were done.

He glanced at Jerusha, surprised to see her eyes on his face. He saw understanding and compassion, and he took heart for another day of this work. She held out Michael Summer's letter.

'I corrected some of his grammar as he dictated to me,' she said, 'then I decided, no, our Prime Minister should hear what I heard.' She looked into that far distance that only those at war saw, which startled him, then humbled him. He had introduced her to dying men, and she now saw what he saw. He looked down at the letter, knowing it would break his heart. He could read it later, and he would, but not now, when this kind lady stood before him, as brave as any of his patients.

'Where do they get such bravery?'

'I don't know.'

Ah, but you do, even if you don't know it yet, he thought. *Courage comes from within, that mysterious place where no matter how the enemy rages, we will defend our homeland.*

As for now, 'Please continue what you're doing,' he told her. 'Let me introduce you to our biggest question mark. Over here.'

She followed him to the bed of the blind man who seldom spoke. He wanted to explain this man, even though he had nothing to tell her. No one did.

'We know nothing,' he whispered. 'Before he turned silent, he told Surgeon Kidwell that no wife needed the burden he would be. They found him floating in the water, nary a ship in sight, after a minor fleet action near Ferrol.'

'So sad,' she whispered back.

'I cannot predict what he will do, but he is harmless. Sit down for a moment and acquaint yourself with him. We've tried everything else except a lovely lady.'

She smiled at that and sat, looking at Blind Man with more curiosity than fear. James watched as she dipped a cloth in warm water, unbuttoned the top two buttons on his nightshirt, and wiped his neck and then his face.

Blind Man opened dead eyes shot with blood until there was no white to the cornea, a sight that still made the night steward flinch.

James almost pulled her back when he cleared his throat, fearing Blind Man was going to spit at her. Instead, he sniffed and relaxed. 'Claudy, *est-ce toi*?' he said in a voice rusty with disuse. 'You?'

Chapter Fifteen

'I wish I were, but no,' Jerusha replied, hardly knowing what she said, but aware of what he had done. 'Does…does your wife wear scented talcum powder, too?'

He nodded and said nothing more. In another moment, he turned away from them, from everyone, burrowing against the place where the blanket and sheet met his pillow, a safe haven.

She had known a parishioner's cat who did that whenever anyone came to call on his mistress, an old widow supported by the parish because all her means were gone. The cat trembled and tried to squeeze himself under her armpit as he shook. 'He's shy,' the widow excused. 'He came to me a stray.'

Jerusha was only a little girl then, and Papa wanted to raise a useful child. She petted what she could reach of the little beast. It growled at her, but nothing more. Every visit, she did that, but nothing changed. She tried it now, putting her hand gently on Blind Man's shoulder. 'I wish she were here, too,' was all she said, before she rose and went to the next bed.

'This is Sam Wycherly,' James said. 'He is our resident artist, at least until his captain misses him and away he goes.'

Jerusha heard the affection, a welcome antidote to Blind Man. 'What do you draw?'

The man eyed her, not in a way to embarrass her, but to regard her as an artist would. He tipped his head this way and that. 'You, for certain,' the man said. 'It's something I picked up on long voyages, after water starts to stink and you've heard everyone's stories. Aye, Sam Wycherly's the name.'

Jerusha thought of the time, years ago, when an itinerant pot mender told her that if she stood still long enough, someone, someday, would surely want to paint her. She mentioned that to Mama and Papa over supper. Mama gasped. 'We're not supposed to sit still in this life of toil and woe!'

She told Sam Wycherly what her Mama had said. He laughed, filling the otherwise silent ward with something unexpected. Jerusha saw smiles on faces that likely hadn't found much to laugh about in recent days, not with war and wounds in plentiful supply.

'Therefore, I do not sit still for portraits,' she concluded.

Sam winked at her. 'I'm no Rembrandy,' he confided. 'I draw fast and make allowances for a ship goin' up and down. You keep busy, miss, but I might snatch a sketch here and there. You'll never know.' He looked beyond her to James. 'In fact, he has one of my drawings already.'

'Aye, Sam, I do,' James said.

A quick glance showed her a red face, and she was too wise to remark upon it, or more likely, too shy, except that she was curious. 'I… I believe I would like to see it, too.'

'Wait here then.'

Everyone in the nearby beds seemed to wait, as well. Jerusha sensed a good-natured silence, as if the sailors around her were healing and reaching that stage of boredom with sickness and were on the mend.

I wonder, she thought, *would you like me to read to you?*

As she considered what book might be appealing to rough and ready men sidelined by wounds, Jamie returned with the little drawing. His face was still red, as if he had been caught in some misdemeanour, but she chose to ignore it. She had never before seen her own likeness, so she held out her hand.

Her eyes widened. 'Sam, you are a man of some talent,' she

told him, as she looked at her likeness on the back of a patient chart, her hand resting on the shoulder of the sergeant of Marines. Her image sat in profile, looking down.

'Not so hard, missy, when I have a pretty subject,' the Welshman said, grinning as her face warmed. 'God blast and damn, you can rosy up!' he declared, which meant smiles from nearby beds. Even Mrs Terwilliger, the matron, traded her usual serious scrutiny for something that softened her eyes.

'I'll draw another,' Sam said. 'Surgeon Wilson, can you find me a larger sheet of paper, maybe thicker, too? I'll only wish I had coloured pencils.'

'Paper, yes, but I doubt I can cajole coloured pencils from the purser,' James said.

Sam shrugged. 'How else can I capture those blues eyes?'

'Really, Mr Wycherly,' Jerusha said. She knew it was time to get her bowl of warm water and cloth and start wiping faces, even if too many of them seemed determined to keep smiling. She reasoned that wasn't a bad thing, not at all.

She devoted herself to the task, not looking around until she thought a glance wouldn't seem out of place. Jamie was nowhere in sight, which made her sigh.

'He'll be back, miss, never you fear,' said a sailor, with his face fine drawn in pain and a leg in an elaborate system of pulleys that made her shudder inside. She sat with him until he slept, then glanced at the watch pinned to her apron bib and turned last to Blind Man.

She sat beside him and did nothing more than wipe around his eyes which he kept closed, even though she knew he wasn't asleep. 'I could read to you,' she said finally.

'You could also leave me alone.'

'Very well,' she replied, determined not to let his words flay her, because she could see and had no worries worse than approaching spinsterhood and employment as a lady's companion, if Aunt Hortensia had her way. He ignored her, but she remained beside him until she knew Jack O'Toole would be waiting for her in his hackney.

Well aware that Sam Wycherly was drawing her, she made a face at him, which made some of the others laugh. She tried not to be obvious as she looked around for Surgeon Wilson, who was nowhere in sight. Ah well. He was a busy man.

Everything followed its normal course at number twenty-eight Finch Street when she returned with the usual luncheon and mail for Lady Oakshott, just roused from slumber. Later, she and Abbie began their onslaught on the sitting room, polishing chairs and the whist table. She heard Napier down the hall, arguing politely with Aunt Hortensia. The tense encounter ended with her aunt muttering something about stuffing bills away if she felt like it.

Who to ask the impertinent question that had been dogging her for days? There was no one to ask but Abbie, currently applying linseed oil industriously to the remaining chair.

'Abbie, it seems to be that Napier and Lady Oakshott are wrangling over unpaid bills,' Jerusha began, in her most neutral voice. 'Has she always done this?'

Abbie was a trusting sort. 'Only since t'master died. Ooh, the wrangles we used to hear from both Oakshotts, coming from the book room then! Now it is Napier reminding her about unpaid bills.' She returned her attention to the chair leg.

'Um…can he exert any influence?'

Abbie shook her head, her eyes sorrowful. 'He's just a butler. He can only remind her.' She leaned closer. 'Between you and me, I don't think Lady Oakshott has paid a bill in donkey's years.'

'But…'

Abbie gave an airy wave. 'I'm sure she knows what to do. Don't the rich always know what to do?'

Possibly not, Jerusha wanted to say, but to what point?

She continued polishing, wondering if her own mother had any notion of affairs at her sister's house.

I doubt we will all be on the street tomorrow, she reasoned finally, because try as she might to manage it, there was no way any of this was her business.

As recently as this morning's return to Finch Street, she had watched a woman with a bleak expression, two small children beside her, sitting upon a well-worn trunk in front of what looked like a boarding-house, probably one of many in a navy town like Plymouth.

Was the lady with sorrow etched on her face a new widow? Perhaps her husband had died at Stonehouse. Where did they go? She knew in her heart that it mattered now, where it hadn't mattered before.

She kept her thoughts to herself as she scrubbed at the sitting room furniture with Abbie. By the time afternoon began to wane, she knew she wanted to spend all day, every day at Stonehouse. The idea was preposterous, of course. Here she was, a gently reared woman destined to remain a spinster and strongly suspecting that a career in nursing was lowbrow and out of the question. Maybe in another generation, but not now, where the only path was marriage.

She asked herself again, *Why am I here? Mama and Aunt Hortensia both seem to think I must become a lady's companion.*

Mama had hinted she could return at the end of summer, but for what? The pity of well-married parishioners? She knew her aunt wanted to turn her into a lady's companion.

No one had ever consulted me, she told herself, as she dressed for dinner at the Beecrofts, an invitation that had sent Aunt Hortensia into ecstasies. *What do I want?*

Jerusha thought about that as she and her aunt walked the two streets farther away from the bay, which gave Sir William Beecroft a commanding view, almost the same view that

Sir Francis Drake enjoyed some two hundred years ago as he bowled and watched the Spanish Armada approach.

So many years had passed since that fraught time, and here they were at war again. 'Amazing what happened here so long ago,' Jerusha said to her aunt, who blew off her enthusiasm with a wave of her hand and one pithy word, 'History,' as if it was something unmentionable.

She slowed her steps, well aware of a deepening chasm between herself and Lady Oakshott, no matter that they were aunt and niece.

I don't know this woman, she thought, and took a careful breath. How to phrase this?

'Au… Lady Oakshott, what do the Beecrofts know of me?' she asked as they turned onto Launch Street. 'I mean, do I address you as Aunt Hortensia or Lady Oakshott? Who am I here?'

'I have told Lady Beecroft that you are the child of my sister, who didn't marry well.'

'Papa is a vicar, aunt!' Jerusha said.

Lady Oakshott gripped her arm. 'At one time, your mother had a baronet mooning over her, and what did she do but marry a penniless cleric in Orders? If my Harvey had not arranged a parish for him, I do not know what would have become of my sister!'

In a startling moment of reflection, Jerusha understood. 'So I am already the poor relation to people in Plymouth.'

'Poor but biddable,' Lady Oakshott told her and released her arm. 'You are along tonight to fetch and carry and arrange shawls that fall off shoulders and help the servants prepare tables for whist. Smile and say nothing. There will be a lady in attendance looking for a lady's companion for her mother. Pay her particular attention and mind yourself!'

What could she say?

'Remember who you are,' Lady Oakshott said, as she turned

around to simper and smile at other arriving guests on the street.

Who was she? Jerusha had a fair idea by the time the end-less evening ended. She noticed a lieutenant who spent a mod-erate, polite time chatting with her, then turning the pages for her when she played a modest Scottish piece on the pianoforte with a fair amount of skill. When she finished to polite ap-plause, she joined the ladies and watched as he chatted with Lady Beecroft. After that little chat, he did not engage her attention again.

Jerusha felt herself sinking inside. She did as she was bid, adjusting shawls for ladies who complained—but politely—of a slight chill. She arranged the whist tables and set the chairs just so.

And she died inside.

Chapter Sixteen

Jerusha cried herself to sleep that night. When she woke, she stared at the ceiling a long while and decided not to cry again. Only a foolish woman would have looked at last night's treatment—polite, yes, but putting her firmly in her place—and felt anything but the hard reality of her future.

She had no doubt that the young lieutenant had expressed some interest to Lady Beecroft and wanted an introduction, and the admiral's wife had set him straight. As for the lady who wanted help with her shawl, or the one who needed lemon in her tea just so, she also had no doubt that Aunt Hortensia had set the record straight there earlier. No one was rude. No one treated her unkindly. They had all passed judgement, but politely.

Jerusha decided that morning to not waste another tear on Plymouth society. She lay there thinking deep thoughts about Bolling, where she had been born and reared. Papa's parishioners already knew her circumstances; she knew word had already circulated that any dowry left to her had been spent on her brother's commission in the army. She could go home, but she didn't want pity from Papa's parishioners.

A dilemma raised its hand and waved it about, demanding that she respond.

Where do you belong? was the question.

The obvious answer was nowhere. She was too poor for the

genteel society in which she had been raised and too superior to the rabble below her to want to mingle there.

That annoying hand kept waving about. 'Very well. What is your question?' she asked herself out loud and answered it. 'Do I really want to be a lady's companion? No, I do not.'

But you are biddable, her other self, that annoying self, reminded her.

It was a fair comment. Jerusha knew she was a quiet sort, obedient to doing good works, because that was what her parents did, and she liked doing good works. It wasn't her fault that she was pretty. Her practical side knew that a wealthy duke or earl, or even a Cit, would never suddenly swoop down and declare that lack of dowry was no impediment. That only happened in bad novels. The plain truth, bold and unvarnished? Gentlemen wanted money, too.

Over breakfast that morning with her companions below stairs, she hadn't intended to whine over the hand fate had dealt. Somehow though, she blurted out her dissatisfaction, then felt deep shame. 'Forgive me. This is a stupid concern,' she said, wondering what these good souls must think of her. They surely already thought of her as privileged. She sat there, wretched with fear that she had ruined her friendships below stairs.

'Jerusha.'

She shook her head, unwilling to look up, even though Napier sounded so kind. 'I'm sorry for whining.'

She heard the butler's chair scrape back, and in another moment felt his hand on her shoulder. He gave her a gentle shake, and she looked up. 'You have our friendship,' he said.

Abbie leaned close to her. 'Maybe things aren't as bad as all that,' she said, the little girl who had fled the workhouse barefoot in winter and was found sleeping by the servants' entrance at twenty-eight Finch Street.

'Maybe things aren't,' Jerusha agreed, heartened to a degree she had not expected.

René cut through any remaining tension in inimitable fashion. 'I'll be happy to spit in Lady Oakshott's soup for you,' he declared, in his finest faux French accent. Jerusha laughed along with the others, relieved that she had burned no bridges below stairs.

If only it were her assigned day to visit Block Four, that safe haven where, for a few hours, she was useful, even if what she did was puny by anyone's standards. Instead, she and Abbie cut up strips of newspaper, dampened them, then scattered them around the venerable sitting room carpet.

She thought of the times she had watched Mama's servants do this. She asked to help once, but Mama firmly stated that her duties didn't include sweeping away carpet dirt with damp newspaper. Mama wasn't here, so she swept and thought of nothing more gratifying than seeing dirt and dust attach itself to the newspaper.

Honest work with Abbie was better than the charade of appearing at Aunt Hortensia's bedchamber at precisely twelve of the clock with mail and a cup of tea, only one cup because Jerusha was never invited to join her.

Aunt Hortensia pounced on the mail first, holding up a letter. 'From Lady Beecroft,' she said, then read it, pausing only to exclaim that Lady Beecroft had addressed her as Hortensia. She shook her head. 'You made a profound impression on Lieutenant Bracknell last night.' She read a little more and chortled. 'Never fear. Lady Beecroft set him straight. I trust he will recover. Isn't that droll?'

Jerusha had no difficulty finding other tasks around the house to occupy her for the day that involved no interaction with her aunt. By evening, Aunt Hortensia was now in transports of delight over another invitation to take tea. To Jerusha's relief, she was not included.

Sleep came easier that night, knowing she would see James Wilson in the morning.

And tell him what? she asked herself, even as she knew the answer was *Nothing.*

She couldn't tell anyone what happened, but she knew it would be enough to see Jamie and the men on Ward A.

Even the hackney ride from Plymouth to Devonport convinced Jerusha it would be a good day. People and commerce were unvarying, which soothed that part of her heart that craved order. To her additional relief, there were no stretchers or bits of bloody bandages on the grass, telling her the jetty bell hadn't rung last night. It was easy to wave goodbye to Jack O'Toole, smile when he raised his whip in return, and hurry inside.

Mrs Terwilliger smiled at her from the matron's desk, where reports piled up and probably always would. Surgeon Kidwell gave her a wave from a bedside where he sat. One of the naughty boys, probably the double amputee at the end of the first row, started a 'Hip-hip hurrah,' at the sight of her that the others joined in.

Jerusha laughed and looked around. Mrs Terwilliger cleared her throat and stacked a few reports, unwilling to meet her gaze. 'Surgeon Wilson left with the tide last night. He's on his way to the inshore station off Brest.'

The sun went out of the day as though Atlas himself had picked up the earth, toyed a bit, then tossed it over his shoulder. Jerusha looked down at the papers the matron had set aside.

He said that would happen, she thought. *Take a deep breath.*

'Then I had better get busy washing faces,' she said. Hopefully, Mrs Terwilliger was a silly woman who would never notice her dismay.

She looked at the matron, who would never be a silly woman. To her relief, Jerusha saw understanding and not derision. 'I wish he were here, too,' the matron said.

Mrs Terwilliger pointed towards the second row. 'This is a stinky bunch,' she said, loud enough for the stinky bunch to hear and laugh and cover Jerusha's disappointment.

'Then that's the row,' Jerusha said.

So there, Jamie Wilson, she thought. *I hope you're seasick.*

It was one thing for the bosun on the sloop *Harmony* to mop sweat from his face and mutter, 'I'm too old for this.' James Wilson felt precisely the same way when the slightly larger *Fleur de Violettes*—such improbable French names—rose out of the fog, so close to the French shore.

Harmony's gunners were better. Trust the Frogs to back off after one well-aimed volley. The only injury on the *Harmony* was to the cook, who scalded his shoulder when he crashed into the stove, extinguished as soon as the *Fleur* hove into view, but still hot. Would that wounds from all sea actions were so easily treated.

Foggy it may have been, but the crossing from Plymouth to Brest had been helped along by a stiff wind. Royal Navy frigates came and went, with the *Harmony* hailing those who were recipients of mailbags. From the grins on the faces of men who received the toss, James knew how welcome mail was to the crews that tacked and wove back and forth across the entrance to the Brest anchorage, with its French and Spanish allies bottled up inside and unhappy.

He watched the mail being handed around. For a brief moment, he wondered what it would be like to receive a letter from Jerusha Langley. Any daydream ended when a sailor tossed him a small package that tinkled alarmingly. To his relief, only one vial of laudanum was broken. The bosun gave the tar a ferocious scold, ending with, 'Suppose you had needed that laudanum after some Frog cannon took off your leg! Ye *hand* stuff to the doctor, idiot.'

So it went as *Harmony* approached the Channel Fleet. Progress slowed as the Fast Dispatch Vessel raised flags signifying Surgeon on Board, sometimes to hand over requested pharmacopeia, and other times to answer signals for help.

There wasn't anything drastic on the voyage out, beyond one duty that always made him shiver. The captain of *HMS Calliope* requested dental assistance, which meant highlining in a bosun's chair across a daunting space to the deck of the frigate. Because of the disparity in the two ship's sizes, this included a climb, with his dental kit slung over his shoulder. That was the easy part.

The captain waved him away. 'Not for me. For my servant,' he said hastily, and led him to his own quarters. There sat the Old Man's terrified servant, his jaw swollen, and his eyes filled with horror.

James assumed a studied air, because no patient liked to see that same horror mirrored in the surgeon's face. It wasn't that he couldn't do the simple procedure. It was the pain he knew he was about to inflict, and the noise, which rivalled that of a man screaming as some assassin ran him through with a dull blade.

The captain had already vacated his own quarters.

Coward, James thought, with an inward smile.

'Open up,' he said.

The servant did as requested. James took a good look, satisfied to see the offending tooth presented no more challenges than usual. He swallowed a few times because this was never easy.

James put his hands on the trembling man's shoulders. 'This will go fast, but you'll think you're going to die. You won't. Open up.'

Startled there were no preliminaries, the man opened his mouth wide. James clamped the business end of the dental key around the tooth, and gave a twist and massive tug. The servant screamed as James yanked, pulling out the inflamed tooth, roots and all. The servant slumped back as his mouth poured blood.

James staunched it quickly with a wad of cotton and pressed down. 'Clamp down hard,' he ordered.

'Ah oo doon?'

'Aye, lad. You were a prince. You and I will sit here a minute. I will change that wadding a few times. I'll tell the captain no duties for you for twenty-four hours.'

He finished in half an hour, satisfied when the hole stopped bleeding. 'Keep the wadding in place,' he directed. He handed the now harmless tooth to the servant, who took it warily with thumb and forefinger, as if expecting the tooth to snap and snarl. 'It ooks oosluss,' he said.

'Aye, it is useless,' James said. 'It will do you no more harm.'

'Ank oo.'

'You're welcome.'

Chapter Seventeen

And that was the worst so far. Happy to leave the servant's drama on the *Calliope* behind, James spent some time on the *Harmony*'s quarterdeck, because he knew the sailing master. He knew him as the proud possessor of a massive suture in Sumatra a few years ago, when the ship fell afoul of pirates and the outcome was in doubt until another frigate hove in sight, belching fire. The master lifted his pantleg and showed off the neat line of fading stitches that James had applied in such a hurry because so many needed his attention.

James remarked on the number of blockade ships he had seen on the way, sailing west, and the sailing master nodded. 'There's been a breakout. Happened during a storm when our inshore fleet crossed the channel to anchor in Torbay.' He shook his head. 'Frankly, I didn't think the Frogs were that brave. Apparently they joined with ships from Cadiz, which meant our little Nelson is tracking them into the Atlantic.'

'Where away?'

The master shrugged. 'Explain the French mind to me, laddie. There's a grand chase on in the Atlantic and we're stuck here and bored.'

They watched the *Calliope* heel to the wind and sail towards France. James stayed on deck when his friend went below, enjoying the lull in duties, the same duties which had no lull at

Stonehouse, where there were patients and the dreaded jetty bell to summon more.

He surprised himself. Usually, the only thing filling his mind were those same patients.

He draped his arms over the *Harmony*'s modest railing and thought about Jerusha Langley instead. The more scientific side of his brain, the side that had bustled in and shooed away anything else, relented enough for her to sidle through the opening. He missed her. Gone only five days, and he missed her.

No one needed him right now, and they were under sail towards the inshore blockade to deliver messages and mail. All he wanted was to return to Stonehouse and see a pretty face in Block Four.

And here he had thought Jerusha Langley would be a real treasure to wounded men who needed to write letters and see a lovely woman. As he stared towards Europe, James Wilson admitted to himself that he wanted to see Jerusha as much as his patients. In fact, he wanted to see more of her.

He knew what women looked like. God knows he had delivered babies at sea and in port. When opportunity presented itself, he had never resisted the charms of the ladies. Now he wanted to know, really know, this charming creature he had met in a fraught moment, then not seen again for years.

James wondered how some sequestered part of his brain had retained that brief encounter, then brought it back with the sight of her walking down the hall in Admin. He shook his head, aware that if he hadn't turned around at the sound of a skirt swishing, he never would have found her again.

The possibility of time with Jerusha sooner rather than later died the day after, as the *Harmony* heeled towards the frigate *HMS Avenger*, answering the messenger's Surgeon on Board flags with, Come on. Urgent.

As he handled the transfer in the usual way, this time carrying his full satchel because he had no idea what the emergency was, James had a moment to consider: Didn't the *Avenger* have its own surgeon?

To his dismay, the answer was yes and no. The surgeon's mate met him on deck, introducing himself only as Silas.

'Where is your surgeon, Silas?' James asked. 'I know you rate one.'

'Just…just come below with me, sir,' Silas said. 'You'll see.'

He followed the surgeon's mate down into the murk and stink of a ship too long at sea, with lanterns giving off a fitful light because the oxygen below deck was limited. Silas opened a hatch where lay the surgeon sprawled on a cot, wearing only a shirt and dangling a bottle in a limp hand. The stench was overpowering. There he lay, utterly useless to the fleet.

'I don't know what to do,' Silas said. 'Please help me.'

With relief, James closed the hatch on the insensible surgeon and followed Silas to another room off the officers' wardroom. There lay his real patient, a man no older than James, but with a leg that had been removed too late. A flick of the sheet covering him showed red streaks moving north from what had been a knee once. They had travelled into his belly, and he was full of death.

'Is…is there anything you can do?' the surgeon's mate asked, even as his eyes told him he already knew James's answer.

'Nay, lad,' James said in a low voice, on the chance the man sinking fast could hear the worst news. 'It's too late. What happened?'

The surgeon's mate turned away. 'Men get careless, sir.'

'Call me James, please.' It was a simple thing, but this overwhelmed man didn't need the bother of protocol. 'What did he do?'

'It wasn't him. T'luff was minding his own business. The

Frogs came out and caused a bit o' trouble. Sent some wounded men below and we was busy.'

'I've seen it, too.' The exhausted look the mate gave James was also familiar. 'Say on, Silas.'

'T'middie in the crow's nest was fooling around and he fell. The lieutenant tried to catch him—a fool move...'

'But a natural reaction.' James could see it all, because he *had* seen it all before. 'The midshipman died, didn't he?'

'Bounced and died. The luff's leg broke in two places. When the surgeon sobered up a day later he took off Lieutenant Gibbon's leg below the knee. Shoulda gone higher.'

'Aye, lad, but even then...' He remembered a similar case near Borneo, only the surgeon had been sick, did his best for another, then both men died, and there he was, James Wilson: young and unprepared.

Silas looked at his patient, who stirred and moaned. 'He's in terrible pain and I can't do anything for him, God damn me.'

'No. God damn the war and gross incompetence from someone who could have done better,' James assured him. 'It's not your blame. Let's see what we can do.'

They returned their attention to the dying man. James took a page from Jerusha's book and washed the man's sweaty face, then his chest. The lieutenant opened his eyes. 'I hurt everywhere,' he said simply. 'End it.'

'Aye, sir,' James replied, as the chill of death settled in his own marrow. There was one thing he could do, and *he* would do it, not leave it to some bewildered surgeon's mate. He opened his own satchel and took out a vial of laudanum.

Silas stepped back in alarm, then seemed to consider the matter. 'There isn't anything else we can do?'

'Nothing.' He leaned over the lieutenant. 'Sir, do you have someone you would like me to write to?'

'Mary Sheffield, number eleven Water Street, Portsmouth,' the man said. He never opened his eyes again, but dutifully drank all the laudanum James poured down his throat. He said something more, and James knew, as he listened close, his ear nearly to Lieutenant Sheffield's lips, that it was meant for him.

'I have…wife…daughter. Mary due again.' He seemed to relax as the laudanum did its duty, as the lieutenant had done his. 'Soon.' More quiet breaths, each with a longer space between. 'Married?'

'No.'

'Good. Don't.'

Shaken, James took out his watch. The lieutenant's face grew slack as the tension melted. He breathed quietly for another ten minutes then stopped.

James called it at fourteen hundred hours, and Silas wrote the time in the dead book, his face calm. As James watched, the mate wrote the lieutenant's name, then his wife's name and address. 'I'll take it to the captain. He'll write her a letter.'

Silas laid a gentle hand on the dead man's chest. 'We'll get him ready for the sea.' The mate's voice hardened. 'Can we get rid of that useless surgeon?'

'We can and will. I'll make my report to your captain and the Navy Board,' James assured him. 'This was a hard school today.'

Silas nodded. 'Did I pass my exam?'

'Quite well,' James said, recalling all his similar trials by fire. 'I can't take the surgeon with me, but he can be confined to quarters. It's all on you now, Silas.'

'I know.'

James found the captain, suggesting—he had no power to order—that the surgeon be confined and not allowed to inflict any more damage. He could do no more for Silas or the lieutenant.

Or for himself. The lieutenant tried to warn him, but no. James Wilson knew he loved Jerusha.

Chapter Eighteen

The dying lieutenant's words lingered in his mind. He was not the first man that James had sent to an early grave, when he knew death was certain. He regretted not one single assisted death.

He had seen other likenesses of wives and children aboard ship, but only now, when there was a woman he cared for, did it occur to him that the misery didn't end with the final breath for married men. Now he knew their agony at abandoning their loved ones, because they had been foolish enough to love in time of war. James knew because now he loved.

He thought of Blind Man in Block Four, the one refusing to tell anyone of his wife's whereabouts. After the death of the lieutenant, James understood it as the desperation of a man completely altered and well aware he could neither support nor perhaps fully satisfy a wife ever again. Whether that was true or not remained moot. The blind man must believe his wife would be better off thinking him dead, and perhaps remarry.

James decided he would be selfish, indeed, to continue his interest in Jerusha Langley, someone beyond his social sphere anyway, even if she didn't quite fit in another, because her undoubtedly respectable parents had not provided any sort of marriage portion. That was her bad luck. His misfortune was to love her during a time of war, when not even he could guarantee he would not end up like the blind man.

And yet… He knew Jerusha was far above the fetch and carry existence of a lady's companion, no matter what her thoughtless aunt imagined. He had to smile when he knew that, provided she was willing and provided he had the courage to *ask*, for God's sake, their only escape was to run away to the United States, where one's social sphere didn't matter. They could find a parcel of land beyond the Allegheny Mountains, maybe on the western frontier in Ohio, and wear themselves out cutting down trees and planting corn. Just the idea made him chuckle and go about his business of healing the sick. He had his life; she had hers.

He won't be there, Jerusha told herself every morning she smiled at Jake O'Toole and let him hand her into his conveyance.

Sure enough, Jamie wasn't. Early in his absence, she attempted what she thought was an offhand remark to Mrs Terwilliger about how long Surgeon Wilson usually spent in his sea duty. What she got was a straightforward answer: 'Hard to tell. One month? Maybe two?'

If Surgeon Kidwell hadn't been there with his affable demeanour and real understanding of his and Jamie's patients, she would have never darkened the door of Block Four again, as one week passed and then another. The one-legged surgeon saw to it there was warm water, washcloths, soft soap, and towels available on the mornings when she volunteered her services. She couldn't call it work. On many mornings he moved from bed to bed behind her, so she was always in his sight, which reassured her.

Sometimes new patients—the Royal Navy had a well-earned reputation—needed to be reminded that she was a lady. One admonition generally served, she noted, especially the morning when a cheeky patient on Monday was a subdued fellow with a black eye on Wednesday. No one ever confessed and Jerusha was wise enough not to ask. Her task of washing faces and writing letters varied little, as the weeks without Jamie Wilson passed. Jerusha worked with a willing heart.

She knew she would always remember the first emergency. She had finished washing the Blind Man's face, humming softly but saying nothing because he had told her not to speak to him, as he told everyone.

'Miss Langley, I need you now. I wouldn't ask, but the steward is elsewhere occupied.'

Surgeon Kidwell's voice was calm and almost conversational. She hurried to his side, aghast to see blood pouring from the arm of a sailor with terror in his eyes. He couldn't speak, even as his mouth open and closed in fright.

'Jerusha, put your finger right where mine is,' the surgeon told her. 'Press down and don't let up.'

Without a word, she did as he said. He quickly tightened down a tourniquet and the flow stopped. To her relief, the patient fainted, which seemed so sensible to her that she almost wanted to try it, too. As she watched in fright, her interest grew.

Surgeon Kidwell threaded a needle with a length of catgut and carefully trimmed the artery, moving aside her finger and sewing the ragged sections together with tiny stitches. 'This happens sometimes, when there has been too much trauma near a vein or artery,' he told her, explaining as he worked. 'Nothing we can't repair.'

She watched in amazement as he sewed and surprised herself by matching her calm to his. 'Surgeon, you can't imagine the tears I shed over embroidery. My mother gave up in utter despair.'

He laughed, pointed to his work, and held out the needle, still attached to the thread and arm. 'Put in two of your own. I'll show you how. Mind you, no fancy embroidery stitch.'

She hesitated until the one-armed man in the next cot

cheered her on. 'Very well,' she said. She took the needle, forcing herself to remain serene. 'I loop it?'

'Yes. That's right. Do it again, then I'll tie it off. Well done, Miss Langley. You have the magic touch. Such a pity that ladies aren't ever surgeons. Now I'll unleash the tourniquet a little at a time and we'll see how good we are.' He looked at his work in quiet satisfaction. 'This will hold now.'

'Aren't ship surgeons any good?' she whispered, not wanting to terrify the sailor regaining consciousness and send him back into oblivion.

'My dear, consider doing what we just did on a ship heaving up and down and maybe dodging about, wearing and tacking, with cannon roaring and a sick-bay full of men just like this one, and worse,' he pointed out. 'Consider that and ask yourself why any sailors at all survive to see us in Stonehouse.'

He touched her cheek, even though his hand was bloody. 'Miss Langley, you're a good person to have around in a crisis.'

'I wanted to faint,' she admitted. 'At least until I discovered how interesting this is.'

'Bravo, little one,' Surgeon Kidwell said. 'I'll send that in a letter to James. I write him every week.' He shrugged. 'Maybe the letters get to him, most often not. I number them.'

Jerusha had to bite her lip to keep from leaping about like a child, tugging on his arm, and asking if you could add a note, too, just a little PS from a friend. She reminded herself how improper that would be.

Still, her minor part in saving a sailor's life warmed her all the way home. So did Blind Man. When she passed his cot, he reached out and tugged on her skirt. That was all. Nothing said. How did he even know she was there? She took a chance and touched his shoulder, then continued on her way, wondering how in the world to convince him to tell them something about the lady and boy in the miniature.

Everything was the same as usual at twenty-eight Finch

Street—Lady Oakshott still abed, and the others dusting, cooking, and managing, as if the house belonged to someone of note, and not an encroaching widow determined to squeeze her way into Plymouth's limited society.

Thinking of the good she did this morning, Jerusha went through the charade of her day, bowing to Lady Oakshott's demands, even as she wondered how to help Surgeon Kidwell the day after tomorrow, when she could return to Block Four and make a difference.

She smiled her way through a boring whist party that evening at someone's house, playing a stupid hand because that was what ladies were supposed to do, so gentlemen partners could 'rescue' them. She arranged shawls, she nodded when expected to, and voiced no opinions of her own when the men discussed the war, even though she had opinions.

The only one who would have enjoyed hearing how she helped Surgeon Kidwell was at sea. She silently admitted to herself—no one would ever know—she needed him, his warmth, his protection, his heart beating next to hers, even as she saw no way in any universe for this to happen. 'Maybe someday' became her mantra, until she tired of it, because it was completely out of the realm of possibility.

True to her upbringing as a vicar's daughter, she petitioned the Almighty for help. Her father had taught her from early childhood that the Lord was available for consolation and remedy. Nothing happened. She knew it was past time to understand that the Almighty had more important petitions to consider, especially with a war on.

Failing that, she wanted to discuss the matter with someone earthly. She came close on the morning of her next visit to Stonehouse, when Jake O'Toole was stalled in traffic. He shook his head and stared at the tangle of horses and wagons, with a street full of chickens in cages dumped from one of the wagons. The drivers had squared off in front of each other, ready to fight.

Jerusha leaned forward, wanting to tell him her dilemma, then sat back, because she had no words for what she was feeling.

Saying, *I am in love with a man inappropriate for someone in my social sphere to even consider*, would probably send him fleeing from his own hackney.

She smiled to herself at her folly and the moment passed. Two stout men in the crowd separated the belligerents, even as several nimble sprites snatched up the chickens, to the crowd's approval. Mr O'Toole laughed and snapped his whip over his horse's head, and they moved on.

Almost to her disappointment—not quite but almost—there was no emergency of wounded men on the grass in front of the admin building. No one needed her to join emergency care on the lawn, which, while terrifying, gave meaning to her belief that this war was her war, too.

But wait. Something she couldn't explain told her something was going on in Ward A. She wasn't wrong.

'There she is!'

Jerusha looked behind her. The good-natured laughter that followed her involuntary action made her laugh, too. They must have been waiting for her. Maybe she was wrong about no one needing her. She put her hands on her hips, saw no Mrs Terwilliger, so exclaimed in her best imitation, 'What are you miscreants plotting?'

Sam Wycherly, the one-armed former gunner, put his finger to his lips, then beckoned her closer. He held out another drawing, this one of Blind Man asleep and facing Sam, whose cot was across from his.

'I want you in the drawing, too,' Sam continued, 'plus a few other, ahem, miscreants. You know, to set the stage this is a hospital.'

'It is,' Jerusha agreed, wondering what the man had in mind. 'What will this accomplish?'

'Mrs Terwilliger—God bless the ladies—thinks we can put two or three such drawings in prominent places in markets where women assemble.' He grew serious then. 'Granted, it's a long shot, but someone might recognise him.'

'What would you write on the picture so people will know what to do?' Jerusha whispered back.

'Surgeon Kidwell said simplicity is best. Something like, "Do you know this man? Please come to Stonehouse Naval Hospital,"' he said, with an enquiring look at her, testing her reaction.

Jerusha considered the matter, unable to avoid her hesitation. 'Sam, I do not wish to be recognised on a poster.'

He frowned. 'Not ladylike, is it?'

'No.'

On the other hand, she considered her small circle of acquaintances among people of her sort in Plymouth. Those friends of Lady Oakshott's did not frequent markets, and this might be the only way to find out anything. 'I will help,' she said, after more thought. 'How do we do this?' She glanced at the sleeping man. 'He mustn't know.'

'Agreed.' Sam motioned to three miscreants who could walk. 'You, you, and you. Miss Langley, you sit over there, and they will group themselves around you.' He gestured to his drawing, propped up before him on his cot. 'I will add you four to what I have already drawn. No one will know you're not beside his bed, even as he faces me.'

Why not? Mrs Terwilliger returned from business in Ward B upstairs and helped arrange them. 'I should be doing something in the drawing,' Jerusha told her, 'something I would usually be doing.'

'I kn...kn...know,' said a patient, who everyone said had

never stuttered before the fleet action that put him here. 'Re… read to us.'

'I haven't a book,' she said.

'I… I…have.'

With some effort, he took a small volume from under his pillow and handed it to her.

'Oh, my,' she said. 'I do like Shakespeare's sonnets.'

Someone groaned. Someone else laughed. 'Hush,' Jerusha said and smiled at the patient. 'You show excellent taste in literature.'

'Yes. He. Does.' Mrs Terwilliger frowned at the lot of them, and the teasing ended promptly.

Jerusha smiled inside. 'Sir, do you have a favourite?'

'Sonnet Eighteen,' the man declared, after a pugnacious look around at his more subdued fellow invalids, now that Mrs Terwilliger had given her opinion.

'My favourite,' Jerusha declared, and cleared her throat, 'Mr Wycherly, are you ready to draw?'

'Aye, miss,' he said.

'"Shall I compare thee to a summer's day? Thou art more fair and temperate…"'

She stopped when Blind Man woke up and rolled over, re-garding them out of sightless eyes. 'Good God, can't a man sleep?' he asked the room at large.

'Mr Whoever-You-Are, I have decided to read Shakespeare,' Jerusha stated, impressed with her own firmness.

He sighed. 'Whether we like it or not?'

Blind Man swore fluently, then closed his eyes, resigned to his lot.

Sam Wycherly grinned and picked up his pencil.

Chapter Nineteen

Jamie Wilson never paid much attention to correspondence received at sea, unless it came as a stamped, sealed dispatch from men farther up the chain of command, which was nearly everybody. He did keep a memo from Admiral Lord Collingwood himself, thanking him for curing his dog Bounce after Bounce ate one too many rats from the hold.

This voyage—perhaps like Collingwood's dog—he would happily have pounced on every memo or note with his name attached. Alas there were none, because the *Harmony* itself was delivering mail and not receiving any, except to forward to ships on the blockade or to the occasional frigate moving towards the Mediterranean fleet.

When they delivered mail to the larger slips, he envied complacent married men who received several letters. He tried not to remember the agony of the dying lieutenant who dreaded the awful letter his wife would receive, noting his death and expressing official sympathy.

Damn him, even with *that* memory, he also tried to forget how much he wanted to court and marry Jerusha Langley, someone who had come out of his past and made him wonder if he had ever really and truly forgotten her, even though he was twelve at the time. He knew enough about the brain to be well acquainted with how little anyone understood that jumble of matter that sat atop everyone's head and dictated…what?

He had no answers, but in a few days, he had a letter. It was one of those rare moments, so unexpected that he stared like an idiot when the captain called out his name after rummaging through a canvas mail sack from another Fast Dispatch Vessel like theirs.

'Ahem, you *are* Surgeon James Wilson?' the captain asked with a grin. 'You *do* read?' He sniffed the envelope. 'Not from a female.' He laughed and handed it to James. 'Go below and read it.'

James needed no more encouragement. He was only slightly disappointed to discover that Surgeon Kidwell had written. He propped his feet on a sack of corn destined for the mynah bird belonging to Captain Hughly of the *Prometheus* and started reading.

To his utter delight, the letter dealt mainly with Jerusha, which made him wonder for an idle moment if Jon Kidwell was interested in her, too. Surely not; the man was a confirmed bachelor and old, nearly forty.

Who could not smile at a letter like this? 'So, Surgeon Kidwell, you taught Jerusha to splice an artery?' he asked out loud, wishing he had been there to watch her eyes. That was what he remembered most about the duck-pond: her determined eyes, as she flailed and tried to reach the edge of the pond, one that probably looked as wide as the Mediterranean to someone whose feet didn't touch the bottom. He imagined that determined look directed at an offending artery.

The letter was mostly taken up with Sam Wycherly's excellent plan to sketch four drawings of Blind Man, with Jerusha behind him, reading to three or four other patients. Sam thought it a brilliant stroke to write in big letters *Do You Know This Man? Contact Stonehouse*, and then distribute the drawings to the four largest markets in Plymouth and Devonport, where ladies shopped.

He wrote:

*Some housewife or servant might know this man. Look
how carefully Gunner Wycherly drew him, with a face
to be recognised.*

James put down the letter, remembering Sam's first little
sketch of Jerusha Langley. He pulled it out of his uniform
pocket, the one where he stored lint and gum plasters. Sam
drew her looking down at a patient. Sam had captured the
softness of her lips and the wrinkle of concern between her
eyes. Sam drew that certain youthfulness about her, the look
of someone untouched by war, which seemed to take the softness out of men and women alike. He wanted her to remain
like that forever, even though he was pretty sure Stonehouse
was already changing her.

Back went the image into its nest of lint. He finished Kidwell's
letter, which was surgical business, then followed the little arrow
to the other side for a postscript.

*The oddest thing. Perhaps Gunner Wycherly should be
flattered. Apparently someone stole one of the four images of Blind Man and Jerusha.*

Surgeon Kidwell had drawn a little frowning face.

*We needed that missing picture. It might be our only way
to identify this stubborn man. Imagine a world where
such images could be churned out in seconds and plastered everywhere. Ha-ha. I know. Almost as fanciful as
your wish for operating theatres so bright that we could
work at night.*

Jamie wanted so badly for the *Harmony* to sail for home,
but there was more medicine to deliver farther south, now that
blockading ships also lurked around Ferrol in Spain.

The only excitement came when *Harmony* was singled out, because of size and dexterity, to move close enough to Ferrol to pick up a spy and get his report to the frigate *Naiad*, which would put on full sail for the Mediterranean and Nelson's fleet.

It was a successful manoeuvre, done in dark and silence. 'I have such news,' the spy said, before he was rowed to the *Naiad*. 'Won't our Admiral Nelson do a jig to know that the Combined Fleet of Frogs and Spaniards is bottled up at Cadiz?'

Three more days—they had been gone six weeks—they delivered mail and medicine and added to the *Harmony*'s growing stack of dispatches for Admiralty and Horse Guards.

Home, please, James thought. *Now*.

If there was anyone more eager to see Plymouth again, James had no idea who it was. Somehow, some way, he needed to find the time—always his chief enemy—to court Jerusha Langley. He closed his eyes to the still-vivid sight of the dying man's regret he had ruined the life of the woman he loved. James decided it would be different with him somehow.

James blamed himself for the next delay. With fire in his eyes, the captain of the *Harmony* woke him too early. 'Get your carcass on deck! Captain Beck of the *Bonne Chance* wants you. It had better not be what it was the last time!'

But it was. 'Bring your little clippers and hurry,' was the message that made James groan.

Shoot me now, he thought, as he pulled on his pea coat, found his thickest gloves and the clippers, and was soon dangling between ships.

At least he thought to bring along twine.

Captain Beck shook his head over the twine when James, soaking wet, was admitted to his cabin on the *Bon Chance*, a frigate captured from the French, which came with a cat that refused to be dislodged. The Royal Navy surrendered meekly enough, and Captain Beck, the ship's next commander, found himself the object of adoration from the French cat.

The cat, now named Booty, as in, prize of war, followed Beck everywhere. The captain succumbed to such devotion, which his crew had to admit, softened him up a little. No harm there.

Six months ago, Captain Beck asked James to clip Booty's nails. The following bloodbath left James with permanent scars, but the deed was done. Booty's nails were trimmed.

Now it was time for another trim. Captain Beck had got word from another blockading ship that James was aboard the *Harmony*.

'Sir, I'm tying this twine around Booty's jaws,' James said firmly. 'Please note that I am soaking wet because your crew dropped and dragged me twice between ships. I am cold.'

'No twine,' Captain Beck said just as firmly. 'Booty will be a perfect gentleman.'

Good kitty, my arse, James thought.

'Twine,' he repeated.

'No.'

When James returned to the *Harmony* an hour later, his cheek bloody and forearm throbbing, Captain Ames clucked his tongue.

'It's just a cat,' he said. 'I know you doctored Admiral Collingwood's dog. That's how the word got around the fleet, eh?'

'I don't want to talk about it, sir,' James said.

Weeks away from Plymouth had never mattered before. He knew Surgeon Kidwell, despite his missing leg, was perfectly capable of managing Block Four. Perhaps that was an exaggeration. Jon Kidwell did tire sooner.

James Wilson knew he was known as a man dedicated to medicine and the fleet. However, he didn't need to look in the mirror to see the longing there for Jerusha Langley. Was he crazy? He barely knew her. Then why… There it ended every time, since love was not scientific and he didn't understand it.

So he thought. Captain Ames disabused him of that foolishness on the voyage home, when the captain joined him at the rail and asked, 'What's her name?'

'Jerusha,' James said without thinking, then stared at the captain. 'How did you know?'

'I looked like you five years ago,' came the captain's dry answer.

'You didn't try to talk yourself out of marriage, war, and leaving her a widow with small children and no income?'

Captain Ames shrugged. 'I tried, then decided I deserved to be as happy as the next man. Marry her. Goodnight, James.'

I wonder, James thought, as he stared after the captain. *Does she even have the slightest idea how much I care?*

Chapter Twenty

~~~~~~~

Jerusha had no qualms about increasing her mornings at Stonehouse from three days to five. Since Lady Oakshott's staff were by no means unintelligent, they had long known how easy their mornings could be, with Lady Oakshott asleep until noon. Going to the market could become a leisurely thing, which meant that René was able to develop a promising friendship with Dolores, a sultry-eyed Spanish candle-maker who sold her wares near the greengrocer.

'I kissed Dolores behind the green beans,' the chef confided to Jerusha as she prepared to leave for Stonehouse. He blew a kiss towards Lady Oakshott's bedchamber. 'No one's the wiser.'

'Thank goodness,' Jerusha said. 'René, for the first time in my life, I am truly useful. If I were not part of Block Four, I wouldn't have known how something as simple as a clean face can change someone's whole day. And a letter? So many of those letters I have written for the men have been answered.'

'No one ever wrote me a letter,' the chef said.

Jerusha laughed. 'Go to sea, receive a grievous wound, and I will write you one.' Her reward was a great rolling of eyes.

She thought her expanded schedule might get an argument from the jarvey, Jake O'Toole, but he gave her none, merely said, 'Five days a week instead of three seems right to me, too. No worries. I'll be here.'

His willingness to help coincided with the day weeks ago that he dropped her off as the jetty bell rang. With no hesitation—even though she knew she would never get over the terror—Jerusha leaped from the hackney and ran to the quadrangle. In a moment, Jake passed her carrying a little powder monkey in his arms. The little lad still clutched a bagged powder charge he had been carrying up to the gun-deck when all hell broke loose. No one had been able to coax it from his grip.

Jake O'Toole helped all morning that day until it was time for him to pick her up for the return trip to Finch Street. 'As God is my witness, I had no idea,' he said as he helped her into the hackney. 'If I hear that bell, wherever I am, I will come.'

Jerusha could have given him several disputes, principal of which was that it needed to work to provide for his family. 'I only hope your kindness isn't taking food from your children's mouths,' was her only attempt, which brought a wistful smile.

'We only had the one son, and he is gone. We'll get by, Jerusha.' He cocked his head towards hers. 'May I take a liberty and call you Jerusha?'

'It's no liberty,' she assured him. 'You're a kind man, Mr O'Toole.'

'You could call me Jake.'

She held out her hand. Only a few months ago, she would have hesitated and wondered if this was a step down from her precarious enough social rung. She knew it for what it was now, a bond with another person trying to live a good life, the same as she was, society be damned. 'Jake, we're equals.'

'I never shook a lady's hand,' he said, the hesitation his.

'Then would you shake a friend's hand?' she asked.

'Aye.' He shook her hand, then stepped back in fake surprise. 'The sky didn't fall!'

She had a friend. Still, five days a week… 'Jake, I can't afford to pay you for five days.'

'No fears! I've noticed that if I drop you off here three days a week, I find more fares on this side of Devonport and Plymouth. Five days will be even better.'

He tipped his hat to her and rode away, his back straight. She watched him a moment, then entered Block Four, moving quickly up the stairs to Ward A, ready to work.

As always, she stood in the door of Ward A for a moment, wanting to take a quick census and see if anything had changed since her visit two days ago. She looked first at Blind Man, wishing that somehow his wife would have materialised overnight. Maybe those paltry four posters hadn't provoked a response.

What are we going to do with you? she thought.

She continued her assessment down the row. The two crushed ribs in Cot Thirty was still there. She sighed with relief to see an older couple sitting beside him, a great hamper between them. Usually that meant food, which somehow managed to be shared around the ward, if there was enough.

Cot Fifteen was empty.

Oh, please, no.

She turned away, determined not to cry this time, as she had last week when a powder monkey died of sepsis. He'd been ten, and had fled a workhouse to join the Royal Navy. As a vicar's daughter, she knew the little fellow was out of pain. As Jerusha Langley, she had wept on the landing, so as not to disturb the others.

But the empty Cot Fifteen meant Sailing Master Kent was no longer. She hadn't thought his injury so serious. Please God, not Master Kent, who, with his rank could have gone to a ward for warranted officers. 'No, Surgeon,' he had told Jamie firmly. 'These are my men. I was one of them once, and here I belong.'

She went to Cot Fifteen for a closer look, in that way of shoppers seeking out a certain produce, who stand there, star-

ing at the place where it should be, even though it is obviously
not there. She dabbed at her face with the end of her shawl.

'Missy, that's not it,' she heard from Sam Wycherly, her
artist across the aisle. 'Master Kent has been reassigned to a
frigate. He told me to tell you ta-ta.'

She closed her eyes in relief.

'Here's something to cry about—a night steward told Mrs
T that one of your posters was pinched from the great market
on Albemarle Road.'

'Who would do such a thing?' she asked in distress.

'Some bloke who likes a pretty face,' he teased.

'Sam, really.' She glanced at Blind Man and lowered her
voice. 'I wonder…we've never told him what we are attempt-
ing.'

'Maybe it's time we did,' Sam said. 'I mean, he lies there
somewhere between awake and asleep, and he says nothing.
Find Surgeon Kidwell. See what he thinks.'

'Where…'

He pointed overhead. 'Ward B.'

'I've never been there. Will it frighten me?'

'It might,' he told her honestly. 'No-hopers upstairs.'

Funny, she thought, as she climbed the stairs. *A month or
so ago I would have thought that nothing could be worse than
Ward A. Stonehouse is a lesson to me.*

The door was closed. She raised her hand, wondering if
she should knock or just run downstairs and out the front
door, becoming the biddable almost-servant her aunt already
thought she was.

Open the door, she told herself. *Walk in.*

The room was a duplicate of the ward downstairs, except
that most of the draperies were drawn at least half shut, turning the bright morning sun dim. The odour was no worse or
better than downstairs.

She was startled to see nuns gliding down the rows, stopping here and there to wipe a face. Jerusha looked closer, then turned away in shock—or what passed for a face. She took a deep breath, and another, aware she was far out of her sphere.

She focused on the nuns, remembering them from the jetty bells, and occasional glimpses. So this was where they laboured, attending those far gone but not quite dead, men with no hope, as Sam Wycherly said. No-hopers.

'Yes, miss?'

Chills ran down her spine as she thought for a small moment that one of the almost-dead had spoken. But no, it was a nun, a sort of person she had never spoken to before.

She saw an ordinary face enclosed in a white wimple and wearing black. 'I was looking for Surgeon Kidwell,' she stammered. 'I… I…'

The woman laid a gentle hand on her arm. 'These are God's children, too. We pray for them.' She gestured down the row to a bed with a curtain around it. 'He is in there, where a man is finally dying. Please follow me.'

The aisle was narrow so she walked behind the nun, seeing with horror the worst of what war could do to the men who fought. She saw vacant eyes and no eyes, one poor boy with no arms or legs, another with his mouth open in a silent scream. Another muttered to himself and kept rubbing at a missing leg.

The nun stopped. 'I'll ask Surgeon Kidwell if he has a moment.' She pulled back the curtain and Jerusha looked at the floor, suddenly ashamed that she had all her parts, a good mind, and a future, no matter how humble it had become since Lady Oakshott took her in hand.

'Jerusha, what are you doing here?' Surgeon Kidwell came out of the tent.

'Sam Wycherly t…told me about the missing poster. We got to thinking that maybe Blind Man doesn't know what we are trying to do for him. Sam thinks I should tell him.' She put her hand to her mouth. 'Surgeon Kidwell! I had no idea about Ward B!'

He regarded her patiently. 'They have nowhere else to go. The Sisters of Mercy tend them until they die.'

She nodded as her mind calmed. 'Should I say something to Blind Man?' She clutched his arm. 'I mean, he could end up here!'

'Do what you think best, Jerusha.'

'That's no answer!'

'It's all you need. I trust your judgement.' He touched her cheek then returned to the curtained off area.

He trusts my judgement? she asked herself in anger. *I don't even trust my judgement.*

She stared at the curtained off area, then looked around and saw the devastation of war. Maybe she could return here another day. Surely that was enough.

She started towards the door, stopping as someone grabbed her skirt.

Don't disappoint Jamie, she told herself.

In that split second, she knew that even beyond Jamie, she didn't want to disappoint herself.

'May I help you, sir?' she asked, surprised at how calm she sounded, when her stomach was doing handsprings. 'Let me get a chair.'

Chapter Twenty-One

Jerusha looked down at a man not much older than herself, but with a massive scar on his forehead. She gently released his grip on her skirt and sat beside him. To her relief, those imps screaming inside her head, telling her to run away, must have sped ahead. Sam Wycherly could wait for an answer. Blind Man didn't want her around anyway. She had time and little else to offer this wounded man.

She held his hand. 'I'm Jerusha. Who are you?'

'T'best foretopman who ever lived,' he said, his words slow and dreamy, as if he were remembering better days at sea. 'Billy Barton is my name. The *Undaunted* was my ship.'

'Billy Barton of the *Undaunted*,' she repeated.

She saw that his eyes were sunken. He opened them as best he could and spoke with intention. 'You won't forget my name and ship?'

'I won't, Billy,' she told him, her voice firm because she understood herself a little better. 'I'll remember you always, you and the *Undaunted*.' In the deepest part of her heart, she knew she would remember.

The look in his eyes changed from urgent to peaceful. His shoulders relaxed and he died. Jerusha stayed where she was, thinking that a Jerusha Langley she barely recognised any more would have run away. Papa told her once that a dead person's spirit lingered after the last breath, which she doubted.

As she sat there quietly, rejoicing in the peace around Billy Barton, *HMS Undaunted*, foretopman, her doubt changed to belief. Papa was right.

She did jump when someone touched her shoulder, except that it was Surgeon Kidwell. 'Everyone else is so busy. What a blessing you were here,' was all he said, before he closed the foretopman's eyes. After consulting his timepiece, he wrote on Billy Barton's chart and pulled a sheet over the best foretopman who ever lived.

'Billy Barton of the *Undaunted*,' she said. 'I promised him I would remember, and I shall.'

'Jerusha, you amaze me,' he said as they walked downstairs to Ward A. He stopped at the door and considered her earlier question. 'Tell Mr Blind Man what we are trying to do for him. I don't care how blunt you are.' He managed a smile. 'He ignores the rest of us. At least he growls at you.'

She gave him The Look, something she borrowed from her mother. He laughed. 'You could chastise children with that someday.'

'My mother excelled in it.'

'Didn't they all?' he commented. 'You seem so obliging, especially when we are making demands.' He looked at the ceiling. 'Or when others feel safe enough to surrender to death, thanks to your serenity.'

Ha, she thought to herself. *Ha-ha.*

He opened the door and ushered her in. Her fear left her as she approached Blind Man. Hadn't she just guided Billy Barton to a peaceful place? She sat beside his cot in silence, wondering if anything could shock her now.

'I know you're there,' he said finally. 'You're wasting your time.'

What to say to this man? 'No, sir, you are wasting *our* time,' she settled on, cringing because it sounded harsh to her. But having said it, she knew this was no time to back down. 'I doubt you will approve of this, but Sam Wycherly across the aisle from you drew your likeness, plus mine and some of the others.'

'Damn him,' Blind Man said under his breath.

'No, bless him for thinking of a way to get your appearance out. Someone, maybe your wife—I think you have one—will see it in the market and find you.' It was the most she had ever said to Blind Man at one time. She didn't hesitate to put her hand on his arm. Billy Barton of the *Undaunted* had so recently offered no objection to that.

She waited for him to shrug off her hand. When he did not, she took heart. 'She needs to know.'

He said nothing for a long time. Jerusha watched his face, tried to look at him as a wife might. She had become used to the scars around his right eye and the longer one that crossed the bridge of his nose and disappeared into his left eyebrow. How sad that affecting one eye affected the other. Perhaps a surgeon—Jamie Wilson?—could explain that to her someday. There was so much she wanted to know.

Blind Man stirred, but still he did not move from her gentle touch. 'Don't you know I want to spare her! Look at me. I am a freak.'

'I've been looking at you,' she replied. 'I think you're a rather nice-looking man. Your ears don't stick out, I like auburn hair, and I like the cleft in your chin. My brother has one of those. Do you have any children, sir?'

'Two,' he said automatically, then cursed. 'I don't want to tell you anything.'

She shrugged, aware suddenly that the ward was quieter than usual, everyone listening. 'Whoever they are, I hope they have your hair colour. It's nice.'

'Mary does. Go away.'

'Very well, sir. I'll leave you in peace. I promised to write some letters. Anyway, someone stole one of the pictures Sam drew, so our chances are lessened.' Oh, why not? She leaned closer. 'Between you and me, I am a raving beauty. I am a bit offended that *all* the drawings weren't stolen. Good day to you.'

Take that, she thought, pleased when he smiled for the first time.

Maybe someday she would write a treatise on managing difficult people. Between Blind Man and Aunt Hortensia, she had plenty of experience.

She finished off her morning taking dictation and wishing Jamie Wilson would suddenly materialise to heal the blind and raise the dead. Surgeon Kidwell took a moment to walk with her from Ward A. 'Did Billy Barton of the *Undaunted* have a family?' she asked, as they walked to the quadrangle, where Mr O'Toole waited for her.

'Not that we know. He came to us as you saw him.' He paused and she saw that faraway look that all men at war seemed to possess. 'We will bury him with others like him, with name, ship and date of death, and we will curse Napoleon and blind ambition.'

He walked her to the street, where Jake waited with his patient horse and hackney.

'One moment,' the surgeon said. 'I should tell you that the *Harmony* is headed back to Plymouth. G'day, Miss Langley.'

She walked away quickly, aware that her face felt warm.

You've been gone too long, Jamie, she thought. *I think I'm finally growing up, after all these years.*

The house on Finch Street was quiet as usual. She wondered what it would be like to sleep until noon, spend an afternoon in idleness, followed by an evening at a dinner, or perhaps only cards, which she feared was her fate this evening. Her aunt confirmed it.

'It is cards tonight at Sir William and Lady Beecroft's,'

Lady Oakshott reminded Jerusha when she brought the mail and breakfast upstairs. 'Sit a moment.'

Jerusha's first thought was that someone had tattled on her mornings, spent in a place forbidden to her, helping, in her minor way, the men of the Royal Navy, also forbidden. Maybe now was the time to own up to her deception, silent and harmless, in her opinion, but deception, nonetheless.

Aunt Hortensia, you would never approve of how I spend my mornings, she almost blurted out, but stopped herself in time.

She poured tea, still only one cup because her aunt had never requested a cup for her, too.

To her chagrin, Lady Oakshott followed her first sip of tea with a command. 'Sit.'

'Yes, Lady Oakshott?'

'Tonight, you will be under scrutiny.'

'Beg pardon?'

'Scrutiny,' Lady Oakshott said, drawing out the word, until it seemed to stretch into four syllables of vast importance. 'Dear Jerusha, Lady Beecroft informed me that she is considering you as a suitable lady's companion for her mother, who lives a restricted life in Yorkshire.' She waved her hand, as if shooing away a fly or a nuisance. 'Apparently her lady's companion eloped with the local butcher, if you can imagine.'

'I can imagine it,' Jerusha said. 'Yorkshire is probably a dreadful bore.'

Lady Oakshott stared at her. 'I told your mother in my last letter that I would find you a suitable arrangement. The Beecrofts are above reproach in Plymouth. For all that Sir William is in commerce, he is a favourite of the Royal Navy apparently.'

She wrinkled her nose, as if the very idea reeked. Perhaps this was Jerusha's moment. 'Mama might not approve of commerce, Lady Oakshott, and I have no desire to go to Yorkshire.'

Lady Oakshott's eyes narrowed. 'Niece, since it is highly unlikely any suitor will appear, Yorkshire is the next best venture.'

'But…'

'Tonight! Do your best to please.' She waved her away. 'Lady Beecroft already told me she was regarding you with great favour. Don't disappointment me, Jerusha.' She delivered the final blow. 'I don't think you have a choice.'

As if to soften the blow, her aunt smiled, perhaps in what she thought of as sympathy, and concluded with this confidence: 'My dear niece, I believe Lady Beecroft is soon to address me by my first name. You may congratulate me.'

Jerusha heard the implied threat, even in its soft form.

I had better not disappoint her tonight, she thought.

Chapter Twenty-Two

Jerusha Langley was made of sterner stuff. She did not disappoint.

Her first inclination was to pack her bags and go home to Bolling, for better or worse, because she knew Papa's parishioners. Bolling already had its share of spinsters. She would eventually fit right in. But there was the matter of coach fare, which she did not possess.

Dinner was a headache, spent in the dining room with Lady Oakshott. Jerusha held her tongue as her aunt reminded her yet again how to behave. She cringed inside at the usual warning: 'I needn't remind you that if there are any young gentlemen, do not encourage them, because you have nothing to offer.'

No, you needn't remind me, Jerusha thought.

She tipped her ear towards Lady Oakshott's continuous flow of advice and quietly shut her mental door on it, thinking instead of Billy Barton of the *Undaunted*, who had died so peacefully. Blind Man had at least admitted to a daughter with his auburn hair, but no, he provided no other useful information.

'You're not listening to me,' Lady Oakshott accused, as Aggie removed the remaining biscuits and stuck out her tongue at the widow behind her back.

'I will be everything you would like me to be,' Jerusha said. 'If Lady Beecroft mentions Yorkshire, I promise to go into raptures.'

The evening went as expected. Jerusha swallowed her heart, soul, personal feelings and performed to admiration as Lady Oakshott's interim lady's companion. She fetched, she listened, she nodded in all the right places and made herself agreeable, not for any hope of employment in an occupation not to her liking, but merely to prove to herself that she could endure anything.

She began to worry, as the evening progressed. She had expected scrutiny because she knew Lady Beecroft was considering her for a paid companion for her mother. This pointed observation was oddly menacing. As she serenely went about helping the older women even before they knew they needed assistance, Jerusha tried to think how she might have offended Lady Beecroft. She could think of nothing, so shrugged off the feeling, or tried to.

The matter didn't keep her awake, except to exult in Lady Oakshott's obligatory self-congratulation on her slow but steady rise in estimation of Plymouth's better citizens. She seemed so pleased with herself that Jerusha asked, 'Did Lady Beecroft suggest that you had arrived at a first-name friendship?'

The self-satisfaction dimmed. 'No, she did not. I thought she would,' her aunt said, then changed the subject.

Before she slept, Jerusha took another look around the mental room where she stored other treasures of the heart. She thought of the pressure of Jamie Wilson's hand on her shoulder as she sat beside Blind Man two months ago. She sighed over his cheerful farewell as he left Block Four for the blockade. Since there was no one around to scoff, she asked out loud, 'Tell me how wives manage such separations?'

Even in the solitude of her room, she blushed to speak of such things. She brought herself to earth quickly with the knowledge that she would never know the answer. She was twenty-five, with no man likely to go beyond smiling and moving on to someone eligible.

'It's a pity,' she said, after she blinked back tears. 'I would have made some man a wonderful wife.'

The matter of employment occupied her as she left the quiet house that morning. Usually she drank tea downstairs first and visited with her friends, but today she wanted her own time and space to consider an occupation, of which there were few for ladies.

She also began a mental letter to her parents, requesting a small amount to get her home. She hesitated over explaining her reasons, and decided the matter could wait. What would have been the harm in Jerusha simply remaining at home, to fade into old maidhood?

As I see it, Mama, she told herself, *you are still mortified at the disappearance of whatever money might have gone to some gentleman as a dowry, because it all went to Reggie. We could have talked about this.*

If she was more quiet than usual on the drive through neighbouring Devonport to Stonehouse, Jake O'Toole made no mention. He addressed his horse instead: 'Walk on, Noble Beast, and we will hope the jetty bell is as silent as Miss Langley.'

She knew he wanted her to at least smile at that, but it wasn't in her this morning. He shrugged and dropped her off with his typical, 'See you at half past ten.'

There was something in the air besides decay and carbolic as she started up the stairs to Ward A. Her first thought was death, followed by the hope that she would see Jamie Wilson sitting with a patient or writing on a chart.

She held her breath as she heard loud sobs and took her hand off the doorknob, not ready for sorrow on Ward A, where she had come to know the inhabitants. She finally opened the door and peeked in, startled to see the stoic Mrs Terwilliger in tears.

'M-M-Mrs Terwilliger?' she asked. 'Who this time?'

Mrs Terwilliger grabbed her and sobbed. 'It's Blind Man.'

'Oh, no,' Jerusha said, burrowing closer to the stiff and professional ward matron, who suddenly seemed as vulnerable as she felt.

She sniffed back her tears. 'See what you and Sam Wycherly have done. Don't be afraid.'

Jerusha took a deep breath and looked down the row, where Blind Man sobbed and held tight to a bonneted woman who sat on his cot, her hands straining as tight as his.

'She was waiting outside Block Four when I arrived,' Mrs T said in a low voice. 'I think she was waiting to speak to a woman.' Her voice hardened. 'The uppity ups in this block probably ignored her.' She gave Jerusha a little push. 'Go on now.'

'He'll tell me to go away. He always does.'

'Not now, he won't.'

Mrs Terwilliger's push moved her towards the sobbing blind man. Jerusha edged closer until the woman looked up, first in surprise, then in recognition. Her expression softened and she held out a shaking hand. 'I know you,' she said.

Jerusha grasped her hand, no words spoken or necessary. Blind Man must have felt her presence. He reached for her skirt and dabbed at his blind eyes with it as his wife scolded so gently.

'Mind your manners, Hal. I *do* know you. You're the lady in the poster,' his wife said. 'There you were, looking down at a book and reading to my Hal. I found the poster in the Great Market in Devonport.'

'Hal?'

'He is Henry Porter,' she said, 'and I am Claudine. He called me Claudy.' She brushed the hair back from his forehead. 'We met in Toulon, back when it was a safe harbour for the Royal Navy.' She made a face. 'It was before the Corsican Monster. He needs a haircut. No, no, not Napoleon. *This* man, this stubborn, foolish man who thought he would disgust me. I hope your husband is wiser,' she concluded, looking fondly at the shaggy man. 'Hal, how could you ever think I would not love you?'

'Claudy, I'm blind!' The words seemed torn from him, as he surrendered the last of his dignity and the rule of society that man earned the living and woman did everything else. 'Don't you see—I hate that word—that I was trying to spare you from all this…this…' He gestured around the ward.

'I'm looking,' she said, her words full of love. 'All I see is a room full of what look like kind people.' She took the folded poster from her grocery basket and spread it open on the bed. 'See here, Mrs… What is your name?'

'I am Miss Jerusha Langley. My father is a vicar in Bolling. I came to Plymouth for…for a reason I have yet to determine, except that I come here as a volunteer to write letters and wipe dirty faces. My aunt Lady Oakshott doesn't know.'

It seemed to pour out of her in one breath. Claudy stared at her with her mouth open and the Blind Man started to laugh. Jerusha sat back, stunned, to hear his laughter, the anguished man who had held them hostage with his silence. She listened to his laughter and knew there was nowhere else she would rather be in all the world.

The feeling grew stronger when she glanced at Claudy Porter, who held her husband's hand to her breast. In another moment, she released his hand and gave her the poster. 'Usually my neighbour goes to the market for both of us while I watch her twins. She likes to get out more than I do.' Claudy ducked her head. 'I am sometimes teased about my accent. There are widows in Plymouth who have lost their own husbands to the French.'

'I like the sound of it, Claudy, *ma cherie*.'

Claudy leaned closed and kissed her husband's forehead,

murmuring something to him that was soft and gentle and not intended for anyone's ears but theirs. 'I went instead this morning early, because her little ones are teething and cross.' She gently outlined her husband on the poster. 'Otherwise, I would never have seen this… And here I am,' she said simply to Jerusha.

When Surgeon Kidwell joined them, Claudy gave him her full attention. 'Sir, please may I take him home with me?' She held Hal's hand to her breast again. 'I promise to take excellent care of him and…'

Hal did not withdraw his hand. 'Claudy, I am blind and useless.'

'You are my husband. We will find something for you to do,' Claudy replied emphatically. She spoke to Surgeon Kidwell. 'Hal comes from a family of millers in Kent. We will find something there.'

'I expect you will,' the surgeon said. 'I'll make the arrangements, if you wish.'

'But I… You can't…' Hal began. Even to Jerusha, inexperienced in wounds and healing and convalescence, his protest sounded hollow. Gone was the angry man who could not see, all because he was with the woman he belonged to, all his ill nature and protestations aside, which were merely barriers against rejection. It was that simple.

Jerusha spent the morning washing faces as usual, then taking dictation from a newly arrived Marine, pale from blood loss. He had come out of that odd sort of half-awake and half-asleep state of the badly wounded and beckoned to her. 'Please, miss, a letter to my sweetheart,' he told Jerusha. She obliged, her heart heavy, as she watched him struggle to say something coherent. Finally, she wrote what was in her own generous heart to Betsy Strider, who need never know that she, Jerusha Langley, had composed it.

She could nearly feel the Marine's exhaustion. He directed the letter to Betsy Strider, Strider Farm, Roads Cross, Yorkshire. 'She'll be here as soon as she can,' he assured Jerusha, then closed his eyes in death. Jerusha sat beside him until her anger at Napoleon subsided into deep hatred. When she rose from the Marine's bedside at Surgeon Kidwell's quiet reminder that Mr O'Toole was waiting outside, she nodded, took one final look at the sergeant whose name she did not even know, and knew she was born for hard things.

And joyful ones, too. By now the Blind Man, a.k.a. carpenter's mate Hal Porter, was sitting up, dressed, and being fussed over by his wife. 'His father is a mill owner,' she said to Jerusha. 'I will write a letter. In a few days I know we will be on our way. Mr Porter will find something for Hal to do.'

Jerusha told Mr O'Toole about Blind Man on the drive to Finch Lane. 'Surgeon Kidwell tells me that such moments as those are the salary he cannot spend,' she said. 'That could have gone so differently.'

The jarvey nodded, as he slowed his horse in front of Lady Oakshott's house. He turned slightly to regard Jerusha with what looked to her like the sort of satisfaction she would have enjoyed seeing on her own father's face, were he a man given to admiration. 'You are doing a great work. See you tomorrow?'

She waved to him from the kerb, ready to take Aunt Hortensia's letters to her and tuck away her deception until tomorrow. Afternoons and evenings belonged to Lady Oakshott, at least until she finished that letter to Mama. It wasn't going to be an easy letter.

Napier must have heard her come in, even though she was ever so silent. Maybe he had been waiting for her, something he never did, because she knew he did not entirely approve of her actions, which he preferred to ignore.

'Napier, see? I am here and your employer and my aunt are none the wiser,' she said, until she took a good look.

The butler was as pale as the Marine. He took her arm and gave her a little shake. 'Napier?' she said again, as a great dread grew in her.

'She knows!' he whispered to her, giving her another shake. 'She knows! Who should storm in here an hour ago but Lady Beecroft herself.'

Jerusha gasped, her stomach dropping somewhere near the vicinity of her shoes.

'She went upstairs with not so much as a by-your-leave, waving around a smudged poster from some market or other!'

As he paused to collect himself, Jerusha saw, through her own sudden fear, an old man grown suddenly older, and knew it was her doing. 'Napier, I didn't mean to cause trouble,' she began. 'I only want to make myself useful. I will explain myself to her.'

He nodded, his eyes troubled. 'Explain to Lady Oakshott why she isn't going to be received in any more drawing rooms in Plymouth, according to Lady Beecroft, who is lording it over her right now! Go explain that away, Miss Langley.'

Chapter Twenty-Three

Jerusha climbed the stairs slowly, hand over hand. She paused outside the door, unable to knock as she heard snatches of '...foolish and stupid...' and '...vulgar behaviour...' and '...nurturing a viper in your bosom...' and '...tending sick men like a common drudge...'

To Jerusha's sudden remorse, she heard her thoughtless, selfish, unkind aunt weep. She realised, to her horror, what she had done to a foolish woman, yes, but not something she deserved. Scathing mortification washed over Jerusha, bringing along its near relative: shame. She opened the door.

Two women stared at her. Lady Beecroft's face registered a cold disregard. Lady Oakshott's eyes were red with weeping, as though a beloved relative had died. As Jerusha looked at her aunt, she knew she stared at social ruin.

'Please, Aunt Hortensia, let me explain...' she began, and was stopped immediately by Lady Beecroft, who crossed the room quickly, waving the poster in her face.

'I knew it was you last night. I knew it!' she crowed in triumph. She held the poster up to Jerusha's face. 'See there, you foolish woman. *This* is your niece. You have harboured a viper in your bosom!'

Lady Oakshott wailed. 'I had nothing to do with this! You say you saw this in the market?'

'I did nothing of the kind,' Lady Beecroft roared back.

'You think I would go to market like a common fishwife? How dare you?' She turned her attention to Jerusha, who up until then hadn't known a person could actually feel blood draining from her face. This woman, screeching like a banshee, terrified her. She edged closer to her aunt, who, to her further dismay, backed away and wept. She stood between them, a target for both.

'I only…how did you find out, Lady Beecroft?' Jerusha asked.

Lady Beecroft turned to glare at Lady Oakshott, returning the poor woman, weeping, to her sodden handkerchief. 'Hush, you old fool! It was a maid who accompanied the chef. She saw you at an earlier whist party, and told the chef, who…er… appropriated the poster. She told me yesterday.'

So that is why you stared at me last night, Jerusha thought.

Lady Beecroft tossed away Sam Wycherly's wonderful poster that had brought together a blind man and his wife only this morning. 'My maid left this on my breakfast tray this morning and I knew it was you,' she said in a softly sinister voice more frightening than her previous sound and fury. 'Lady Oakshott, how could you be so common as to let her do this in a hospital full of…of…'

'Wounded men,' Jerusha concluded. 'My aunt had no idea what I did each morning.'

Lady Oakshott gasped, perhaps wondering if she could work her way back into Lady Beecroft's fast-vanishing good graces. 'Deceiver! You told me nothing of this! You…you… took advantage of my great leniency…'

'I took advantage, yes, of the fact that you never get up before noon each day, to do something useful in a place where *you* sent me initially, to deliver a basket of useless things,' Jerusha said in a firm voice, even as her insides roiled about.

Both women were silent, so she continued, knowing in her heart and mind that neither would understand what it meant to be useful. 'I wiped off dirty faces. I held the hands of dying men. I wrote letters on behalf of those unable to write, either because of wounds or because they never learned.' She forced herself to cross the room to pick up the discarded, forlorn poster. 'One of the wounded men—he has only one hand— drew this, in the hope of putting several like it in the markets in Plymouth and Devonport to help locate a blind man's wife.'

Silence, then, 'Oh, good for you,' Lady Beecroft said, and Jerusha heard all the venom. 'I suppose there was a touching reunion.'

Jerusha chose to ignore cruel sarcasm. 'As a matter of fact, there was. The poor man had not wanted to be found, because he knew he would blight her life.'

'I don't care,' Lady Beecroft said. 'It was beneath you. For shame.' She came closer to Jerusha, who dug her toes into her shoes, determined not to let this woman frighten her. 'I was going to offer you a position as my mother's companion in Yorkshire. I wouldn't dream of it now.'

'I couldn't dream of it before,' Jerusha replied calmly. 'I would never have accepted.'

Lady Beecroft gasped as if Jerusha had struck her, then Lady Oakshott stuck in her oar, too, perhaps in a vain attempt to remain in that vile woman's good graces. 'Jerusha! Apologise!'

'Never,' Jerusha replied. 'I never wanted to be a lady's companion, Aunt Hortensia. That was your idea.' She should have stopped then, but she couldn't. 'I have done more good on Block Four in three months than either of you have done in your entire lives.'

'Leave this house at once,' her aunt said.

'I wipe my hands of both of you,' Lady Beecroft announced. She narrowed her eyes as she glared at Aunt Hortensia. 'To think I was going to address you by your first name.'

'She's only my niece...barely a relative,' Aunt Hortensia

stammered. 'A few months ago, I wouldn't have recognised her on the street!'

'I doubt another door of any consequence will open to you.'

Lady Beecroft marched across the room to the door. She slammed the door, the feathers in her hat also trembling with righteous indignation.

Jerusha knew she owed her aunt a massive apology. She had been deceitful, without question. Perhaps Lady Oakshott meant well by seeking out gainful employment for a lady gently reared, but with no prospects.

'Aunt Hortensia, I am so sorry,' she said, and she meant it.

'That is supposed to make everything right?' Aunt Hortensia replied, biting off each word.

'I know it cannot.'

'You have ruined me forever in Plymouth,' her aunt said.

'Send me home,' Jerusha said quietly, even as her heart broke. She knew she belonged in Block Four.

To her astonishment, Aunt Hortensia grabbed her arms in a grip that belied her age. 'I wouldn't spend a penny on even the mail coach, you fool,' she hissed. 'Get out of my sight!'

Jerusha left the room, closing the door quietly behind her. She stood there a moment, listening to Aunt Hortensia weep. She put her hands over her ears and stood there until she knew she could go to her room, where she sat as the afternoon passed.

What to do? Aunt Hortensia had turned her off. She had no money. She had no doubt that her aunt was even now composing a letter to her easily influenced little sister in Bolling. Papa might take her back, but preach a sermon about ungrateful children, because she already knew he was somewhat lacking in forgiveness.

Lady Oakshott would probably return to Oaklands when the tenant's lease ended. There might be enough society there to placate her, if the word did not spread of shameful goings-on in Plymouth.

When shadows lengthened, Jerusha washed her face, tidied her hair, squared her shoulders, and made her way below stairs, uncertain of her reception there. There they sat in the servants' hall. Jerusha stood there, waiting for Napier to motion that she join them. When he did not, every fear returned.

'I caused a terrible scene upstairs,' she admitted. 'I am certain you heard it.'

'I think the neighbours heard it, too,' Napier replied, sounding like a stranger.

'Lady Oakshott and I were never close, but I do regret what happened. I suppose now she will return to Oaklands as soon as the lease is up.' Their expressions were unreadable. 'Have you been keeping something from me?'

Again the others looked at Napier, who appeared years older since this morning. 'Lady Oakshott did not lease the house to that mushroom from the City,' he said. 'She sold it to him.'

Jerusha couldn't help her intake of breath. Napier stared straight ahead. 'Sadly, the old place was already deeply in debt. It took nearly all of the purchase price to pay off her creditors.'

She saw a spark of anger in his eyes, this man who had probably been trained from birth to show no emotion. 'Sir Harvey gambled, wenched, and drank. He ruined whatever prospects either of them had. Lady Oakshott only has this house and a small pittance.' He looked at his co-workers. 'None of us have been paid in months.'

'I had no idea,' Jerusha said, when she could speak. 'I suppose my situation is not important to you, is it?'

'Not really,' René agreed, but not unkindly. 'You at least have a home to go to.'

I doubt it supremely, Jerusha thought.

'We shall see. Excuse me, please.'

She went upstairs again, as an idea took hold. She squelched her thought of borrowing money from Napier to get home; they had less than she. Lady Oakshott told her to leave.

What to take? She had come with a sturdy grip and her portmanteau, which would have to remain behind, because she could not afford to cart it anywhere. By folding and rolling, she managed to get two dresses, petticoats, camisoles, nightgown, robe and shoes into the grip, plus smaller items, and her treasured hospital aprons, given to her by Jamie Wilson, who was somewhere between here and France.

There was only one place to go. No one enquired after her as the sky turned dark. When she knew no one would notice, she moved quietly down the stairs and out the door without a backward glance.

She avoided Devonport's streets with grog shops where sailors hung out, and which Mr O'Toole drove past with no qualms. It was strange to hear only silence from the dry docks where warships came for repairs. She walked with purpose, as she watched Mrs Terwilliger walk, confident in appearance, even as she quaked inside, wondering if she was doing the right thing, but knowing she had no choice.

The front door of Block Four was locked, but her momentary panic left her when she saw one of the nuns from Ward B coming out of a side door. When the woman was out of sight, she tried that door, sighing with relief when it opened. It was an easy matter for her to store her grip in the broom cupboard by the morgue.

She put on her apron and walked upstairs to Ward A, where, to her relief, Mrs Terwilliger was supervising the end of supper. Quickly and quietly, she explained her unexpected appearance. 'I will do tonight what I do during the day,' she said, 'if you will let me. Do I know the steward who will be on duty?'

She did, an older fellow who put her to work tidying the men she already knew so well. Sam Wycherly, her dear artist, swore a mighty oath when she told him what had happened.

The word passed quickly, and soon she was left to tend these friends.

Blind Man's bed—no, Hal Porter's—was already occupied by another patient, a frightened powder monkey. She found a book to read to him, loud enough for all to hear. Little by little, she knew that somehow, someway, this would work out.

Chapter Twenty-Four

Jerusha knew Mrs Terwilliger left at seven of the clock. She had no idea what tomorrow would bring, when Surgeon Kidwell returned, and the admin building filled up with men who made decisions. She could think about that tomorrow.

I am in everyone's black books and I have become a burden, she told herself.

When the powder monkey slept, she washed faces as the hospital steward helped the patients who needed urinals. For a rough-looking fellow, he was delicate in his duty and also careful to make sure she did not see anything a tender young woman should not witness. She silently thanked him for this kindness.

On the steward's advice, she took dictation on a letter from another new arrival, who wanted his mother to know where he was, and how fast she could bring a hamper of food. They both laughed over that one.

'Gor, miss,' the gunner said. 'I didn't think I'd laugh again.'

Neither did I, she thought.

When she finished and the ward was full of drowsy men, or patients dosed with laudanum to stop pain for a few hours, Jerusha sat at Mrs Terwilliger's desk. She leaned forward and rested her head on her arms. What a dreadful day this had been, a day when she declared a small measure of independence, with little, really, to show for it.

She started in fear when a firm hand rested on her shoulder.

'No worries, Miss Langley,' she heard, and sighed in relief. Surgeon Kidwell stood there, Mrs Terwilliger beside him. 'Mrs T told me of your dilemma.'

'Had to wait for him to leave Ward B,' the matron said. 'Don't mind admitting that Ward B gives me the willies.'

Personally, I feel closer to God there, Jerusha wanted to tell her.

But that would be presumptuous, and she had caused enough problems for herself and others today. Better to remain silent. God knew she was penitent.

The surgeon sat down with his own sigh of relief. 'Long day. Good night, Mrs T. I'll take it from here. I promise her back to you in the morning.'

'Verra well, sir. G'night, you two.'

'She told me what happened,' he said, with no preliminaries. 'You're in a bad spot, but I can help.' He appraised her, as if searching for courage. 'Or rather, Surgeon Wilson can help, even though he doesn't know it yet. Come along.'

She followed him without question. He waited while she retrieved her grip by the morgue, then followed him out the side door.

'Surgeon Wilson and I are quartered in two houses behind the Admin Building,' he said. He held the lantern higher. 'See there?' He stopped before the second house. 'It would be highly improper for you to stay in my house.'

She nodded, grateful the darkness hid her rosy face, which turned even warmer when he gestured to the other house, lit inside. 'Surgeon Wilson is still at sea, so we are going to take a chance for a few days. You may stay here. I've already discussed the matter with Margaret McDonald, his housekeeper.' She saw his smile. 'Mags found the whole thing entertaining. There is no accounting for the Scots, is there?'

She had no way of knowing any such thing, but she nodded, suddenly aware of just how tired she was. It had been a long, awful day.

She stood back as he knocked on the door, which opened almost immediately to reveal a short and plump woman, neat as a pin and wearing an apron.

'Here she is,' Surgeon Kidwell said simply. 'I know you'll make her welcome.' He nudged Jerusha. 'I'll stop by tomorrow morning at eight, and we can walk to Block Four.'

'I am a lot of trouble, Surgeon Kidwell,' she said. 'I didn't know what else to do.'

'You're only a little trouble, not much over five feet, I think,' he said with a smile. 'I can use your help, oh, my word, I can.'

'But when Jamie—Surgeon Wilson—gets here?'

'He and I will arrange something. Goodnight, Miss Langley.'

He left, then turned back. 'My mother used to say to me, "Things most generally work out." I still believe her.'

'Miss Langley, are you hungry? I am,' Mags McDonald asked, also with no preamble. Jerusha was discovering that medical personnel didn't waste words.

She doubted she would ever eat again, but the chicken stew was perfection. And since Mags—she insisted Jerusha call her Mags—always took a little grog before bed, Jerusha did, too.

'Two parts water and one part rum,' Mags told her. 'Simplest recipe I know. You'll feel better after a snootful of this.'

Jerusha doubted this, too, but her shoulders did relax after she downed the grog, and her eyes grew heavy. Dutifully, she followed Mags up the stairs and into one of three rooms. 'I'm downstairs, and there's only that one small chamber off the kitchen,' the housekeeper explained. 'You'll be fine here.' She gestured. 'The surgeon sleeps across the hall, and he has a wee office in the other room.'

Jerusha looked around the small chamber, with its bed,

bureau, and washstand. 'I'm so tired,' she admitted. 'This will never *ever* do once Jamie—Surgeon Wilson—returns...'

'Then it's a good thing he's not here,' Mag concluded cheerfully. She shook her finger, but Jerusha saw nothing unkind in the gesture. 'Remember what Surgeon Kidwell told you?'

'Things most generally work out?'

As she closed her eyes mere minutes later, Jerusha sincerely hoped they were right.

The deck of a Fast Dispatch Vessel like *Harmony* was no place for a worried man to walk back and forth, but Jamie Wilson had done it before, stepping around rope and other deck accumulation. This time the worry was a lieutenant of Royal Marines below deck with a broken leg that might set correctly with proper pulleys, if he could get him to Haslar Hospital in Portsmouth soon enough.

The wrinkle in that plan? Stonehouse in Devonport was closer, but *Harmony* also carried dispatches from Admiral Nelson cruising off the Strait of Gibraltar, with orders to get them as soon as possible to London. The leg had to wait to Portsmouth.

The able seaman with the shattered collarbone died last night and had been given a burial at sea this morning.

You should have lived, Jamie thought, as he bowed his head with the others and sent the man sewed into his hammock to the depths.

It was a careless accident, as so many were on the blockade, when the tedium of service made crews lax and silly.

But orders were orders. The amputation was doing well, with no red streaks or bad smells to warn of worse to come. The ensign still had most of his lower right arm. He could be fitted with a hook and continue his career on the quarterdeck. He seemed content, and more to the point, alive.

James still wanted to pace back and forth on the deck,

and not solely because of his miniature floating hospital and its patients. Only yesterday he had received a note from Jon Kidwell, tossed aboard *Harmony* with a bag of mail from an outgoing messenger sloop. The message had ended up in the water, and the ink ran. All he could make out was:

Jerusha...bad spot... We're making...

Making something? The rest was illegible except for either *tears* or *fears*.

Although not a message designed to comfort him, it meant Jerusha was still in Plymouth, and must have reached out to Jon Kidwell for something. He added Jerusha to his long list of worries. The longer he practised medicine, the longer that list grew.

Even worse was the overwhelming, all-consuming exhaustion that worked its way into his mind and body never to leave. He had forgotten what a peaceful night's sleep felt like. By the time he returned to Plymouth and saw to his patients aboard the *Harmony*, he would be away again to the blockade.

Usually, his wishful thinking ended right there. This time was different. Nobody on board *Harmony* had any idea he was wondering how nice it would be to lie down with Jerusha Langley, her head tucked into his chest, his arm around her, and sleep. Nothing more. He had never been a man to ask for much, not during this generation of endless national emergency.

And there was this: What could he possibly offer the gently raised daughter of a parish vicar and his well-bred wife? Jamie knew his origins and they were humble; Jerusha knew them, too. She had already told him she had no dowry and was destined for the single life. He also knew her dilemma was none of his business. Better he look forward to a deep sleep in his own bed, and not a hammock that swayed.

To his relief, no fickle wind or additional duty stopped *Harmony* from Portsmouth. The sloop sailed into the bay and the dispatches for Admiralty were handed off to a courier. Captain Ames took *Harmony* directly to Haslar. God bless the architect who knew precisely where to put a naval hospital. Hospital runners waited with stretchers for the broken leg and the amputated arm. Jamie saluted both men, and returned to *Harmony*, where Captain Ames slept on the deck next to the mast.

And God bless you, Captain Ames, he thought, looking down at a man who had come up through the ranks, same as he.

No wonder *Harmony* suited him. There was none of that posturing plaguing other ships. Everyone aboard *Harmony* was as common as ducks in a pond.

A day later in the waning afternoon, the sloop docked in Devonport, snugging right to the wharf because of its small size, and not anchoring in the bay. A bleary-eyed Captain Ames already had orders to sail in two days with the tide. Jamie had prepared his list of medications for the next voyage. He would slip it under the apothecary's door in Block Four and hope it would be ready in two days.

Jamie started towards his quarters behind Admin, ready to collapse in his bed, when the jetty bell began to ring. Too tired to even curse, he turned towards the quad, where the newest crop of wounded would soon litter the ground.

He raised a tired hand to Jon Kidwell, coming slowly from Block Four on crutches, telling Jamie worlds about his fellow surgeon's own exhaustion, when his peg leg pained him. He started towards Jon, until he was grabbed by his night steward and directed towards The Hopefuls, as he called those likely to survive. He worked without stopping.

Two hours later, Jamie pressed his hand into the small of his back and watched the hospital administrator finish assigning the wounded to wards. With a sigh, he turned towards The

Hopeless, to see what, if anything, he could do for those who would never find a bed inside.

In the near darkness, he stared in open-mouthed amazement to see Jerusha Langley, her dress and apron stained with the blood of The Hopeless. Surely he was imagining things, but no. He watched, humbled to the dust, as she carefully wiped what remained of a sailor's face, and held his hand. Her own face was calm. She had eyes only for the dying man.

'Come along. I'll tell you what happened to her,' Jon Kidwell said behind his back. 'She's been staying in your quarters. Her aunt turned her out.'

'What on earth…'

Jon stopped him. 'If I'm misreading the signs, I'll find another place for her tomorrow,' he said. 'If not, then you have been given a rare opportunity.'

If he had been more alert and less exhausted, Jamie would never have said what he did. 'This is war and no time for… for what I am not certain of.'

'It's all the time you have, James,' his superior said. 'Think hard.'

Chapter Twenty-Five

Bless her heart. Mags McDonald had bean soup and bread ready when Jerusha dragged herself back to Jamie Wilson's quarters. It was a simple matter to strip naked in the kitchen and wipe herself free from the blood and unmentionable debris of the dying.

So tired, she barely watched as Mags pocketed a note and turned a cheerful look her way, which startled Jerusha. Surely the old lady had heard the jetty bell ring? To her further surprise, Mags took the comb from her hand and extracted the rest of the detritus of war and wounds from her hair.

'There now,' the housekeeper said in her usual brusque way. 'I'll get my robe. You look too tired to climb the stairs.'

The robe was miles too big, but Mags helped her by tying the belt snugly enough and then touching up her hair again. 'Sit and eat,' she said when she was apparently satisfied. 'If I don't help you up the stairs, someone will.'

It was already their little joke. Mags had assured her it was the joke in many a British household where the men were at war, and wives and daughters left to fend for themselves.

She was halfway through the bowl of beans—vaguely surprised that she could tend to dying men with unspeakable wounds and then knock back a meal—when the front door opened. 'I hope to goodness that isn't someone needing me,' she said to Mags.

'I think it is,' the housekeeper replied, then went into her quarters off the kitchen and closed the door.

To Jerusha's delight, agony, consternation, joy, relief, longing, and total confusion, Jamie Wilson came into the kitchen. As she watched him, her hands folded in her lap, he leaned against the doorframe and smiled, as if he could not get enough of merely seeing her sitting in his kitchen. She knew she was no prize at the moment, but it didn't seem to bother him.

She remembered her manners, as in, 'May I get you a bowl of beans?' and then forgot beans when he wrapped his arms around her.

'I am so tired,' he said, which did not surprise her, not after his weeks at sea. Then she wondered. 'Were you…were you in the quadrangle?'

He released her, which she thought a good idea, since Mags's robe was starting to gape a bit. He sat down, looked at her bowl, and appropriated it without asking, which touched her heart. 'Mags makes the best bean soup,' he said. 'And I have rag manners.'

'You're hungry.'

'You have no idea the depth of my hunger,' he told her.

To her heart's delight, she understood him perfectly because she saw it in his tired eyes. Still, he needed to know. 'My aunt turned me out because she found out my deception.'

'You mean the deception of becoming indispensable to Wards A and B in Block Four? That one?' She heard the tease, despite the exhaustion.

'Aye, that one,' she replied. At least Jamie Wilson might not scold her about the mess she created, all by herself. 'I was wrong to deceive her, when everyone told me to avoid the navy.'

'Would she have given permission for you to help us on Block Four?'

'Certainly not. She considered it beneath me.' He might

as well know more. 'Jamie, she was training me to become a lady's companion, since no man of my society would ever want a wife with no dowry.'

'Men need that bride money, I suppose,' he told her.

Her heart failed her at that simple statement. Better not to show it, so she turned towards the kitchen range. Maybe something needed stirring, except that it was midnight and the stove was clean.

He needed to know everything. 'The worst part is that my deception ruined her in the eyes of those fribbles she has been toadying up to, seeking entry in Plymouth high society.' She had to smile. 'Plymouth *has* no high society.'

'Not that I've ever observed,' he agreed.

'I ruined her, nonetheless,' Jerusha concluded. 'She turned me out. She was counting on her inclusion amongst the wives of admirals and bankers, I suppose.' Oh, why stop there? 'She hid from me that she sold her late husband's country estate, and the purchase price was just enough to discharge Sir Harvey's great debts. All she has is the house on Finch Street and a pittance left for her to live on and no, she has no friends, thanks to my deception.'

That was the worst of it. She dabbed at her tears with the end of the tie on Mags' robe. 'No matter how she treated me, she is worse off because of me.'

'Those friends would have turned her off anyway, once they discovered how poor she is,' he said reasonably. 'It's hard to keep secrets when you're broke.'

'Custom and tradition, Jamie. She tried to hide her ruin, and I made it worse,' she said, tired now and wanting her bed.

'That's out of *my* social sphere,' he assured her. 'Surgeon Kidwell told me how you and Sam Wycherly found the blind man's wife.' He sighed. 'I doubt Lady Oakshott would have approved.'

She felt on safe ground, now that the talk had turned to

Ward A and not her predicament. 'Jamie, he was so determined that his wife not know he was even alive, and she was so happy to find him. Why would a man do that?'

'He wanted to spare her the burden,' he said too quickly, which made Jerusha wonder if this long-forgotten, apparently never-forgotten friend of hers had considered the dilemma himself.

He stood up and held out his hand. 'Let's sit on the back steps. It's chilly out there and I'm falling asleep in here.'

'Then go to bed,' she said, practical again, now that he knew the worst about her. She could figure out where to go in the morning. Mags might know of a position.

'Not yet,' he told her.

She suddenly felt too shy to question him. Maybe he wanted to tell her of his weeks on the blockade, going from ship to ship.

'Why this?' she did ask, when they sat on the outside steps. She had no plan to ever tell him that all she wore was Mags's robe, and the cold from the stone step cut right through. He at least wore a wool cape.

'I like the peace and quiet back here. Nothing is creaking or moving, and no one is going to ask me for anything.'

Oh, dear. This squashed her tentative plan to ask him for mail coach fare home to Bolling. Still, he was probably the only one she knew well enough to help her. She realised she had nothing to lose in the asking. Perhaps she could joke about it.

'Jamie, your statement entirely ruins my feeble plan to ask for the loan of mail coach fare to Bolling. I cannot stay here and…'

'Why not? You're so useful in Ward A, according to everyone,' he said. 'Even our dragon lady, Mrs Terwilliger.'

She looked at him in amazement. 'Mrs T said something nice? Surely not.'

'Surely yes. She told me you are fearless.'

If I never get another compliment in my life, I can die content, she thought.

'I had no idea.'

'What will happen if you go home?' he asked, when she was starting to wonder if he had fallen asleep. He seemed to be leaning against her, or maybe she was leaning his way.

'Mama will weep and sigh, and Papa will deliver a lengthy sermon about the sins of deception and ingratitude.'

'That's wicked,' he said in a tone of voice that made her never want to cross him.

'I will find out when I get home.'

His arm went around her and she leaned in. 'Jerusha, do you really want to leave?'

The question hung in the air, delivered in total seriousness. Something sweet and certain told her he was really asking, 'Do you want to leave me?'

Did she want to leave him? Never.

Jerusha Langley took a deep breath and changed the course of her life. She held his hand to her cheek and kissed it. 'No, I do not,' she said firmly, the right answer.

He tightened his grip on her shoulder, which more than suggested that for the rest of their lives, this man would protect her, and if she was lucky, love her.

'We'll manage, Jerusha,' he replied. 'We'll manage.'

He relaxed his grip, and she burrowed closer. 'I have to return to the blockade immediately.'

When she started to cry, he handed her an already used handkerchief, all he had. 'Blow your nose. I can get a common licence for eight shillings today. I believe it is after midnight.'

'But the banns...'

'Nae, nae lassie, listen a moment. The Royal Navy has certain prerogatives. Banns don't matter.' He held her off and took a good look at her. 'Are you prone to seasickness?'

'I have no idea,' she answered honestly.

'No matter. Whatever ship I am on is my parish. Right now, it's the *Harmony*, Captain Ames commanding. I am going to pay a persuasive visit to Plymouth's bishop, whose son I tended successfully at the Battle of the Nile. I think I can convince him to marry us on the deck of the *Harmony*. That is another prerogative. I'll help you down the gangplank like a real gentleman, and I'll sail away like a cad. What an offer! Aye or nay?'

She smiled at that, then watched his face, seeing exhaustion. Perhaps when he had some sleep, he might shake his head at this folly and call the whole thing off. Until that happened— if it did—she was ready and willing. 'Aye.'

He pulled her up and kissed her soundly, which did amazing things to her body. He led her up the stairs and pointed to the left. He went to the right.

'Lass, when you come down for breakfast, I'll be gone,' he said. 'Go to Block Four and help all you can. Can you locate Mr O'Toole?'

She nodded.

He seemed to understand her shyness. 'Ask him to meet us at the dock and come aboard, too.'

'Surgeon Kidwell and Mrs Terwilliger, as well?'

'They'll probably have to do a coin flip, one or t'other.' He kissed her. 'Find a better dress. Mags's robe is a little casual for a wedding.'

With that, he yanked the tie off and chuckled as she tried in vain to cover herself. 'G'night, my bonnie lassie.'

Chapter Twenty-Six

He had huge doubts the next morning; maybe that was what two hours sleep did. In the middle of the night, Jamie opened his bedchamber door several times to stare at Jerusha's closed door, but went no farther. He lay down again, revisiting the sight of Jerusha's beautiful body in the half-light of the upstairs corridor, then went over every medication he needed to cajole from the apothecary. He scolded himself for thinking a wartime wedding like this was even remotely a good idea. His doubts didn't vanish, but did slink away to a dark spot, maybe to jump out later and yell 'Boo!'

Mags didn't seem surprised at his announcement. 'I thought this would happen.'

Between toast and tea, he told her about his and Jerusha's back step decision, which made her laugh. On her advice, he gathered up his papers identifying him as a naval surgeon, place of birth, and other proof that he was not a drooling idiot. With those, and a visit to the bishop, who remembered him and couldn't stop thanking him, he acquired a common licence. Minus eight shillings, he arrived at Block Four a few hours later.

He nodded to Jerusha, who sat beside one particularly obnoxious purser's mate who was barely wounded and taking up bed space, then sat down to write a quick note to Captain Ames aboard *Harmony*. He sealed it and before he lost his nerve, handed it to the runner who had followed him into Block Four and now relieved him of another shilling as he darted away.

He wanted to sit down with Jerusha Langley, apologise for his hasty proposal last night, and see if she felt the same way. They could end this mad business with no one the wiser. On the other hand, his Scottish soul reminded him that he had spent eight whole shillings on permission to rapidly wed and eventually bed a wife.

A moment came during the noon meal, when Mrs Terwilliger and her assistants passed around food, helping where needed. He rose to seek out Jerusha, but annoyingly, she was helping someone already. He got close enough to see that her eyes looked tired, suggesting that she had suffered a restless night, too. He needed to say something to her. No time.

Then it was an afternoon of setting bones, and performing an amputation there in the ward with a curtain separating them from patients probably trying to studiously ignore the noise, tears, and rasping of saw. At least it was quick.

He was assisted by Jon Kidwell, who looked at him with merry eyes once the worst was over, and the patient, lighter one foot, dozed with the blessing of Surgeon Laudanum. Still behind the curtain, Jamie poured out his doubts. Kidwell stopped him. 'This is the smartest thing you have ever done.'

'What? Ruin someone's life? I could die at sea tomorrow.'

Kidwell shrugged. 'War is the hand we have been dealt, I would remind you, Surgeon Wilson. Look around you.'

Jamie had one last, weak card to deal in that hand of death, something feeble about sparing the woman he loved. He thought about a sweet face on a crowded dock, waiting for him to return, a sight he longed for, if he was honest, because he had no one, either. Was it fair, though?

'I'm a coward,' he said simply.

'Hardly. You see right here the consequences of war. That

doesn't make you a coward, because you *are* going to marry Jerusha this afternoon, in spite of what you know about suffering and death.' Kidwell clapped a hand on his shoulder. 'I envy *you*.'

Jerusha bided her time quietly all that long day, with Jamie so close but busy, and when he wasn't busy, in intense conversation with Surgeon Kidwell. She knew he must be having second thoughts, and she did not blame him. She took her own census of her defects. All she brought to marriage was a pretty face. Yes, there was silliness about a dip in the duck-pond, possibly the only thing they had in common. She thought of all the reasons this was nonsense.

She told herself to stop. There was work to do, and time between their walk from Stonehouse to *Harmony*'s dock to sort this out and end it. He would sail away.

The matter became simpler. Cot Fourteen's mother enlisted her to hand out soft bread and jam to those who could eat it. Jerusha marvelled at such goodwill in a sad place. She glanced at Jamie's broad back a few times—he had a marvellous back—and knew this turmoil would amount to nothing.

She had distributed the last of the bread and jam when Jamie gestured to her by Mrs Terwilliger's unoccupied desk.

This is it, she thought, because he had removed his surgeon's apron.

She glanced at the clock and knew it was over.

You're not waiting to walk me to the dock.

He spoke with no preamble, because that was Jamie Wilson. She braced herself, then wondered. 'I am to supervise my pharmacopeia order immediately,' he told her. 'There's no one else to get it to *Harmony* and I need it. I must leave now.'

Over and done, and neatly, too. 'I hope you have a successful voyage,' she said.

He gave her a strange look. 'What I mean is, I won't be

able to walk with you to the dock. I'll meet you there. Do you need directions?'

She shook her head. He handed her directions anyway, written on the back of a prescriber's pad. 'Your handwriting is illegible,' she said, which made him chuckle.

'Just look for a small ship with one mast and a quantity of naval stores being loaded aboard. See you in an hour.'

And he was gone like that, a surgeon intent on getting his medical supplies on board his second home, doing battle with Napoleon. She returned to her duties, well aware that if she didn't show up at the dock, *Harmony* would sail anyway, no matter what. He might be at sea for another six weeks, and she could be home in Bolling. A grovelling letter to Mama would provide mail coach fare.

Except for one thing. She surveyed Ward A and found herself looking at Blind Man's cot, occupied again. Still, the sight remained of Blind Man and his wife, their arms around each other, ready to do battle with an enemy besides Napoleon, but together for the fight. In that moment, Jerusha Langley knew that if she did not walk to the *Harmony* and know for sure, she would regret it the rest of her life.

She walked by herself, head up, shoulders back, and no target for lounging sailors. The air was brisk and cold, and the water had a chop to it. The sight of a row of docked ships stopped her. She looked in the bay where the larger ships of war anchored. It was a world foreign to her, but she felt the energy and the need for speed, with the turning of the tide soon.

There was *Harmony*, so small that it dismayed her.

A big wave will swamp this wee thing, she thought. *What can the Royal Navy be thinking? That's my man on board.*

She stood still with that realisation. *Her man on board?*

She saw other women waiting, some with little ones, some

alone. She was about to join a sorority of those who waited, feared, and hoped.

How do they do it? she asked herself, even as she knew she had committed herself.

Uncertain, she stood by the ship, watching the loading of the last cargo, winched up efficiently, the ropes soon to be stowed. Men were already climbing the rigging, heading to furled sails. Was she too late?

'Jerusha.'

James stood near the wheel. He motioned her closer and started for the gangplank, a narrow affair that made her frown. When she hesitated, he came down as calmly as if he strolled along a wide boulevard. He held out his hand and she grasped it.

'Watch your step. They're still stowing things,' was all he said.

'This boat really looks too small for the ocean,' she said. He ended all argument by holding her close. She turned her face into his uniform, which smelled of brine and camphor.

'It's a sloop, not a boat, dear lubber,' he said.

She remembered something she wanted to tell him from their first encounter since Bolling and a duck-pond. She held herself away from him, noting his disappointment at that, but wanting to see his face. 'I should have told you this sooner,' she said, laughing inside at his wary look.

'Should I worry?'

'Not at all,' she replied. To her delight, Mrs Terwilliger came puffing up the gangplank.

'I taught myself how to swim,' she said quickly. 'I can float and paddle about. I promise I won't sink ever again.'

He laughed and gave her a loud smack of a kiss, then turned her around to face Captain Ames, who eyed them with a smile of his own. The bishop stood beside him and opened his prayer book while the first lieutenant bellowed, 'Stow the noise, ye fiends of hell!'

'I don't have a ring,' Jamie whispered in her ear.

In sudden, unexpected silence on a ship preparing to get underway with the tide, they were married. It was a brief ceremony. A sail thundered down as the bishop said, 'Kiss your wife, Surgeon Wilson, then see her over the side.'

He kissed her and held her close. 'I had the coldest feet this morning,' he told her. 'All day, if I'm honest.'

'So did I,' she said. 'I changed my mind three or four times.'

'And here you are anyway. I'll see you who knows when,' he told her, after they signed a registry and then the sailing master's log. 'There's a war on, my love.'

'Say that again,' she asked impulsively.

'A war on?' he teased.

'Oh, you…'

He pulled her close and put his hands on her neck. 'My love,' he mouthed, then kissed her, to the general enjoyment of the crew, the bishop, and Captain Ames.

He helped her down the gangplank as the ship's crew cheered. 'I'm a particular favourite,' he confided, 'except when I wield a dental key or treat one of them for the clap.'

'That's hardly loverlike conversation,' she told him, even if she wanted to tug him back to his house and see what happened in that bedchamber across the hall.

'Wait till I come back,' he replied, his face serious now.

Sniffing back tears, Jerusha stood on the dock until *Harmony* sailed out of sight.

Mrs Terwilliger walked her back to Stonehouse, then told her to go home.

Home.

She looked down at the wedding papers Jamie Wilson had put into her hands, along with a pouch. She opened it, looking inside to see shillings, a key, and a note, which was—true to form—scribbled on a prescriber's pad.

She read it.

This is your house. My bed has an excellent mattress. Remember me, my dearest duck-pond girl.

Chapter Twenty-Seven

Jerusha set about becoming a wife without a husband, a husband she knew she wanted more every day. She lay in bed the next morning after her hurry-up wedding, hands folded together, watching the day come. She enjoyed the luxury of there being no one in the house, Mags a possible exception, to tell her what to do.

That realisation lasted briefly because she knew duty summoned her from Stonehouse. There were never enough people to help Mrs Terwilliger, an awesome dragon who frightened pursers and bosuns, but was tender enough to sit beside a frightened Marine until he died.

And those letters Jerusha wrote for others weren't going to write themselves. She got up, made her bed, then padded across the corridor to her husband's empty chamber. She was almost afraid to open the door, so palpable was his presence.

'Such a tidy man I married,' she said, marvelling at the order. The bed was neatly made. It touched her heart to see that his pillow still bore the indentation of his head, telling her he must have lain down for a moment after he made his bed.

She came closer to observe the book on his bed, with a folded note on top. There it was, addressed to *Jerusha Wilson*.

She sat down and read it, her hand to her cheek, whispering the words.

Dearest Jerusha,
If you wish, read this book first. It's basic and contains
information to begin your own medical education, if I
am not overstepping any rights and privileges I might
have as a husband. I regret that likely no one will allow
your intelligence to be considered in its true light, but
you will be knowledgeable all the same, and surpass-
ingly useful.

She followed the arrow with her finger, laughing softly as
it meandered all over the page, then indicated she turn it over.

Or don't read it. The choice is absolutely yours. If you
wish to stay here and tend our home, I will be equally
satisfied. The choice is yours and no other's.
Love,
Your husband

'You dear man,' she said, and ran her finger lightly over
those three words. 'I will always be safe with you,' Jerusha
said.

She kissed the letter and put it in the book. She dressed and
went downstairs, hoping not to wake Mags, but pleased to see
her in the kitchen anyway, porridge and tea ready.

'Mags, I could do this, and you could sleep,' she said, which
earned her a stare over the older woman's spectacles, followed
by a finger-wag and a smile.

'It's what I do for the master,' Mags said. 'You are his mate.'

'I am, aren't I?' she asked, still filled with the wonder of
it all. She blushed then, aware in her mind at least, that she
might be married, but she wouldn't be Jamie's wife until there
was time to consummate the matter.

Mags seemed to understand her red face. 'Give it time,
lovey. He'll be back.'

Without asking, the housekeeper fixed her a luncheon of meat and cheese, with one apple, and wrapped it in a large handkerchief. 'I'll tell you what I tell the master: Take the time to eat and don't just throw it away on the way home and tell me a fib.'

'Surely he would never…' Jerusha started, then laughed. 'I promise.'

She began her morning as she usually did, cleaning up after breakfast and washing faces, Mrs Terwilliger supervising, which meant that the matron looked up from her paperwork every few minutes and stared intently.

Letters came next, which more and more led to quiet time to merely sit and listen as some of the wounded sailors told her how they earned their cots in Stonehouse. Some were matter of fact and cheerful, others embarrassed that the hated Frenchies caught them off guard. Still others tried to tell her, but ended up in tears. She cried with them.

She made herself eat her sandwich and apple, then asked Surgeon Kidwell what he wanted her to do. 'Jamie said I should make myself useful,' she explained. 'He…he even left a book for me to read.'

The surgeon considered her request. 'Follow me. Watch. Then read for an hour.'

And that became her day, and then her week. After lunch, she followed and watched, eyes filled with sympathy and sometimes horror as the one-legged surgeon stumped from cot to cot, tweaking there, mending here, observing everywhere.

Her test came at the end of the first week of her marriage, when he drew the curtains around a man with burns on his leg. Jerusha knew him as Hank from Sheffield, a bosun who had tried to drag out one sailor too many from a burning bomb kedge before it exploded. Two days before, Jerusha had watched Surgeon Kidwell and his steward remove the dead tissue with tweezers. She winced as the burned man winced and sniffed back her own tears when he cried.

'Here,' the surgeon said, handing her his tweezers. She looked around for the steward. Nowhere in sight. She took the tweezers from Kidwell, and then looked into the eyes of the bosun. 'I... I really don't want to hurt you,' she said. 'I promise you.'

'Pluck away,' he told her cheerfully, 'as long as you promise me a kiss when you're done.'

She smiled at that, imagining what Jamie would say, and began her work gently and carefully. She pulled away the burned skin as the bosun swore quietly under his breath. He grabbed at her hand once and she turned her hand to hold his, fingers twined together.

Surgeon Kidwell watched the whole thing, guiding her hand where needed, then readying the ointment when she finished. 'Spread on a light coat, and we'll cover it with this gauze.'

She did as he said, relieved to be done. Hank lay there with his eyes closed. She kissed his cheek. 'There now. I'll do better next week.'

'I have a daughter. She's about your age now.'

She kissed his cheek again. 'This one is for her,' she said, then moved to the next cot with Surgeon Kidwell.

'You're a cool one,' he said.

'Thank you, Surgeon Kidwell,' she said, feeling far from cool.

'Call me Jon,' he said, which meant Jerusha gained admission into the society of suffering.

She wrote about it that evening in what became her nightly letter to Surgeon James Wilson, Ship FDV *Harmony*. Channel Fleet, Ship to Shore.

Mags reminded her to put a number on the back of each. 'That way the men know what has gone astray, as most do.'

Every morning Jerusha took each letter to the Administration Building and left it in a box marked Channel Fleet. Once she learned that there was something to write about every day, she hoped she wouldn't make her husband the fleet's laughingstock. She said as much to Jon Kidwell.

'He's the envy of nations, providing any of the letters find their way to a little sloop always on the move.'

She contented herself with that, and so she told the comatose man in Ward B, where she always ended each long day. 'I don't know what they hear, if anything, but sometimes I think I see a spark in their eyes,' Jon told her earlier on a ward walk through cots with dead men still alive. 'Talk to them. What can it hurt?'

She lost her fear of death in Ward B. The nuns kept the men clean and fed the ones who could eat. The others died quickly enough. The comatose man—according to his chart he was a gunner—lay there with his eyes open, blinking now and then. Feeling like a silly woman complaining, Jerusha told him what had happened to her at number twenty-eight Finch Street. Now and then he frowned, and she wondered.

Something happened as she told her own story to him. The sting of her rejection by Aunt Hortensia left her, as she realised that her trials were nothing compared to what these heroes, these men who kept her safe from Napoleon, had suffered. 'I'm sorry I complain so much,' she whispered to the gunner as she said goodnight at the end of her second week.

It must have been her imagination, but she thought he managed a slow wink. 'What you must think of me,' she told him, and left after straightening his coverlet, all with the approval of one of Ward B's Sisters of Charity.

That next evening, she came home to two letters addressed to Mrs James Wilson, Stonehouse, Quarters D, Devonport, England. Mags, all smiles, had set them beside her dinner plate. They were number One and Four. She read them in silence while Mags busied herself in the kitchen. 'He hopes you are doing well, Mags,' she said, after blushing over Letter Four that ended with his longing to see much more of her anatomy in a few weeks.

'Mags, how do people manage when they are so far away?' she asked. 'How did you manage with your foretopman gone so often?'

'The same as you're doing.' Mags's voice lost that brisk tone, which threw off years and miles as nothing else could have. 'I kept very busy. Eat your dinner now, or I'll scold!' Her tone softened again. 'Mark my words. He'll show up when you least expect him.'

Chapter Twenty-Eight

I am a well-trained surgeon, professional and concerned about my patients to the exclusion of all else.

Over a tankard of *all* parts rum—no one's idea of navy grog—Captain Ames had so expressed himself to his first mate and Surgeon Wilson one night after a near collision with a frigate in a freezing rain off the Brest blockade. Of course, Captain Ames had said 'captain' and 'crew' instead of 'surgeon' and 'patients,' but Jamie heard the message clearly. All *he* wanted to do—professional or not—was to go home and crawl in bed with his wife.

'We're to do our duty, gentlemen,' Captain Ames added, raising his middle finger to that careless frigate that nearly mowed them down. 'What do you say, gentleman? Shall we not leave HMS *Brawler* any mail?'

They all laughed, men well acquainted with both danger and duty, and now it was definitely pea coat weather on deck. Jamie draped his arms over the railing in lubber fashion, impervious to hoots and catcalls from his fellow seamen.

Captain Ames joined him at the rail. 'Heading home and high time, Surgeon.' He nudged Jamie. 'I reckon you are more eager than most.'

For six weeks he had been teased about his remarkable wedding on the deck of HMS *Harmony*. There were no blushes left in him. 'I am not the only eager husband aboard this sloop,' he corrected.

'Perhaps, but you are the envy of all. How is it that you get a letter or two with each passing messenger sloop?'

'She likes to write to me,' Jamie said. 'She writes every day.'

'How she can possibly think of something to write about every day is beyond me,' Captain Ames said. 'My wife can only manage a letter or two a month.'

'Anyone working at Stonehouse always has something to write about,' he replied and stared at the water again. He could tell the captain about her latest medical education, but would he understand? Jamie read Letter Number Twelve several times, marvelling to himself how someone so quiet, shy almost, could debride a burn and not slump into a dead faint. It was not women's work, not at all. She wrote how it terrified her, but she learned anyway, because Surgeon Kidwell was overworked, and the jetty bell rang all the time.

The *Harmony* worked her way through the fleet, laden with dispatches and mail and bound for home. They were five days out from England when Lieutenant Simpson, grimmer of face than usual, burst into the sick bay as Jamie was tying off a final stitch on a gunner's laceration.

'Topside!' he shouted.

Jamie followed him to the deck, where a frigate was backing her sails. 'Look.' Simpson pointed to the signal flags snapping in the cruel wind that seemed to roar down the Channel.

Extreme Distress flew. There was more to follow, and he waited for it, knowing that one captain's idea of extreme distress differed from another.

'What is it?' he asked the bosun's mate, who stared in surprise.

'I'll be damned, sir. It's Baby.'

Jamie grabbed his satchel and rooted about for some cloths.

He had no small blanket, but he found a towel. He mentally rehearsed what to do, since it had been three years since he had delivered a baby. Still, babies were babies.

On deck, he slung his satchel across his body and wrapped the cloths under his new pea coat, a gift from a grateful Dutch mariner he had cured of piles. He wasted not a moment in settling into the sling and nodding to the bosun's mate, who lowered him always too close to the water.

The distance was short. As soon as he was aboard the frigate *Naiad*, the *Harmony* backed off and waited.

The captain himself waited on the *Naiad*'s deck. He took Jamie by the arm and hurried him to the companionway. 'It's a damned sad business,' he said, his voice soft. 'The wife of our sailing master is dying in childbirth.'

'Let's hurry then,' Jamie ordered.

He ran down the companionway with the captain and into the wardroom. 'This is Master Whittier,' the captain said, motioning to a man with sorrowful eyes who stood by an open hatch in the wardroom.

'Please, surgeon, can you do anything?' Master Whittier said. 'Our surgeon is in the middle of a malarial relapse—damn the Caribbean anyway.' He started to cry. 'Maudie insisted on coming along to the blockade. She's done it before, but this time… Oh, God. In here.'

Jamie stared down at a woman mere seconds away from death. Her eyes were already sinking back into her head. Ear to breast, he listened for a heartbeat. As he listened, it stopped.

He waited not a second, pushing the master and captain out of the stateroom and slamming the hatch shut. His concentration fierce, he whispered, 'I will save your baby,' and went to work with his capital knives.

Not until the infant was out and screaming at the top of her lungs and the cord cut, did he close his eyes for a tiny moment of peace. Not until he opened them did he notice a wide-eyed young man crouched in the corner. 'Are you the surgeon's mate?'

The lad nodded, tears on his face. 'I tried to help. There was nothing I could do.'

'Nay, lad. It was a terrible presentation. I want you to wrap this little lady in that blanket over there and take her to her father. Don't let anyone in here.'

The mate did as asked, and hurried with his screaming bundle through the hatch. Jamie sewed up the woman. He made her presentable by smoothing back her still-sweaty hair. He marvelled at the peace on her face now, as if she somehow knew her baby was alive and well and noisy. Such a pretty lady. He thought of Jerusha and vowed she would never follow him to sea, as some wives of masters did.

In another moment he had bound the pretty lady into a blanket and knotted the ends. No need for the sailing master to see anything. He washed his hands, removed his bloody apron, and stowed it, then opened the hatch.

The sailing master, tears streaming down his face, held his daughter. 'My wife was a bonnie lass,' he said. What he said next did not surprise Jamie. He knew sailing masters were generally the smartest men on a ship. 'Surgeon, obviously I cannot take care of her, but I have a sister and brother-in-law in Cornwall who would love this little one heart and soul, because my sister is barren. Will you get her to them for me?'

'Aye, sir,' Jamie said.

'Thank you from the depths of my heart. I… I don't know how you're going to feed her, even with the—what—four days from here to England,' the father said, as he held his daughter close to his chest. 'I just don't know.'

Beyond the fact that his daughter was alive and well, there was another good piece of news Jamie had for the bereft man. 'I'm on a Fast Dispatch Vessel. We have, of all things, a mama goat aboard.'

'You're jesting me.'

'You would be amazed what we haul back and forth,' Jamie said. 'It belongs to a lieutenant aboard a warship at Ferrol whose goat ate his captain's best wool stockings. It was apparently the last straw.' No point in telling a sorrowing man that the lieutenant sneaked the goat and her kid aboard the *Harmony* before his captain ate the thing in revenge.

The master managed a smile. 'I suppose we have seen it all, on blockade.'

'Aye, sir. Your daughter will be in good hands from here to Cornwall. Just give me the address,' Jamie said, his own heart full to bursting. 'I have eyedroppers and syringes. No fears, sir. No fears.'

And so it was that Jamie Wilson carried a baby to his house a week later in the middle of the day. Between his medical duties and 'round the clock tending of an infant on a dispatch vessel, he could not remember when he had slept last. Captain Ames gave him a long and mournful look as they disembarked from *Harmony*. 'Four days only and we sail again. I'll expect you back from Tweazel.'

'Aye, sir,' Jamie said. He understood duty, as much as he sometimes hated it.

'If I were a braver man, Jamie my lad, I would apologise to your new bride myself. She still isn't going to see much of you.'

Mags McDonald met him at the door, her mouth open and her eyes wide. Barely able to keep his eyes open, Jamie told the whole, sad story to his housekeeper.

When he'd finished, she held up her hand. 'Wait right here,' she said. 'Don't move.'

'I probably couldn't,' he said, mystified. Still, he had grown somewhat attached to the little one, who was stirring now, probably hungry, and ready for goat's milk through an eyedropper.

Mags darted out the door, moving faster than he had ever

seen. He watched her out the window as she ran towards the littlest house on the row, the one belonging to a hospital steward on Block Three.

She came back more sedately, arms linked with the wife of the Block Three steward. He opened the door for them. 'Well, Maisie Brower, you've been kidnapped,' he teased.

'Aye, sir,' she said, and took a long look at the infant, wrapped in a towel, that he held close to his chest. 'What's she been living on?'

'Goat's milk.'

'Hand her over. I have plenty.'

He stared in amazement as Mrs Brower opened her bodice, gave the little one a nudge, and smiled as she latched on. 'There now, there now,' she crooned.

'I still have to get her to Tweazel,' Jamie said. 'In God help us Cornwall.' He sat down, his eyes closed, and his head dropped forward.

'Don't be so certain about that,' his own dear Jerusha told him only spare minutes later, as she arrived on the run, breathing hard. She shook him awake, gave him a smacking kiss, and blew a kiss to Maisie Brower now burping the baby.

He doubted he had ever seen a more beautiful woman, and she was his. 'I wish I could stay here, my love, but I have four days to get this babe settled. Then it's off to the blockade again.'

As tired as he was, he saw the silent message pass from Mags to Maisie Brower to Jerusha, the secret code of women that he knew he would never understand. He knew enough to gently remind them that the baby was promised elsewhere and he had a duty to get her there.

'Of course, dear man,' Jerusha said. 'Can you, Mags? And you, Maisie?'

'I'll go home and bundle up my little one,' Maisie said. 'There's milk aplenty for both. Keep your goat.' She handed the sailing master's baby to Jerusha and was out the door in a moment. Jamie could only stare at them in befuddled, exhausted amazement.

Jerusha took charge, the baby asleep on her shoulder now.

'Surgeon Kidwell can make arrangements for a post chaise. You know how he is. Mags, you'll be on your way within the hour. Go pack. I'll tuck in the surgeon.'

'Wait… I…' He what? Jamie couldn't think of how to end a sentence. 'But…'

He wasn't sure how Jerusha steered him upstairs, but he made no objection when she pulled back the bed covering and helped him from his clothing. When he was bare, she kissed his shoulder and pulled up the blanket.

'Nighty-night, sleep tight,' was the last thing he remembered.

Chapter Twenty-Nine

Jamie Wilson slept for twenty-four hours. Jerusha watched him for an entire luxurious hour, sitting in the comfortable chair in his bedchamber, knowing that when she looked up from the medical text she read, he would be there. In itself, that was bliss.

The silence of the house was also bliss, not that she or Mags McDonald were noisy women. She tried to imagine how peaceful this must seem to a man either at sea, with the constant creak of a ship, or in a hospital, with people moaning in pain.

The exhaustion on his face saddened her. She knew he must be twenty-eight or so, if she was twenty-five, but between ocean winds and constant medical emergency, he had earned the lines on his face. She thought of other sailors she tended on Ward A, and silently thanked them—and this man asleep before her—that she and others like her were kept safe from the warfare on that tortured continent across the English Channel.

She watched his whole body relax as he stretched out on his back. She watched the rise and fall of his chest and found herself breathing along with him in perfect rhythm. She found herself relaxing, too.

There was work to do. She returned to Block Four, explaining the situation to Surgeon Kidwell, requesting he arrange a post chaise now and assuring him that she would return in a day or two. 'When he wakes up, he will want to attend here,' she told him without a blush. She added, 'I intend to be an obstacle for his appearance in Ward A. I offer no apology.'

Surgeon Kidwell nodded, grinned, and started for the stairs. 'Post chaise first,' was all he said.

'My husband is back,' she told Mrs Terwilliger. 'He is mine for a while.' This earned her an unexpected smile and a shooing motion towards the door, which made them both laugh.

She spent the afternoon and evening reading and taking notes, pausing when Jamie muttered to himself, disturbed by dreams. With humility, she wondered how any man in a world at war could escape the danger and terror, even in slumber. She thought of the letters she had written for her wounded patients, letters that spoke of amusing incidents and mundane duty. She had watched enough of them to know their nightmares belied all the simplicity of their letters, written to reassure loved ones. She thanked God for their resilience.

Jerusha thought he might wake up as night fell, but he slumbered on, telling her worlds about his need for rest. When it was full dark, she stripped and put on her nightgown. She knew she would never get to sleep, but she did, lulled to slumber by the warmth of another person so close.

At some point during the night, she draped her leg over his legs. He murmured something, but did not wake up. Neither did she, until morning. She woke up to stare at his back and admire the width of those shoulders. She smiled to see freckles there, as she thought she might.

After breakfast of boiled eggs and toast, Jerusha washed herself thoroughly, wondering if she should take a tin of water upstairs. Jamie was bound to wake up eventually. As it was, she marvelled at the sturdiness of his bladder.

Not inclined to ever wake a sleeping person, Jerusha made herself comfortable in Jamie's chair again, continuing her vigil. It lasted until mid-morning, when he opened his eyes at last.

'Oh, Jerusha,' was all he said. He closed his eyes, then opened them. 'You're still here,' he joked, which made her laugh.

'Let me give you a moment's privacy,' she said, much as she would say to a patient in Ward A, where Mrs Terwilliger told her not to attend to anyone's pissing.

'I've heard you say that a time or two.' With no embarrassment he got out of bed and went into the adjoining room.

Jerusha set aside the book on her lap. The wave of shyness that washed over her surprised her. This beautiful, naked man belonged to her. She considered the matter in her practical way and knew what to do.

When he returned, she ushered him back to bed, fluffing the pillow behind his head. Amused, he patted the space beside him. She sat, after bringing over that tin of now warm water from the kitchen and a cloth.

'See here, this is what I do, because Mrs Terwilliger has trained me well.' As he smiled, she washed his face. 'I'm good around the ears,' she told him. 'You get a neck wash, too. Mrs T only lets me wash a man down to his waist, because she is circumspect.'

'Aye, she is. We can't have any wild notions,' he said. His smile widened. He stretched, then grabbed her and rubbed his unshaven face into her neck, which made her shriek and then laugh. 'What follows?' he asked. 'She's trained you well.'

You dear man, she thought. *You are putting me at my ease.*

'That's simple,' she said and went to his desk, returning with paper and pencil. 'You tell me what I am to write to a loved one. Don't be shy.'

He put his hands behind his head. 'How about this? *Dearest Jerusha, I love you more than I can express in mere words.*' He looked over at her. 'Well?'

Her face rosy, she wrote what he said. 'That's a short letter.'

'There's more.' He regarded the ceiling. 'Add, *Kindly re-*

move your clothing and get into bed with me. Yours most sincerely, Jamie Wilson. Will that do?'

She set down the pen and pencil, stood up, and slowly unbuttoned her bodice, her eyes on his. Her dress crumpled at her feet. Her camisole came off next, after a little hesitation. She knew how abundant she was, and she hadn't bothered with a corset today. From the sigh she heard, her favourite surgeon didn't seem to mind, even if fashion dictated smaller bosoms.

Like most women, she only bothered with small clothes during her monthly flow, so when she slid off her petticoat, that was that. She looked deep into her husband's eyes, liked what she saw there, and got in bed when he raised the coverlets.

At first he did nothing but hold her close, running his hand down her hip. 'You're wondrous soft,' he said. 'You realise this entire thing is preposterous and unbelievable and yet here we are together.' He kissed her breast, then raised teasing eyes to hers. 'And glory be to God, you can swim!'

She laughed then, and gave herself completely to him, her shyness gone, unable to resist a lover with a sense of humour. She touched him, admired him, held him close and made room for him inside her when he stretched out on top of her. Joy had never been something she anticipated, especially since she had given up on any man wanting her. Joy was the only thing she could think of now.

He was gentle, but equally focused on filling his needs, and hers, too, even though she didn't really know what those needs were until he was deep inside, and they were doing a rhythmic slow dance. 'I love you,' he said into her ear. 'Hug me with your legs.'

She did and felt her own urge mount. 'I'm feeling distinctly unladylike,' she managed to say between gasps and a moan that surprised her.

'Good! And you know I'm not a gentleman,' he replied.

Then he was past words as his love for her spilled out of him and she felt like the most privileged woman in the universe. She wanted the feeling never to end. When he finished, spent, she urged him to a little more effort and he obliged, until she truly knew what it was to be complete.

'My word, Jerusha,' he said. He didn't move from her body, and she didn't want him to. He kissed her hair, sweaty now. 'Here's the nice part: we can do this again and again.'

He stayed where he was, growing heavier as he returned to sleep. She ran her hands over his back, enjoying the rhythm of his heart as it slowed to normal cadence. Heart to heart, she loved him in silence now, where before love murmured to them both.

At least we didn't keep anyone awake here, she thought, enjoying the bliss of solitude with the one person in the universe that she knew she could not do without, not ever.

She edged out from under him and moved him onto his back. She washed him below the waist this time, admiring his now peaceful anatomy. Amazing. She wondered how to inform Surgeon Kidwell that washing down to a wounded man's waist was still her limit. This man sleeping soundly was all she ever wanted to see. 'I am yours only,' she whispered.

There didn't seem to be any point in putting on her clothes. The house was empty, and she knew this man would want her again when he was able. She curled up beside him and slept, too, even though the sun was high in the sky. She willed the jetty bell to remain silent, and it did.

Jerusha woke up and found herself gazing into blue eyes. She kissed him, which began all manner of tumult. She was no more of an expert than she had been the first time, but it hardly mattered. Jamie was slower this time, almost leisurely as he caressed her body, then covered it with his. She was better at the rhythm of love this time, her senses more alert to what was happening. She savoured every moment, knowing in her heart that her man was only here for another day or two, then it was back to the blockade.

Go away, war, she thought, as he kissed her here and there. *Go away.*

Later, lying beside her, he was inclined to talk, his arms around her as her head rested on his chest. 'Jerusha, don't let me embarrass you…'

'I am noticeably past embarrassment, you might have observed,' she teased.

'The sight of you coming out of that camisole nearly made my heart stop,' he said.

'I think we'll muddle along, whenever you make port.'

'I'll be a source of envy when I'm back aboard the *Harmony*, a husband with a stupid smile on his face.' He turned serious. 'Too many men are too long gone on the blockade.'

Too many, too long. 'But you are here, and I rejoice,' she said simply.

Chapter Thirty

Jamie knew he would cherish forever the fluttering of Jerusha's eyelashes against his chest. Her words touched the deepest part of him. He looked down at her, marvelling over sudden joy in his life, where before there was only duty and hard things. She was right; he rejoiced, too.

Duty tugged at him to go to Stonehouse. Jerusha's long lashes tugged at him to stay in his bed. He stayed where he was, content this time to remain awake and watch the loveliness of his wife in slumber. *How often will this happen?* he asked himself, and knew the answer.

Stonehouse could wait, except he knew that it shouldn't. He didn't usually resent his duty, but he resented it now. Jon Kidwell was overworked and should have retired years ago. Mrs Terwilliger was overworked. The stewards were overworked. What right had he to dawdle here and delight in soft eyelashes against his chest? At least he had the good sense to store up that little detail about her to comfort him when he was at sea again, stewing over some medical problem, wishing for more knowledge, craving an end to war: Jerusha's eyelashes.

He patted her on the bottom—storing up that little pleasure, too. 'Up and at 'em, wifey,' he said, sounding cheerful when he knew precisely what he wanted to be doing. 'I propose two things today.'

'Oh, do you?' she asked. Her drowsy voice suggested there hadn't been much sleep involved recently. 'Suppose I disagree?'

He clutched his chest in mock surprise. 'What? Dissension in the ranks?'

'Aye-aye, sir,' she teased back. 'What is your wish?' She sat up and stretched, not remotely shy about showing her assets this time.

'That we stay in bed and pleasure each other,' he said promptly, 'except that I believe we need to pay a visit to your aunt.'

My, but that changed things. She lay down again and curled up close to him. He kissed the top of her head. 'Dear lady, I want her to know that I am not an ogre. True, I am no gentleman, but I should meet your relative. Do you think she is amenable to change in her society?'

'I do not think that is a wound we can heal,' she said, her voice muffled against him. 'I have written to my parents, and they have returned no reply.'

'You're cut off from them as well?' he said. 'I am so sorry. Jerusha, it might take years. It might never happen, but I don't want anyone to think we did not try.'

She was silent and he knew she was thinking over the matter. He got up, found his clothes, and dressed as she stared at the ceiling and thought. When he tried to tackle his neckcloth in a room without a mirror, he heard a rustle behind him. Dressed as far as her petticoat and camisole, Jerusha finished tying it for him, her eyes half slitted in that determination he remembered from the duck-pond.

Her shyness returned as they left the house. 'It is midday. People will know what we have been doing,' she whispered to him, her face rosy.

'That makes me the envy of nations,' he replied. 'Let's stop first on Ward A. I want Jon to know I will be back here soon.'

It was his turn to blush when Mrs Terwilliger looked him up and down. 'I believe you are the last person I expected to see here,' she said, and returned her attention to the papers in front of her. 'Before you leave, sign here and here and here. Jerusha, sit down a moment.'

Jerusha remained at Mrs T's desk, their heads together in a whispered conversation. At the end of the first row, Jon Kidwell debrided a nasty leg wound. He nodded when Jamie said he had an entire day to spend here.

'Jerusha, too?' John asked. 'Someone has been asking for her on Ward B.'

'I doubt you could keep her away.'

But first, Lady Oakshott. Jerusha wanted to walk to Plymouth. Although new to marriage politics, Jamie understood she was trying to put off the ordeal of Lady Oakshott. He agreed with her. They walked slowly past Devonport's dry docks, noisy with hammering and sawing, and the long ropewalk, where men twisted cotton cords, turning it into rigging.

She slowed down, the closer they came to Finch Street. She stopped altogether at the front steps of number twenty-eight. 'You're never alone, Jerusha Wilson,' he told her as he knocked. 'Remember that.'

The butler—Napier? — answered, drew himself up, and announced, 'Tradesmen go through the servants' entrance below.'

Jamie stepped aside so the butler could see his wife. 'Good day, Napier,' she said, crowding close to him. 'This is my husband, Surgeon James Wilson. We want to speak with Lady Oakshott.'

He gave her points for including his rank. After an intimidating glare on the front step, the butler motioned them in. He drew himself up, stared over their heads, and announced, 'Lady Oakshott has told me to say that she is not receiving visitors.'

'I'm her niece,' Jerusha said quietly. 'I am going upstairs anyway. Please don't try to stop me.'

You're braver than I am, Jamie thought, as she released his hand and climbed the stairs.

He waited below with the butler, who wouldn't look at him. It was too much, finally. 'Napier, I am a good man, serving a useful function in the Royal Navy,' he said. 'My father is a respected steward of a laird in the Highlands.'

'You are not good enough for Miss Jerusha Langley,' Napier replied. 'You are no gentleman.'

Jamie strained to hear some sympathy, and there was none. He heard a loud voice drifting down from upstairs. 'Excuse me, Napier,' he said. 'I believe I need to rescue my dear wife.'

'But…'

Jamie took the stairs two at a time, listening. He opened the door on a woman who might have been beautiful at one time, berating the dearest person in his orbit.

'Who are you, to barge in here?' Lady Oakshott demanded.

He was at Jerusha's side in a moment, hauling her close, saddened to feel her trembling, angry that a witch in a dressing gown was making her cry.

'Let's go to work, Jerusha,' he said. 'Let's go where we are both wanted and needed.'

She nodded, calmed herself, and took a step towards the old woman. 'Aunt Hortensia, my only regret is that I did not tell you immediately what I was doing. That was deception and I apologise. I will never apologise for marrying the dearest man in my universe.'

'Your parents have washed their hands of you, too,' Lady Oakshott retorted, her eyes blazing with indignation. 'Augusta is beside herself. Selfish, foolish girl!'

'I know my own mind,' Jerusha said in a calm voice that Jamie knew he could never begin to master, in the face of such vitriol. 'Good day. I wish you well.' With that, she turned on her heel and head high, left the room holding his hand.

Down the stairs in silence and out the door. He could only walk beside her in amazement at her courage. At the corner, she stopped and looked back at the house. 'I would rather know than not know, and now I can continue with my life,' she told him. She accepted his handkerchief and blew her nose. There in the street she put her hands on his arms. 'I love you, James Wilson. Yes, let's go do some good.'

Her husband was a man of good sense. He hailed a hackney, helped her in, and let her sob into another of his handkerchiefs. He apologised for dragging her to Finch Street. 'I should have listened to you, but I wanted to know where we stood,' he told her. 'Now we know.'

'I might cry about this again,' she admitted to her man, 'but I will mend.' The look he gave her she knew she could store up in her heart against the hard times.

Ward A was quiet, some patients napping while others stared into great distances that disturbed her at first, until she realised the wounded belonged to a fraternity of warriors.

'I am to assist with two amputations,' Jamie told her. 'Someone upstairs on Ward B wants to have a word with you.'

'I heard too many words on Finch Street,' she said.

'I'll go upstairs with you.'

She saw Jon Kidwell beckoning to him. 'No need. I can outrun anyone on Wards A and B,' she reminded him. She blew him a kiss that made a sailor put his hand to his cheek and flop back on his cot.

'You rascal, you're ready for discharge,' Jamie said, but his voice was mild. The others laughed and Jerusha went upstairs to another place that both frightened and humbled her.

She had been away from Ward B for two days, enjoying

herself in the arms of her husband. As she looked across the aisles of quiet men, she knew her heart lay here, too.

My darling could be here someday, she thought, dismissing the Aunt Hortensias from her life. *I must serve where other ladies cannot.*

A man sat beside her patient that she told about her day, every day. He had opened his eyes now and then, which startled her at first, but no longer. The visitor had opened the book of Shakespeare's sonnets that she kept beside the bed.

Should I bother him? she asked herself.

She came closer and cleared her throat. 'Sir?'

'You must be Mrs Wilson.'

She hesitated, then covered her mouth to hide her smile. 'You see, sir, I haven't been Mrs Wilson too long. I… I'm still getting used to it.'

He pulled up a stool from the bedside of another silent patient, and she sat. 'This is my son,' he said. She clearly heard all the pain.

She put her hand on his arm, then hoped he didn't think she was a forward little piece. 'I read to him nearly every day. I talk to him, as well. He knows everything about me.'

'Then I thank you. I am Sailing Master Roger Kent, and this is Alec. I have been on the blockade for months and this is my first opportunity to see him.' She knew better than to interrupt his thoughts as he looked at his son. 'He was a sailing master's mate in the Baltic, learning the family trade. Then this happened.' He bowed his head.

She understood. 'I wash his face and talk to him. I am not a medical person. I come to wash faces and write letters and read to them. It isn't much.'

He covered her hand with his own. 'It is everything. Keep doing it, please.' He managed a smile. 'No one will ever recognise your service, but Alec knows somehow, some way.'

'Yes, sir.'

'No medals for you.' He kissed his silent son.

She walked him to the door of Ward B. When she promised, 'I will tend him,' the sting of Aunt Hortensia vanished.

'I will return the favour someday.'

Chapter Thirty-One

September began with a gust of wind that blew Mags back to Plymouth two days later, minus a baby, and her own story of the sailing master's sister in tears when she put the infant in her arms. 'You know I am not the tearful type, Surgeon Wilson, but that whole village was full of gratitude. Two of her friends lined up for wet nursing. You did a kind thing.'

Jamie nodded and walked upstairs, while Mags unpacked and asked Jerusha to tell 'that silent boyo' thank you for her adventure. 'Maybe I needed to get away for two days, myself,' she confided. 'I trust you and t'master used your time well.'

'That we did, Mags,' Jerusha said. She heard the door to his study close. 'Now he has turned quiet.'

'He sails in the morning. He always turns quiet.'

'Mags, I've never sent a man to sea.'

'It's hard. Just remember to cry after he is gone.'

Jerusha debated only a moment. She went upstairs to knock on the door cautiously, wishing she knew what to do for this man suddenly silent.

'Come in, Jerusha. You never need to knock.'

He leaned back in his chair with his feet on the desk and his hands behind his head. She came up behind him and he stared up at her breasts.

'Now that is a sight to behold,' he said and put his feet

down. He patted his legs and she sat, her arms going naturally around his neck.

'I have lots of similar wonderful sights,' she told him, which made him chuckle.

'I need to see every one of them between now and tomorrow morning.' He put his hand against her head in a protective gesture, this man of hers. 'We had a meeting in Admin after you left the ward, someone from Admiralty telling us what lies ahead.' He looked around elaborately. 'If you share any of this with a spy, I will have to shoot you.'

'Cross my heart.'

'I'll cross it for you.' He ran his hand across her breast. 'Sworn to secrecy. It seems that our little admiral is determined to dislodge the French and Spanish ships from Cadiz. Napoleon is jumping up and down in Boulogne, trying to pry Villeneuve—he of the Combined Fleet—out of Cadiz.' He tightened his arms around her. 'The Frogs are ready to take small boats across the Channel to our fair sceptred isle. And the blockade of Brest wears on. It's unfair that such nice people as we are must live in perilous times, eh?'

She put her hands on his face. 'The only place in the world where I feel safe is right next to you in our bed.'

'That's a simple solution to England's problems!' he said, and kissed her palms. 'We'll get in bed and hunker down. I like it, too.'

He held her close for a long and satisfying moment, then, 'But we must sail. I doubt you will see me again until winter, or until after Villeneuve decides to peek out of Cadiz.' He sighed. 'That's why I turned quiet. I would rather be here, too.'

How did one say this casually? She had no idea. 'There will be a battle?'

'Everyone wants it, except perhaps Villeneuve.' He looked around again. 'Spies say Napoleon is sharpening a guillotine himself for Villeneuve. I suppose that particular naval Frog is trying to decide who he fears more: Old Boney or Admiral Nelson. It will be a huge and decisive battle.'

'So it makes you quiet.' She kissed her husband, thinking of the night to come. 'Remember this: I will always be waiting here for you.'

'I hope I will return. There are no guarantees.'

If she lived to one hundred, Jerusha knew she would never forget that final night before her husband sailed back to war. At first, she hoped they weren't noisy and disturbing Mags below stairs, and then she didn't care. 'Good heavens,' she said once, after a particularly exquisite moment that left them both exhausted and sweating. 'Where do you *learn* this?'

'Wifey, you forget I am an anatomist,' he said. 'I must also admit to prior experience. I am a Royal Navy man after all, and we do have a certain reputation.' He returned to kissing her in places she never thought to be kissed, and forgot any commentary.

They must have slept a little, but only enough to regroup and return to that exquisite place, forgetting everything except each other, two insignificant people in a world gone mad. She knew the pleasure ended when he cuddled her close as the sun rose, and turned practical.

'Dearest, you will find all my important papers in the second drawer of the desk in my office,' he told her. 'There is a letter explaining who you are to see to release my savings into your custody, should the matter arise.'

'I don't want to think about it.'

'You must. Everything is in order. I've accumulated some prize money through the years, and I've been frugal. So must you be, as well. Be wise and you'll never be destitute.'

'Please stop,' she whispered.

'Don't hesitate to remarry, should you find another fellow as charming and wise as I am.'

He held her close as she cried. 'There now. Don't see me

to the docks. Just stay here and let me imagine you cosy in my warm spot.'

He dressed quickly, then flicked a little water on her from the basin, which catapulted her out of bed to thrash him with her pillow. As a consequence, they were both laughing when he shouldered his medical satchel and slung his duffel across his back. She followed him into the little street that ran behind the administration building, grabbed him for another kiss, then covered her eyes until he was gone.

Mags was banging about in the kitchen when Jerusha dried her tears, squared her shoulders, and stood in the doorway, feeling both amazingly shy and so sad. Mags handed her a cup of tea.

'Nothing makes it easy,' Mags told her. 'Get to work.'

Surgeon Kidwell helped the time pass. Every morning, he knocked on the door, and Mags ushered him in, serving him breakfast, too, over weak and then no protestation. He walked Jerusha to Block Four, discussing his cases with her as if she were Jamie. She found the notion flattering.

The real test came when he asked her to assist in an amputation. 'We see this too often,' he told her as they walked to Block Four in the rain, moving slowly because Jon couldn't move fast anymore. 'A surgeon at sea is too busy to notice what needs to be done in the moment. Part of him wants to wait and see, but he hasn't that luxury. We must do what he should have done.'

September sped or dragged towards October, depending on how active she was, or how much time she spent brooding on the empty space in their bed. She couldn't help her tears when Surgeon Kidwell handed her a note with familiar handwriting.

Mrs Terwilliger sent her into the linen closet for a quiet space.

Dearest, I am in Portsmouth, delivering patients to Haslar. I have no time to take a coastal carrier to Plymouth. Keep that cosy spot warm. With love, your surgeon.

'I hate the navy,' she told Mrs Terwilliger when she came out of the closet, the note stuffed down her bodice, and her arms full of sheets. Her work went on.

She had to credit her mother, quiet self-effacing Augusta, with giving her something else to worry about. Mama showed up, proper and unannounced, on Block Four.

Jerusha saw her as she finished wiping the face of a new patient from Ferrol, where more Royal Navy blockaders sailed, reinforcing what Jamie said about Admiral Nelson tightening his grip on the enemy coast.

'Mama?' She hurried to her mother, a women used to doing good for others that required no exertion, standing bewildered in the middle of a ward reeking with exertion. Jerusha gratefully accepted Mrs Terwilliger's offer of her little cubbyhole as a refuge for two.

Jerusha braced herself for a scold and Mama wasted not a moment, berating Jerusha for her slapdash marriage. To Jerusha's surprise, Mama abandoned the topic almost at once and moved to what Jerusha discovered was the real reason for the visit: her sister, Hortensia.

'Daughter, last week a Young Person named Abbie—I suppose she has no last name—arrived at our house.'

'Abbie?' Jerusha repeated, startled.

'She had a letter from my sister, Hortensia,' Mama continued. 'I won't bore you with it, but Hortensia went on at length about your deceit, consorting with a person beneath your notice.'

'Surgeon James Wilson is my husband.'

'Don't remind me,' Mama snapped.

Jerusha rose, her mind calm. 'If you have come here to scold me, kindly leave.'

Mama put a hand on her arm. 'No! It was a wild letter, full of vituperation and malice, then vast self-pity that no one cares about her and that her prospects are ruined.'

'She blames me. I have apologised to her for my deception,' Jerusha told her. She sat down again. 'Mama, did she tell you that she sold Oaklands, the family estate, because her late husband's debts were alarming? She is eking out the barest living in her last remaining property, and trying to hide it.'

'It all came out last night when we arrived. She showed me mounds of unpaid bills and cried, blaming everyone for her trials,' Mama said. 'It is vexing.' Mama regarded Jerusha with something that at least resembled understanding. 'She decries your deception, little bothering to mention her own, trying to represent herself as a woman of wealth and position.'

'Did she fool you, too, Mama?' There. She had to ask.

'She did, and for years,' Mama admitted. 'I suppose I have always been a little afraid of her. You know how she is.' Her tone hardened. 'Now she is an embarrassment.'

Poor mama. Jerusha regarded her with more compassion than she might have imagined only weeks ago, when Mama didn't bother to answer her letter. In a flash of recognition, she saw her mother as she was, a lovely lady who managed life well, as long as there was nothing to disrupt her ease.

And she saw herself, too, someone willing to break rules to follow her own path and forge a different life. Whether that was wise or not, only time would tell. 'What will you do about Aunt Hortensia, Mama?'

'Your father is here, too, talking to an estate agent to sell that property on Finch Street,' Mama said. 'Papa has a bilious stomach. You know how he hates to be troubled.'

'I do,' Jerusha said with serenity, certain now that she had chosen a far better path, even with all its uncertainties. Poor Papa. 'What will happen to Aunt Hortensia?'

'She is coming home with us. No one need ever know how poor she is.' Mama sighed, and Jerusha heard all the resignation. 'I suppose this is my penance for spending what money I had entirely on your brother and leaving you in a situation where, in desperation, you had to lower yourself in society.'

Mama would never understand. Ah, well. Perhaps someday she and Jamie would be invited to visit the parish in Bolling, although she had her doubts. 'I am quite content where I am, Mama,' she said firmly. 'Perhaps you had better return to help Aunt Hortensia pack. What happened to little Abbie, who brought the message?'

'She is a jewel and will work for me,' Mama said. '*I* will pay her for her services!'

It was too much to hope, but why not ask? 'And Napier?'

Mama put her hand on Jerusha's arm. 'My dear, he has kept Hortensia out of the poorhouse, paying her bills out of his savings. He is looking for another position.'

'There is a French cook, too.'

'He scarpered off, the scamp!' Mama leaned closer. 'Napier said his name is Robby Blair and he is a scoundrel.'

'He will land on his feet, I have no doubt.'

'And you?' Mama asked, her face anxious.

She didn't have to consider the matter, even as she mourned that her husband had no time to sail from Portsmouth to Plymouth because there was a war on. 'Mama, I will do very well with the man I love. Depend upon it. Depend upon me.'

Chapter Thirty-Two

Jerusha was never too tired to write to Jamie, no matter how often the jetty bell clanged, or how many wounded men poured into all blocks at Stonehouse. The visit from her mother had been an odd interlude, reminding Jerusha briefly of a life she had left behind, one she did not miss.

In three weeks, she received a hurried note from her husband on the *Harmony*, as it made its way through the blockading ships with medicine and messages.

Tears started as she read that his ship-to-shore life had ended.

I am going to Revenge, a seventy-four whose surgeon has died of disease.

She ran to the linen closet after the last line.

Dearest wife, I do not know when I will see you again.

After weeping every tear in her body, she dried her eyes on a sheet, squared her shoulders, and continued her work.

Wounded men passed though Ward A. Some died, others flourished and left—in her opinion—too soon. 'That is the vexation of writing letters for so many of them,' she grumbled to Jon Kidwell as they walked from their quarters to Block A one morning. She walked slowly to accommodate his painful progress on one leg and a peg, as he put it.

'How is that?' he asked, his eyes merry.

'By writing letters, I come to know the men,' she replied. 'I briefly meet sisters and sweethearts and mothers. I want to know more, and I care.'

She saw the shadow cross his face and wanted to ask about his own life, which he never discussed. She maintained her silence. Jamie had told her once about a wife and child dead of cholera, and that leg gone at the Battle of the Nile. 'That's all he ever said,' Jamie related.

'I suppose there are depths to people I will never know, Surgeon Kidwell. Perhaps I am nosy.'

'Jerusha, you are involved in mankind, and I thank you for your bravery.'

She felt all her bravery desert her the morning she sat beside the comatose son of Sailing Master Kent and watched Alec Kent fade from life. Surgeon Kidwell had warned her he was failing. She could have told him that herself, because she knew the signs—his eyes sank further in his head and he stopped eating. She knew death was only a matter of when.

Alec Kent seemed to know when she was there. How that could be, she had no idea. She had moved from Shakespeare's sonnets to *Pilgrim's Progress*, not that it mattered what she read. This week she brought her Bible.

That afternoon, Sister Mary Martha whispered, 'It won't be long. Please don't leave him,' so Jerusha settled in, knowing she would not leave until he was gone, no matter what time it was.

He died in Micah, Chapter Seven, his breathing softer and slower. She rested her hand on his shoulder, as she often did, and looked at the words, thinking of nations at war and her love sailing into trouble. '"*Rejoice not against me, mine enemy,*"' she read. '"*When I fall, I shall arise; when I sit in darkness...*"' She paused, wondering how or even if his comatose world was dark. 'Is it dark for you, Alec Kent? What do you see?' she asked the silent man. 'I wish I knew.'

She watched his chest rise and fall and continued, *'"When I sit in darkness, the Lord shall be a light unto me."'* She closed her eyes when his chest rose, fell, and did not rise again. 'You dear man,' she said. 'I hope it is light where you are.'

Later that night, when she should have long been asleep, she sat at Jamie's desk and through her tears wrote a letter to Sailing Master Kent, serving aboard the *Protector.* She assured him that she had been with Alec to the end. She wrote that his son's body had been taken to the family burying ground at Plymouth's oldest church, according to his instructions.

No fears, she concluded. *I did as you wished.*

She wrote a much longer letter to Jamie and took both letters to the usual box in Administration, mindful as she did so of a recurring nightmare, where over and over she dropped letters into a box that opened at the bottom and dumped them into the ocean.

October came with no letters from Jamie, not even a note. Jerusha kept her thoughts to herself as she ran with the others to the quadrangle when the jetty bell rang, and did all that was asked of her, even if the wounds seemed to grow more terrible as each day passed. She soothed her heart with a small thing. Every night after supper with Mags, she took a hot water bottle to her bed and put it on Jamie's side.

When she was too exhausted to do anything else except sleep, she took out that hot water bottle and lay down in Jamie's warm spot. That was the only way she could sleep, and it comforted her…one little warm spot.

Each day turned into the one before, except the day it didn't, the day she received a note from Sailing Master Kent. She changed bloody sheets and forced herself to joke with the patients when she really wanted to go somewhere and hide. Mrs Terwilliger called to her and waved a letter.

Thank God, she thought, running to the ward office.

She grabbed the letter, but she frowned to see Master Kent's handwriting, much neater than her husband's.

Buck up, Jerusha, she told herself sternly. *It's a letter.*

She sat down in Mrs Terwilliger's chair. 'My goodness,' she whispered, and read it again.

'What?' the matron demanded.

She handed the note to Mrs Terwilliger. 'Sailing Master Kent is aboard the *Protector*, here in Plymouth! He cannot come ashore—they have to leave again so soon—but if I don't mind being rowed out to his ship, I can hand him a letter for Jamie. He can find the *Revenge* on the blockade and hand it to him personally.'

Mrs T read it quickly, then slapped a sheet of paper in front of Jerusha, and moved over her ink and quill pen. 'Hurry. Tides don't wait.'

Jerusha started to write as the matron read out loud.

'You missed the postscript: *"Look for a little fellow name of Cornell to take you to the* Protector *in one half hour. I hope you are not prone to seasickness."*' The matron laughed. 'I think you can manage a sail in the harbour.'

Jerusha wrote as fast as she could, knowing it might only be a matter of three weeks or so before Master Kent delivered the letter to the *Revenge*. She wanted to add something of a deeply personal nature, but there was no telling how many eager eyes might read the letter, too. It could wait.

Surgeon Kidwell stopped by as she wrote, and Mrs Terwilliger filled him in. 'There's nothing like a little voyage around the harbour to make you appreciate land,' he teased.

Tugging on her cape because the wind blew cold, Jerusha tucked the letter in her apron pocket and hurried to the harbour.

She went directly to the wharf. 'Are you Cornell?' she asked one promising-looking youth. A blank stare sent her to the next small craft, this one with a sail. Her 'Are you Cornell?' earned her a nod, smile, and a hand down into the dinghy.

'Sit ye in the middle, miss,' was all the instruction he gave.

Cornell navigated expertly between other small craft and gigs, narrowly avoiding a gig filled with crates of chickens loudly protesting. They passed a cow, head down, mooing a sad refrain. This was a sight of the Royal Navy she hadn't expected, although there was the mama goat on the *Harmony*. It was something to remember when Cornell sailed her back to Stonehouse.

The ships thinned out and then she saw *Protector* spelled out in gilt paint on the stern of a two-decked ship of the line. Cornell expertly brought his little craft close to what looked like a wooden swing dangling down from the deck, which suddenly looked so high above them. 'Here ye are, miss.'

She looked at it doubtfully. 'If you tie up, I can hand you the letter and they could pull *you* up instead.'

'No, ma'am,' he said. 'Orders were for you to do it. Master Kent wants to see you.'

'I would like to see him, too,' she admitted. 'Up I go.'

She looked up to see smiling faces, Master Kent's among them. 'Just sit in the swing, Mrs Wilson,' he called down. 'Hang on tight!'

When she was secure, Cornell backed away his small craft. 'Don't go too far,' she called to him, as the men on deck expertly towed her up the side of the ship.

Master Kent reached for her and helped her off. 'You barely weigh a thing.'

'I'll warn you that some ship out here is about to get a load of irate chickens,' she teased back. She reached into the pocket on her surgeon's apron. 'Here's the letter to my Jamie. Thank you so much for doing this, sir. Now if you'll help me back…'

She looked towards land to see Cornell in the distance. At the same time, the sails dropped and filled with a loud *whoosh!*

and the *Protector* started to move. 'Wait a minute,' she said, her heart in her throat. 'What…?'

Master Kent kissed her cheek. 'Jerusha, I couldn't think of a better way to thank you for how well you tended my son in his final hours. I'm taking you to the *Revenge*. We'll be on the blockade in five or six days, if the wind is right.'

She stared at him.

'I planned this with Captain Ames on the *Harmony*. I know roughly when he will pass the *Revenge* on his return to Portsmouth. What's the harm in spending one night aboard with your husband?'

Chapter Thirty-Three

'Are we still friends?' Master Kent asked Jerusha, when the laughter died down and the crew returned to their duties.

His expression was so earnest that Jerusha had only one answer. 'Master Kent, we are.'

'Call this the adventure of a lifetime, and something to tell your children. Come below. I'll find a spot for you in the wardroom.'

She followed him below deck, picking her way past coiled rigging and mysterious bits of equipment. The rocking motion of the ship was making her queasy, but she told her stomach to behave.

Master Kent opened a hatch and ushered her inside. 'Our second luff is laid up in Stonehouse with a terrible case of hives, so here you are in his quarters.'

She looked around the tiny cabin, touched to see a miniature of an older couple and another of a dog, tongue lolling out, eyes bright. She picked it up. 'Just think, Master Kent: There is a side to every man on board that we lubbers never see.'

'Aye, lass. You're getting a rare glimpse.'

Her rare glimpse expanded during the five days the *Protector* sailed to the blockade. The officers of the wardroom kindly admitted her to their mess table, an offer she declined the first day because she spent it in her cabin, heaving into a vomit tin.

The ship's surgeon, obviously in league with an apothecary

from Hades, concocted a brownish brew that smelled worse than broccoli—her least favourite vegetable—with overtones of rum.

'Hold your nose and drink it,' he said, in the tone of a doctor who seldom heard anyone disagree with him and wasn't about to start with this female.

She drank. To her astonishment, the smelly mass stayed in her stomach. To her further amazement, she felt well enough the next afternoon to come on deck, pleasantly surprised that she was alive.

It was a rare day of sunshine, considering that they were into October now, and she knew the English Channel was fickle. She debated what to do until she saw Master Kent above her on the quarterdeck. She started towards him, but he put up his hand, palm out, to stop her. He conferred with the man with gold epaulets on his shoulders. The captain gestured her up himself.

Jerusha made her careful way to the quarterdeck. The captain was obviously the man to thank, and she did so with a small curtsy. 'I gather I need your permission to be here, sir.'

'I'm happy to grant it,' he said, 'unless you become a managing female who thinks she knows more how to run a ship than I do.'

'I would never…'

'My wife would,' he replied with a smile. 'Welcome aboard.' He glanced at Master Kent. 'Since that man is held in high regard throughout the fleet, you'll always have a welcome on the *Protector*.' He lowered his voice. 'Thank you for tending his son so well, in his final moments.'

'I did it gladly,' she replied.

Jerusha learned other lessons that day, taught by Master Kent, who seemed to have made her his project. She spent a pleasant morning with him at the quarterdeck railing as he pointed out other ships sailing in the same direction, the French coast of embattled Europe. From her hours in Ward A, she knew enough about sailors who liked to joke when she asked nautical questions.

'Sir, I have been teased by rascals in Ward A,' she told him as they watched the water. 'My questions may seem silly to you, but I am a nautical novice.'

'We all began that way, Jerusha,' he said. 'You…you don't mind if I address you by your Christian name, do you?'

'Not at all, sir.' She looked towards the open sea. 'I would have given the earth to hear your son say it, or say anything. I know he wanted to.'

When he put his hand on her shoulder, she steadied herself. She knew people spoke of iron men in wooden ships, and it seemed a glib statement to bandy about. At this moment, she knew these *were* iron men.

'Thank you for what you do, sir,' she said.

He did not reply, but the pressure on her shoulder increased. Some instinct told her he was struggling, too; perhaps they all were. 'No fears. We'll get you to the *Revenge*.'

Good winds bore them towards France as she remained prudently below deck, helping in the sick bay by rolling bandages and scraping lint. The ship's surgeon was a shy older man with a sure touch. On the third day, Jerusha watched him suture two small wounds. 'Watch closely,' he told her. On the fourth day, he handed her the needle and catgut when a third sailor managed to lacerate his forearm and showed up at Sick Call.

'Such a lovely wound, all neat and orderly,' the surgeon declared, which made his patient stare at him and edge towards the companionway. 'No, lad, come in, come in. I have here Mrs Wilson, who I am instructing in the fine art of suturing. Sit down.'

'Beg pardon, miss,' he whispered when the surgeon turned to his medicine chest to rummage about, humming to himself. 'Can you…?'

'I can,' she assured him. 'I'll probably flinch when you flinch, because I have a soft heart, but I can do this. Steady now.'

The surgeon watched as she dabbed and stitched and dabbed some more. When she said, 'I am not certain of a final stitch to close it,' he took over. She sighed with relief at the same time her patient did. After she bandaged her handiwork, he gave her a small salute and left, a happy man.

'Let's practise that final closure,' her mentor said. 'I have here a slice of condemned beef. I'll slice it in half and you will suture and close. Watch me. It's simple.'

On the fifth day, the *Protector* reached the blockade. Jerusha watched with interest as ships signalled, wore, and tacked. She jumped to hear gunfire, and the first luff was quick to reassure her.

'No fears, Mrs Wilson,' he said. 'The gunners practise all the time. It's our strength.'

Right then, she prayed in her heart that this lieutenant would live long in service to king and country. She had prayed that way at night for years, kneeling by her bed, but as she heard his conviction, she also knew he had a young wife in Hampshire and a son he had not seen yet. She had learned this only last night in the wardroom after dinner.

I have come to know you better, she thought. *I also know what can happen to you, because I run towards the sound of the jetty bell.*

The *Protector* passed one ship, then another. In mid-afternoon as clouds gathered in the west, the first luff handed her his glass. 'Here you are, Mrs Wilson.'

She looked, steadying her arm on the railing, and looked again to see *Revenge* across the stern of the closest ship to port. The lieutenant spoke to the signalman and flags rose in orderly fashion.

'What is he signalling?' she asked.

'Stop. Bosun's Chair. Medical Supplies,' he said. 'Here's what you have to do...'

* * *

'Sir, you're wanted on deck. The *Protector* is dropping off supplies.'

Jamie looked up from his contemplation of an angry tooth in the mouth of a terrified cook's mate. There was no medical matter that bothered him more than the removal of teeth, and this felt like a reprieve for both of them.

Jamie gave his full attention to the messenger, who seemed to be stifling a laugh. 'I didn't know the *Protector* delivered pharmacopeia,' he said. 'Are you certain?'

'Oh, sir...oh, sir,' was all the man said.

Idiot, Jamie thought mildly.

'Seaman Lafferty, stay here,' he said to his almost-patient. 'I am certain you want this tooth removed. I will only be a few minutes.'

'Aye, sir,' his victim said promptly, only it sounded like 'Uh...er...' because of the gauze in his mouth.

'Or this could wait another day,' Jamie said.

The sailor nodded vigorously and began removing the gauze. Jamie unstoppered his oil of cloves and dabbed it on the renegade tooth. 'This will hold you.'

The man beat him up the companionway in his urge to be elsewhere immediately. Jamie followed more slowly, until he saw a cluster of officers around a small person and his heart melted.

His captain was smiling. 'Sir?' he asked, as he hurried to his wife.

'Surgeon Wilson, you are the victim of a conspiracy between Sailing Master Kent, a man I greatly admire, and apparently your own Captain Ames of *Harmony*,' the captain said. He led Jerusha across the deck. 'She is yours until *Harmony* hails us in a day or two to return her to Plymouth.' He tipped his hat to Jerusha. 'Go on, dear, he won't bite.'

He heard the cheers and laughter, and saw Jerusha's smile

so wide that it lit the deck. 'Master Kent engineered this,' she said just before he enveloped her in his cloak and held her close, pressing her head, bonnet and all, tight against him.

He doubted anyone had ever been kissed in the sick bay of the *Revenge*, but it happened as soon as he got Jerusha carefully down the companionway and into his medical domain, which smelled strongly of cloves now.

She sniffed and said, 'You're so sweet, my love,' which made him laugh, then kiss her thoroughly. 'I love you,' she managed, before he locked the hatch, picked her up, and set her down on the cot he used when there wasn't time for a proper rest in the officers' wardroom.

He had no plans at all for a proper rest, and apparently neither did she, considering how eager she was to help him out of his uniform. 'It's easier for me,' she told him as she concentrated on his trouser buttons. 'All I really have to do is raise my skirt and petticoat.'

'Then do it, wife,' he ordered.

She'll think I'm a beast. I've been so gentle with her before, were Jamie's last coherent thoughts, before he performed the most unorthodox bit of medical relief ever attempted in a Royal Navy sick bay, as far as he knew.

There was nothing gentle about it. To his intense gratification, Jerusha matched his own desire, her hands tugging him down onto her, as if he needed encouragement, which he didn't. And thank goodness there were plenty of the usual nautical noises that masked her moan of complete satisfaction, or maybe it was his. He neither knew nor cared. His wife was here and he was the world's most complete man in this longitude and latitude.

When they finished the first instalment of what he hoped were several before the arrival of the *Harmony* to ferry her back to Plymouth, he fetched another blanket and made a more comfortable nest beside the medicine chest. Oh, why not? He was as bare as a new babe, so he divested Jerusha of all her clothes and cuddled her to him, enjoying every curve, nook, and cranny.

'How in the world...' he started, then listened with growing appreciation as she told him of the kindness of one sailing master.

'He sent me a note telling me to write to you, and that I would have to go on a small boat out to the *Protector*, since he could not leave his ship,' she explained. 'It sounded logical. He kidnapped me!'

He liked the way she burrowed so close to him. His heart broke a little when she whispered to him how she used a hot water bottle every night to trick herself into thinking it was his warm spot in their bed. He couldn't help his smile when she fretted that everyone on the *Revenge* knew what was going on in the sick bay. She was a lady to the end and he adored her.

It seemed a waste, but they slept off and on through the afternoon, lulled by the unmatched well-being of coitus noninterruptus. No one needed his services except his wife, who became insistent, along about time to gather in the wardroom for supper. As it turned out, she was far more delicious than any meal of stringy beef, beer, and hard bread could have been.

By the time morning came many hours later between sleep and utter magnificence, he was ready to tidy up and prepare the sick bay for morning Sick Call. 'I am a surgeon, after all,' he told her. There was no lack of water to clean themselves, and plenty of soft cloths to blot at tender parts, which almost became his undoing, because he wanted to do more than blot.

Duty called; in fact it cleared its throat and tapped its foot, speeding the process of becoming presentable. When he unlocked the door, he saw the usual number of sore throats, lacerations, black eyes and coughs. Morning had come on the blockade.

Another day followed, with equal parts bliss and business.

He discovered how proficient Jerusha was in suturing wounds, a skill he had not expected. He worried, but no one smirked or made snide remarks as Jerusha helped him. She did have a chance to show off her suturing skill on a small wound, impressing both him and the recipient.

And later, when everyone was tended and gone, no emergencies arose to ruin another perfect day. There was more leisure this time to talk. He dabbed at her eyes when she told him of Alec Kent's peaceful death and his father's gratitude.

In turn, she listened to his tally of injuries both real and imagined and laughed when he groused that one of the Articles of War should include a flogging around the fleet for hypochondria. It was the kind of silly talk he never thought they would have time for, not when Napoleon breathed down everyone's neck and they lived in a world at war.

'I will never dare show my face on deck again,' she said, when Jamie opened the hatch to see some kind soul had left them food with a note.

Make sure she eats, Surgeon. You can spare twenty minutes for that. Yrs. sincerely, the Wardroom

The next day began the same as the others, troubling Jamie, as he knew the *Harmony* was due today or if he was lucky, tomorrow, on her return journey through the blockade fleet to England. Jerusha knew it too, because she became more quiet.

In silence, she folded their blankets and set the sick bay to rights as he doctored and admonished today's crop of patients. 'It will be good to put on another dress in Plymouth and wash my hair,' she said halfway through the morning. 'I'm feeling a little dingy.' Jamie's only consolation was that she didn't sound too cheerful about leaving.

He went on deck, thinking to himself why it would be a useful thing to train women for actual medical work in the fleet. It was wishful thinking—such events probably waited for another, more enlightened century—but it gave him food for thought besides the reality that Jerusha was leaving, and he would be alone again.

He asked for and received permission to climb to the quarterdeck, then wondered at the gathering of officers with their telescopes trained on the nearest blockader, still some distance away.

'It can't be.'

'You're not reading it right.'

'Look again. See there.'

'By God, at last.'

The captain was closest but preoccupied. Jamie looked at the first luff and raised his shoulders in a questioning shrug. The lieutenant motioned him closer. 'As near as we can tell, the dons and the Frogs have left Cadiz and come out to play. Hoorah for Nelson!'

They both turned as a signalman in the rigging shouted, 'Full speed for Cadiz! All haste. Prepare to join battle.'

'There we have it, gentlemen,' Captain Moorsom said calmly. 'Our wait is over. To your stations.' He turned to the Royal Marine sergeant standing alert. 'Tell the drummer it's "Beat To Quarters."'

'Sharpen your knives, James,' the first luff said.

Jamie stood still as the drummer beat out the familiar rhythm.

God help me, I have a wife aboard.

Chapter Thirty-Four

The full implication of her husband's words sank in immediately. 'I'm sailing into battle, too.'

Her covered her hand with his. 'The navy has been waiting for this moment. It will be big and decisive.'

'I'm afraid,' she admitted.

'That's two of us.' With the sound of 'Beat To Quarters' drumming in her ears—she knew she would never forget the steady, unrelenting cadence—he pulled her down the companionway, then farther down, to the deck above the hold, the orlop deck.

She looked around the poorly lit space, crowded with unused sails, tar in buckets, nails, and other naval gear that looked like clutter to her, but she knew must have a purpose. 'Why are we here?' she asked, speaking loudly to be heard above the sounds of men running on two decks to the continuous drumroll.

'This is the safest place. When the bleeding starts, the wounded are taken here. This is my office in battle.'

She didn't mean to start shivering. God knows her husband was soon to be far too busy to worry about her, but she shivered anyway. She had the good sense to keep her lips tight together. There was no sense in giving him one more person to fret about.

She saw his worry for her in his eyes and knew she had to

say something, even as her stomach churned and she wanted to run…where? Deep breath. 'Then it is my office, too,' she told him. 'Tell me what to do, and I will do it.'

That was all her husband needed. He became the reliable, dependable man who had caught her attention in a duck-pond. 'We are aft in the midshipman's portion of the ship,' he told her. 'The only thing below us is the hold.'

Jerusha couldn't help what she knew was her sceptical face. 'I say that in relative meaning,' Jamie said. 'We're in deep water, and we will be fired upon.' He pointed to a mess table. 'That becomes my operating table.'

'It's so dark here. No portholes, no…how can you see to…'

'My mate is gathering lamps.' He pointed to another dim corner. 'Let's clear a wide space to work there.'

'Why so far?'

He took her by the shoulders and gently pulled her to him. 'When the fleet action starts, that is where my assistants and the ship's crew above us—whoever can be spared—will lay the wounded.'

Jerusha nodded, unable to speak.

'You won't recognise it by the end of the day.' He released her and pointed to what looked like sails. 'I have never been to battle in this ship. Hopefully, this is…ah, aye. The surgeon before me knew his business.'

Jerusha knew he was talking to himself, and she listened, sure to glean information and spare him the time of repetition. He raised several portions of sailcloth. 'Aye, aye, Surgeon Westin, you kept it tidy. Jerusha, we will cover this table with one of these sail portions. They're old sails, but clean, and still useful. When I ask you for a new one during battle, toss aside the bloody one and replace it with one of these.'

She couldn't help but suck in a deep breath and another, and he saw it and understood. 'Remember that this is the safest place on board. I'll make you work hard, doing things that on an ordinary day would terrify you. It's fast work and that will occupy your mind, believe me.'

She didn't, but she nodded anyway, and he saw right through her. He gave her lips a hearty smack and shook her gently by the chin. 'And you're thinking I'm completely barmy, and how can you overlook all the blood and gore, and why on earth did you marry me? Trust me here, my love, you'll be too busy to worry until it's over.' He touched her body in a popular place. 'You know, like the first time we did the marriage dance.'

What could she do but laugh, pat him gently in another popular place, and get to work.

As the *Revenge* raced along with the other blockaders, free at last from their numbing, boring duty in front of Brest, she helped her husband and Paddy, the surgeon's mate, a boy younger than she was, move most of the sick bay's contents a deck above to this tight space below. They were joined by the ship's purser, that officer who doled out supplies with a thimble, according to Paddy. 'He's quiet and a bit barmy, but I trust him,' Paddy whispered.

She helped Paddy clear off that part of the deck by the ribs and piled up more of the sail fragments. 'That's to cover the dead,' he told her, his voice so matter-of-fact. 'We may end up stacking them, too.'

She took his arm, hoping he would overlook how her own arm trembled. 'Paddy, have you been in battle before?'

'Aye, miss,' he said with a grin. 'My first was the Battle of the Nile. I was fifteen.'

'I'll stop complaining then.'

He gave her a wink, the Irish kind she had seen a time or two in Ward A. 'Ye don't complain *now*, Mrs Surgeon.'

The reality of the ordeal to come came home to roost on her shoulder like a vulture when two sailors came below deck, bouncing a canvas sack down the companionway steps. They lugged it near the table, opened it, and with tin pails started spreading sand.

'For the blood,' one of them explained. 'You won't slip this way.'

Numb with fear, she waited for her husband to return from his summons from the captain, who had ordered all officers and warranted officers to meet him on the quarterdeck. 'He calls it a "consultation,"' Jamie told her as he went topside.

When he returned, he carried some clothing, which he handed to her. 'It's the smallest I could find in the slops chest, but I'd prefer you belay that dress you're wearing for these.' He took a lingering look at her dress, a dark one entirely appropriate for her Stonehouse days. 'I recall undoing all those buttons quite recently.'

She couldn't help laughing, even though she knew that was precisely his intent. She shook out the clothing he handed her. 'I am to wear trousers and a heavy shirt of some sort that will wrap around me twice?'

Again, the reality of what lay ahead brought her down to earth. 'If you end up in the water, it's likely easier to swim in trousers instead of a dress,' he said, and then because he was Jamie, 'You already have your surgeon's apron. Cinch it tight.'

She found a dark corner—orlop decks had plenty of those—and changed into a shirt and trousers that worked well enough when she rolled up the pantlegs and found a length of rope for a belt. When she returned to the improvised operating room, Jamie was leaning on the table, reading what looked like a well-used text. She looked away. There were bloodstains on the pages.

When he finished, he got another bit of sail to cover a smaller table and spread out his capital knives. Paddy brought over a small brazier with a kettle and water. He started a fire and put in a wicked-looking saw. 'Put in two,' Jamie said.

He saw the question in her eyes. 'Lord Nelson's orders.

When he lost his right arm at Tenerife, he said the worst part of the amputation was a cold saw. Hence his mandate to all surgeons: warm saws.'

'I need to sit down,' Jerusha said.

Jamie led her to a stool beside the table. 'That better?'

She had to know, needed to know. 'What will you expect of me today?'

'What you already do best, but this will be hard. When the guns start, every gunner will quickly be covered with block soot from gun discharge. Ah, here it is.' He pointed to another brazier Paddy had toted out from a dark corner. 'This is warm water for you. I know we will run out of towels, but do your best. Wounded men will be bloody and blackened with gun smoke.'

'I'll get them clean.'

'I know you will, my love.' His hand went to her shoulder; she loved the firmness of his touch. 'If we're down to the wire, I'll need you to suture.'

'Oh, my.' What else could she say?

He appraised her, then snapped his fingers. 'One more thing.' He selected a length of muslin from his bandage chest and wrapped it around her hair. 'That'll do.'

'You will never be a lady's maid,' she scolded, and rewrapped the muslin. 'I still refuse to look repellent, and you haven't a clue where to knot anything except a bandage.'

He shrugged. 'I am no hairdresser. I prefer to rumple it.' He held her close. 'My lady, you're amazing. I am going to try you to the limit.'

'Not you,' she said quietly. 'Napoleon.'

Shortly after noon, because of a light wind with greasy swells on the water, Admiral Collingwood's line of battle sailed slowly, majestically, towards the combined fleet of French and

Spanish warships parallel to Admiral Nelson's line. Jerusha sat on the lower deck in her husband's lap.

She had been listening to guns and gunners on the decks above, the trample of feet and gun carriages rolling in and out. 'What will battle sound like?' she asked.

'Loud, so loud. What's harder might be the way the ship will roll with each barrage, in addition to the ship's movement towards the enemy. I need scarcely add that it is hard to amputate limbs or suture under such circumstances.'

'How in the world do you do what you do?' she asked, touching his face, caressing it, even as Paddy looked on with interest.

'To the best of my ability. What else can I say?' He managed a laugh. 'We can both tell our children about this battle outside of Cadiz someday.'

Was this the right time, considering that once the action began, she did not know if he or she would survive? Maybe she should have said something sooner. She knew herself well enough to know that, married or not, she was always going to be a modest woman.

'You should know something,' she said finally, as shouted commands from far above them grew louder.

'Hopefully I'll remember it,' he told her, giving her an extra cuddle. 'Right now I'm wondering if I have enough retractors and if I should have had Paddy roll more bandages.'

'You need to know this. I think—not totally sure, mind you—but I think we started a baby the last time you were in port.'

There was no stunned silence, because the ship noises seemed to get louder, even as she whispered right in his ear. 'You know, in the family way?'

'Oh, Jerusha,' he said, his voice suddenly so tentative. 'Oh, Jerusha.'

'I'm dreadfully inconvenient.'

'I love you anyway. I think both of us are dreadfully in-convenient, unless it was another lucky fellow who surprised you some night when I was gone serving king and country.'

She heard the humour in his voice and marvelled at this man of hers. 'James Wilson, do you have a middle name?'

'Andrew. Is this the dread three-name dress down?'

'It's too late for the tri-scold,' she teased back, astounded at this silly conversation when the *Revenge* could be blown apart at any minute, if things went precisely wrong. 'I was wondering, that's all. Andrew might be a nice name for a son. Aye, Andrew Wilson.'

'And if it's a daughter, I'm partial to Mary.'

She nodded, fearing what was coming soon. She burrowed into his chest and nearly through to his backbone, or would have if she could. She straightened up when Paddy clambered down the ladder into the orlop, his excitement palpable. 'Sir, Captain Moorsom wanted you to know that when the carron-ades fire, it's the general signal for a broadside.' He rubbed his hands together. 'Sir, looks like we're heading smack in the middle of the southern end.'

'Thank you, Paddy,' her husband said calmly. 'Are you ready?'

'As ever I will be,' his mate said.

Jerusha closed her eyes. If she could have run home to Plymouth, she would have. 'Carronades?' she asked, hoping to sound merely curious, and not terrified, too.

Jamie had no trouble sensing her high reticence for bat-tle. He rubbed her cheek with his. 'Those smaller guns on the quarterdeck. We must be nearly into the Combined Fleet lines. I can't prepare you for the sound of cannonballs hit-ting the *Revenge*, or maybe sails or a mast struck and falling. Bear it the best you can. That will be followed by men bring-ing the wounded down here to us and Paddy. We're going to be busy. Hang on.'

Chapter Thirty-Five

Hardly had Paddy assumed his position beside the operating table when Jerusha heard the carronades far forward on the *Revenge*.

'That's it,' Jamie said so calmly. God bless the man she married. The surgeon she adored checked his timepiece, as though pronouncing a death in Ward A, even as she knew they were about to be engulfed by death far outmatching any hospital ward. 'A quarter to one of the clock. Here we go, my love.' He grinned. 'Not you, Paddy.'

The mate laughed.

These men are crazy, Jerusha thought.

She braced herself.

She wasn't prepared. Not at all. Every cannon on the lee side of the *Revenge* blasted death into the enemy. The force of the broadside threw her against the operating table. Jamie grabbed her, righted her, and sat her down on the deck. 'That's going to leave a bruise,' he shouted above the sound of the mighty gun carriages rolling back as gunners swabbed and reloaded.

Her ears rang, but she heard someone on the deck above yelling, 'Fire at will!'

Poor Will, she thought, then realised she had enough lunacy to match that of the man she loved. *Poor Will*.

Jamie was precisely right. Once the wounded men came down, assisted by other gunners or spare men on the gun-deck, she was too busy to be terrified. It was as though a hundred jetty bells clanged for medical help pouring from Stonehouse to assess, patch immediately, and send wounded men into the wards to live or die. No, a thousand jetty bells, and there were no wards to send the men, only this orlop deck.

In no time, there were ten, then fifteen, then twenty wounded men groaning, crying, and screaming on the sail-covered orlop deck near the operating table where her husband worked with his knives. Some bore their agony silently. She decided silence was worse.

Jerusha wasted not a moment, wiping blood, gun soot, and other bits and pieces she didn't want to think about from those men waiting their turn. She cleaned as gently as she could, which she quickly understood would never do. She increased her tempo of wash and wipe as more wounded surrounded her. On her knees, she moved from one man to the next, cutting off their clothing when she could, at Jamie's command, and wiping blood and bone around shattered arms and legs.

To the side of the orlop deck, she saw where other men were placed, those men who had no chance of survival. She thought of her silent patients on Ward B, Sailing Master Kent's son among them, and wished with all her heart she could sit with them, as she had sat day after day with Alec Kent. Maybe there would be time later.

In a momentary lull, she heard noise of chests being dragged across the deck and looked up. His face grim, his expression set, Paddy tugged three midshipmen's sea chests into the marginally better light next to her husband. The Irishman slung down a bit of sailcloth and nodded to two other slightly wounded men who must have helped take their mates below deck. She couldn't hear what was said, but those sailors carried their wounded to Paddy. She watched another moment. Jamie must have assigned him to suture wounds requiring no amputation.

I can do that, too, she thought. *Maybe when Paddy tires.*

She cleaned the men as best she could, assisted by a uniformed officer she did not know. He must have noticed her questioning look. 'I'm Bailey the purser,' he said. 'Pleased to meet you. I can help here.'

Was this Paddy's man? He sounded like he was addressing her at a garden party. She nodded and returned to her task, and he to his, after he poured out the already bloody water and refilled the brazier from a keg.

After what seemed like hours but was probably only minutes, Jerusha gasped to hear the *Revenge* firing cannon from both sides now. They must be surrounded. She wept in utter terror, stopping only when the wounded man below her put his hand on her arm.

'No worries, missy,' he consoled her, even as his gunnery mate tightened the tourniquet near his shoulder. 'Thank 'ee, mate.'

'But we're surrounded!'

'Never you worry,' the gunner said. He grinned, his teeth white in an otherwise black face. ''Tis the way our little admiral likes to fight. Hit hard, then divide into skirmishes. Pell-mell, he calls it.'

'I think you're all crazy,' she told him, which made him laugh.

As the guns roared, the *Revenge* shook and shivered, and more wounded men joined her sea of patients on the orlop deck. Jerusha ran out of towels.

I haven't a single scruple left, she thought as she pawed through discarded clothing for any cloth that looked remotely clean.

She took solace in watching her husband standing with legs wide apart to balance himself as the *Revenge* did its own battle dance. He barely paused from one patient to the next.

This was no time to complain or hold back, even though

her stomach revolted against the sight of one more drop of blood, or one more man looking at her with hope in his eyes. There would never be enough surgeons for a battle such as this.

To comfort herself, she thought of their baby, nestled deep inside and so tiny, evidence of a wife's love for a husband so often gone, because he had no choice. She wondered if their little one, no older than six or seven weeks, if that, could hear the terrible sounds, or feel the constant shaking of a ship tried to its limit. She hummed a lullaby and realised she wasn't only humming to Andrew or Mary inside her but soothing the Andrews on the deck around her. The notion pushed the heart back into her breast.

When Jerusha began to wonder if every man aboard the *Revenge* was below deck with her, she sensed something different. She became aware that the *Revenge* was not surrounded anymore and the guns fired on one side only, and not as rapidly.

'Jamie?' she said in what she thought was a normal tone of voice. 'Jamie?'

He didn't turn around, so she went back to cleaning dirty men with equally dirty towels and no clean water anywhere now, in hopes that somehow the god of battle would take pity on them.

She noticed that Paddy was rotating his shoulders and turning his head from side to side. To her relief, she saw no new patients on his makeshift operating table. She returned to her duty, aware that the smallest hope was peering at her, its eyes bright, as though it were a living, breathing entity and not just a wish in her heart. She knew she imagined it, but the thought kept her working steadily through the endless afternoon.

When her husband demanded Paddy's aid at his table, Jerusha wasted not a moment, stepping to Paddy's table to continue stitching up what even she recognised as more minor wounds. When Paddy finished, he examined her work and nodded. 'Mrs Wilson, you're amazing.'

'Hardly,' she said. The compliment buoyed her as she returned to wiping away soot and grime.

She finally became aware that she was wiping down one of the remaining wounded, this man a Royal Marine. He seemed alert so she asked, 'Please, sir, what is happening up there?'

'Many ships on fire,' he told her in that cryptic way of the wounded, doling out as few words as possible, because everything hurt, even grammar.

'Ours?'

'Theirs. I pray…'

Suddenly a loud explosion shook the *Revenge* so hard that Jamie threw himself across his patient on the table. Only hours ago, such a noise would have sent her screaming around the orlop. Jerusha waited in silence for a falling mast, or water pouring down the companionway, but nothing happened. Above the appalling odour, she smelled something on fire, and close by.

'Paddy, go have a look,' Jamie ordered, as he continued with an amputation.

Paddy came back soon enough. 'It's a French ship! There's a huge flame!'

'God rest their souls,' Jamie said, he who had been working for hours to save those Royal Navy men near death because of French warships like the one in its death agony nearby.

'It's drifting away from us,' Paddy added. He darted up the ladder again and came down just as quickly. 'Come look, sir!'

'I can't. You go topside, Jerusha.'

Topside was a strange world. Her mouth open, Jerusha stared at bodies in the water, ships dismasted and drifting, others locked together as if in mortal combat. She watched what remained of the explosion, an orange fireball that spread as she stared, transfixed.

But that was almost nothing compared to the death so close

around her on the *Revenge*. She stared at men who never made it to medical aid on the orlop deck.

'Wh-what did you want me to see, Paddy?' she asked, when she could form words again.

'The little ships, one a schooner.' He pointed across the rail. 'It's the *Pickle*.'

'Such an odd name,' she murmured, half to herself. 'Ship to shore, like my husband's usual office at sea?'

'Sometimes. See there? They're picking up survivors.' He squinted in the failing light. 'Good God, they're naked.' To her surprise, Paddy nodded his approval. 'Easier to swim with no encumbrances.'

She jumped involuntarily when more explosions battered her already tired ears.

'No fears, miss,' Paddy said. 'It's just guns still cooking off.' He watched the nimble ships darting in close, too close, to reach for Frenchmen floundering in the water. 'Go below and tell the boss we'll be tending the enemy soon.'

Jerusha stood a moment longer, taking in the sight of so much carnage and mayhem. She gently patted her belly. 'We're still here, little one, you and I,' she whispered. 'Someday, you can tell Admiral Nelson your mama served in whatever place this is.'

She made her way carefully down the gun-deck ladder and farther down onto the orlop deck, slippery with blood. She watched her husband as he put the last few stitches into a flap of skin covering an amputation, and summoned the purser to clear away a spot on the deck for a sailor lighter now than when they laid him on the table.

Maybe Jamie sensed she was watching him. He turned around and leaned against the operating table, where in better times young midshipmen gathered for meals. 'Jerusha,' was all he said.

She came closer, suddenly shy, even though she knew this

man as she had never known another human being before. With humility earned in a terrible afternoon, she thanked God Almighty, Ruler of the Universe and even this sorry spot off the coast of Spain for the best man a wife could have.

He smiled at her, but she could tell he was too tired to move. He looked at the patients on the deck, men he had saved, and men who couldn't be saved. His glance went to the dark corners as if wondering if those men still breathed, those sailors and Marines taken there in the beginning because no power outside of a miracle could save them. She could almost hear his brain working, apologising to the dead that no one alive knew how to heal them.

She came to him and looked, too, where death had come calling, despite the surgeon's best efforts. Jamie's arms circled her from behind.

'What have we been a part of?' she asked.

'Something I hoped you would never see,' he told her. 'But now you know what I do.' He rested his blood-crusted cheek against her blood-crusted cheek. 'We never see the battle, but here we are, fighting the worst of it below deck.'

Her tired brain remembered Paddy's message. 'That explosion? It's a French ship close by. Paddy says you—we—will have more work here soon.'

'I expect we will.'

He spoke so calmly.

How do you manage? she asked herself.

She leaned back against him. For a small moment in a crowded day, maybe it was enough right now to be held close and feel his heartbeat against her back. She squinted into the darker corners where Jamie had looked, and felt an overpowering urge to check on them.

Of the many, she found one still alive, and sat by him. He still breathed, so she sat and took his hand. 'Felicity,' he said, content. 'Felicity.'

Call me whatever you want, she thought, as Nameless One finally breathed a peaceful sigh and left her.

As she sat there, she heard silence, blessed silence. The guns were stilled at last.

'Surgeon? Surgeon?'

Who was calling for her husband? She moved towards him, careful not to step on any of the wounded. She sensed something worse, some news she didn't want to hear. That was folly. What could possibly be worse than this entire day?

Black with gun smoke from hat to shoes, a midshipman picked his way down the companionway.

'Aye, son, what? Who needs me?'

'Captain Moorsom. He's in a bad way.'

'I'll come up now,' Jamie said. 'Move aside.'

'Wait, sir,' the middie said. He straightened up, eyes ahead, as if in recitation. 'One hour ago, our glorious little admiral died on the *Victory*, struck down by a sniper. Lord Nelson lived to know we had won.' He turned away and began to weep. 'What will we do?'

'We carry on,' Jamie told him, a comforting hand on the lad's shoulder. 'As he would wish. Take me to our captain. Now!'

'I don't think I will ever forget this day, sir.'

'None of us will, lad,' Jamie told him. 'Neither will England.'

Chapter Thirty-Six

'Come with me.' Jamie took her hand, so Jerusha followed him topside. She already knew how horrible the deck looked, but barely recognised the congenial captain who had insisted she join the officers in the wardroom when she came aboard— Was it yesterday? The day before?—as part of a good-natured prank. His eyes were two coals in his head, and he was as filthy as his men. She saw the wound by his ear, which seemed to be hanging on by a thread.

He pointed towards the still burning French ship. 'Wounded from the *Achille* are coming here,' he managed to say. Then, 'Lieutenant Hole is now in command. You two there. Take me below deck.'

'Aye, sir.' As two grimy gunners took Captain Moorsom below deck, Jamie went to the rail and stared down as the much smaller *Pickle* and a cutter came closer, carrying wounded men. 'Lieutenant Hole, the quartermaster needs to rummage around quickly for some trousers, at the very least. These Frogs are as bare as Adam in Eden.'

'I've already sent for him,' Captain Moorsom called from near the companionway. Jerusha wondered how he could manage his casual air, with such a wound. 'Close your eyes, Mrs Wilson.'

Where did Jamie find the energy to joke? 'I hope he hurries, Captain. I can't have my wife looking at naked Frenchmen and making any comparisons. I'd hate not to measure up.'

To her astonishment, Captain Moorsom laughed. 'We do have a certain reputation to maintain, madam.'

'Do either of you ever lose your sense of humour, Captain?' she declared, amazed that after all she had seen today, she could still blush.

'Just exhausted. Get me below deck, gunners.'

She looked across the water to see the *Achille* blazing everywhere, with burning sailors too done for to jump. She covered her face with her hands, but that was no reprieve. She still saw them on fire. 'Will I ever not see them?' she asked Lieutenant Hole.

'If you are lucky,' he replied. 'Carry on, Mrs Wilson. I have work to do.'

He looked so young. As Jerusha watched him take calm charge of the disaster on deck, she knew she was seeing a junior officer turn into a commander of men, and it humbled her.

Working with Purser Bailey, she scrounged below deck for more sails. Mr Bailey found a place in her heart forever when she just stared at the wounded already crowded together and wondered where to put Frenchmen, too. He brought her a glass of wine.

'It's a fine Bordeaux from my own stash,' he assured her with no little pride. 'I'm saving some for our captain over there.'

It went down her throat like, well, good Bordeaux. 'Heavens, but that was splendid, Mr Bailey. You have a knack.'

He beamed with delight, and casually brushed a bit of someone's nameless body part off his sleeve like the gentleman he obviously was. He flicked something from her hair. 'My pleasure,' he said, as courtly as if he were her host at an elegant dinner. What a strange place this orlop deck was, she decided, as she returned to her labours, energised.

To her surprise and then her relief, two other women joined her on the orlop deck. She recognised one as the wife of the quartermaster, and the other as the sailing master's wife. Without a word, they continued her homely task.

She had to know. 'Have…have you ever seen anything like this?'

The quartermaster's wife, whose hair was already greying, shook her head. 'Not in all my years at sea.'

She watched as Paddy and the purser made room for more wounded, Frenchmen this time. In record time, Jamie rearranged and stitched until Captain Moorsom was patched as well as he could manage. In record time, the captain was taken to his own quarters across the *Revenge*'s stern. Over Jamie's protest, Jerusha sat her husband down and wiped his face. 'There now,' she said, hands on hips. 'Time for Frenchmen.'

And they came, some protesting, but more of the enemy from the *Achille* seeing only help and hopefully relief from their burns. Jamie went to work.

He called for her quickly, gesturing her closer for a look. 'Surgeon Kidwell told me he taught you how to debride burns,' he said.

'He did.' She looked and turned her head away. Lacerations were one thing; burns, quite another. 'I've helped with burns,' she managed to say. 'What do you want me to do?' she asked, terrified but game because she had no more choice than the others. He had a good shoulder. She rested her chin on it as he leaned there on the operating table. 'You stink,' she said, which made him chuckle.

'I've stunk worse,' he assured her. 'I sent Paddy to forage for olive oil, any kind of oil. And praise God, I found some gauze. When the burns come in, I want you to put a generous bit of oil on the burn and drape gauze on it. Wait here.'

She nodded. 'I hate war,' she said softly. She knew Jamie's

dreadful task was to decide who of the burned French sailors even came below for such puny aid as they could offer.

She and Purser Bailey stretched the olive oil as far as it would go, helped by the two uncomplaining wives. Hours passed and they were reduced to water only. The more alert among the French prisoners talked, but she could only shake her head and wish she spoke their language.

She thought of all the letters she had written for her patients in Ward A, certain they would be delivered to loved ones. These injured Frenchmen had no guarantee anyone would know where they were. The thought saddened her as nothing else could have.

The purser and quartermaster found trousers and some sweaters, but most of the barely covered patients shivered until their teeth chattered. It went against all her sense of respect for the dead, but she and the wives took the canvas coverings off the English dead to preserve the shivering French.

The moment Jerusha thought she could not stand another patient, a weeping Frenchwoman arrived, towed down the companionway by a Royal Navy officer Jamie introduced as Captain John Lapenotière.

'He skippers the *Pickle*,' Jamie said. 'Who is this noisy baggage?'

'Jamie, don't be rude,' Jerusha scolded.

She reached for the woman, who was dressed oddly in trousers and a jacket with a Royal Navy insignia.

The woman, her black curly hair wild around her face, drew back, then declared, *'Vous êtes une femme!'* She threw herself into Jerusha's arms, sobbing.

Seeing the utter pointlessness of trying to coax rational thought out of the woman, Jerusha did the logical thing and hugged her back. Soon the woman's sobs turned into hiccups, and then she was silent, her head down.

'Captain Lapenotière, why us?' Jamie asked.

Looking as sorely put upon as probably everyone else in the fleet, the captain shrugged. 'I took her to the *Belle Isle* first, but they're in far worse shape than the *Revenge* and they waved me off.' He leaned closer to Jamie. 'She was as bare naked as the others, but some kind soul on the *Belle Isle* gave her some trousers and another man took off his jacket. Surgeon, she has a burn on her neck and back. Can you help her?' He started for the ladder, his mission complete, apparently. 'By the way, her name is Jeannette. That's all we could understand.'

Jerusha coaxed Jeannette to sit on the operating table and held her hand while Jamie probed her burn. She flinched, but did not shriek, and bore it patiently, her eyes on Jerusha's. She talked at length, gesturing with her hands, her face a mask of worry and uncertainty.

Using the slender store of olive oil, Jamie dabbed at Jeannette's shoulder and back and bandaged it loosely. 'I wish we knew more,' he told Jerusha. He cleared his throat. 'Does anyone here speak French?'

No one did, or no one would admit to speaking French, until Mr Bailey returned to the orlop deck, bearing a flask of olive oil. 'I stole this from the quartermaster,' he said. 'QMs are the curse of the world.' Jerusha hid her smile when the quartermaster's wife fixed him with a malevolent stare. He flinched at the stare, shuddered, and turned his whole attention to Jeannette. 'Where did you find her?' he asked.

'She's from the *Achille*,' Jerusha said. 'No one speaks French here.'

'I do,' he said. *'Bon soir, madame,'* he said, which produced more tears and gestures. By the time she finished, they knew Jeannette had been working as a powder monkey with her husband's guns. She gestured a *whoosh* and a *boom*, then more tears.

Through it all, the purser listened intently and with sympathy. When she finished, leaning against Jerusha in her exhaustion, Mr Bailey shook his head. 'The poor dear cannot find her husband.' He was a proper man. He blushed, much to Jerusha's delight. 'She had perched herself near the rudder. When the lead started to burn her, she took off her clothes and leaped into the water.' He spread out his hands. 'My quarters are untouched. I will clear a space for her there. Back soon,' he said, and left as quietly as he had come.

James and Jerusha looked at each other. 'I'm too tired to laugh,' James said at last. 'I believe I will never underestimate pursers again. How does he know French? Jerusha? *Jerusha!*'

She heard his voice from a peculiar distance. Jeannette grabbed her as Jerusha Wilson had all she could manage on this day of crushing, grinding battle. She either fainted or fell asleep. She didn't care which it was. She and either Andrew or Mary were done with this endless day.

Chapter Thirty-Seven

When she woke, Jerusha found herself on a pile of sailcloth, tucked in a dark place. She looked around in wild alarm, wondering how many wounded she had displaced, then took a closer look. Where was she? And what was the *Revenge* doing? She curled up and made herself small as the ship pitched and yawed wildly, caught in the grip of a monstrous storm.

When she cried out in fear, Jamie knelt beside her, gathering her close. She held on just as tight. 'We're all going to die,' she whispered.

'Not yet,' he said, 'although Captain Moorsom muttered something about the wind and waves being allies of the French. And I thought I had heard every curse word possible in the Royal Navy. Silly me. Thank God he is still alive.'

As her vision accustomed itself to the dim lighting, she stared hard at the deck. 'Where have they gone?' she asked, as terrible dread assaulted her. 'The deck was covered with wounded men.'

It was his turn to gather himself together. She had seen him do that on Ward A when something didn't go well; she dreaded it. 'This storm has proved too much for some,' he told her. She rested her cheek against his hand. 'Those men needed a hospital, and not the orlop deck. Look over there, though.'

She looked where he nodded and saw the survivors of rough and ready surgery aboard a ship under attack, some sitting up, others curled tight as though trying in some weird way to make themselves smaller targets for shot and shell. She heard low-voiced conversation, and to her relief, the quiet slap of cards on the deck. God bless the Royal Navy.

'It's not quite Ward A, but it's close,' she said. 'I should be up and helping. I didn't mean to shirk my duties.'

Her doctor disagreed in firm tones she had heard him use with his patients in Stonehouse, where the floor didn't heave and threaten to toss everyone around. 'You've shirked nothing. No, little mother. You had all you could manage last night. You slept through the day.'

She smiled at that, even as the *Revenge* pitched and tossed like a wild horse unbroken to bit and bridle. 'I know I was tired.'

'Aye, lass. Now will you go back to sleep?'

Not yet. She struggled to sit up, to help, to do a thousand things, because that was what this situation demanded. Drat her sneaky, duplicitous husband. What did he do but what she had seen him do to cranky patients at Stonehouse? He held her close until she felt herself relax in his arms.

'All right, have it your way,' she said finally.

'Why, thank you. That's my intention.'

Jerusha tried to bargain her way to a few more moments of awareness. 'The other ships? Tell me we're not alone.'

He humoured her. 'We're not alone, but several of the Spanish and French prizes of war have escaped or wrecked. Admiral Collingwood is in charge of the fleet and we are heading to Gibraltar to refit.'

'Not home?' she asked, disappointed.

'Some of the larger ships took a terrible beating and will never survive to the Channel without repairs. Admiral Nelson's flagship was badly damaged, and Admiral Collingwood is determined that Nelson will be returned in the *Victory*. First Gibraltar, then home. Go to sleep. You're getting tedious.'

She smiled at that, then closed her eyes. The last thing she remembered was her husband tugging the sailcloth higher on her shoulder and kissing her cheek.

The storm raged for days, so wildly destructive that the cooks couldn't light fires and feed the men anything except ship's biscuit and hard cheese. There was nothing for Jamie's patients except ship's biscuit dipped in wine and then ale, when the wine ran out. Jerusha thought of the low diet that wounded men needed in order to heal, and her heart broke.

Revenge's Lieutenant Hole—obviously cut from the same cloth as his commander—restored all the order he could. The next day, Jerusha heard the temporary walls go up again in the officers' wardroom, which were broken down during battle. She spent a better night in Jamie's tiny quarters, curled up in his swinging cot and prayed not to be dumped out on the deck.

Despite the storm, more order came to the orlop deck. The *Revenge* seemed to have an unlimited supply of vinegar in kegs. Sailors not busy on deck were put to work mixing a little seawater with a lot of vinegar and scrubbing the orlop deck to remove bloodstains.

From somewhere, Jamie managed to actually heat some strong tea, which she managed to keep down. 'I will always smell vinegar,' she gasped, as he held her hair back as she puked into a bucket, because he wouldn't allow her on deck.

Against his protests, she returned to tending the wounded, wiping faces and then simply holding hands with those men as frightened as she was from the storm that continued to rage. Now and then one of the masters' wives joined her, as she soothed and commiserated.

They inched closer to Gibraltar, a wounded, limping fleet that looked nothing like conquerors. Jerusha made her way topside to see the remains of enemy ships, some with men clinging to them, knowing there would be no rescue, no hope.

They may have been the enemy, but this was a cruel death and she couldn't watch.

Jeannette proved to be useless. Even the calm-tempered, courtly Mr Bailey was ready to throw her overboard. 'All she does is weep for her missing husband,' he complained over a luncheon of ship's bread dipped in rum. 'I would happily chuck her over the side, but there is probably a rule of war against that,' he said morosely.

Jeannette cheered up slightly when Jerusha gave her the dark dress she had been wearing when she came aboard the *Revenge* as part of a lovely prank Sailing Master Kent played upon her and James Wilson. It pained her not at all to give away her own dress, because the events of recent weeks faded into nothingness, when the battle they'd been through together loomed so much larger. Perhaps it would stop Jeannette's complaints. It didn't.

In the directive Admiral Collingwood managed to compose, even with his writing desk heaving like a living thing as he put pen to paper, he declared this fleet action to be called Trafalgar, after the nearest cape south of Cadiz and not far from Gibraltar. Jamie told her that some of the officers were already calling this a battle no one would ever forget, when her most fervent wish was to forget it. Men and their battles...

'And here you are, a part of it,' Jamie told her. He kissed her, complimented her on her ability to keep tea and hard bread down in this raging storm, and began his midnight ward-walking among his patients.

No one wants to be here, she thought as she watched him, *but I would gladly stay, as long as you are here, my love.*

She marvelled at her husband, working in a tight, storm-battered space, with almost no medical resources except an active mind and well-honed resourcefulness.

He stayed with her as she wiped down one particularly hard case, a bosun who suffered no fool gladly. The one-eyed brute glared at her, then his gaze softened. 'Surgeon, who is this pretty lady who winces when I wince?'

'That's my wife,' he told his patient. 'She has a tender heart, and she is mine.'

'I had a wife like that,' the bosun said. 'Gone these five years. Keep blushing, little lady. I'm enjoying the memories.'

'That is more kindness than I have ever heard from him,' Jamie told her later, which only made her sniff back tears and work harder.

At Jamie's insistence, she spent the next day swinging in his cot, blanket warm, her hand resting lightly just below her belly, acquainting herself with her little one. She had no larger task than the greatest task: to simply *be*, so another could grow.

The next day seemed no better than the four that had preceded it, as the storm raged and the fleet limped towards Gibraltar.

She was feeding the wounded their pitiful hard biscuit soaked in only water, when Jamie called to her from the companionway. He draped a woollen cape around her as she came to him. His face expressionless, he led her up to the main deck, cleared now of debris and almost tidy.

'You're going to hate this. You're leaving this ship don't argue with me, Jerusha.' He turned it into one rapid sentence.

He held her close. 'What are you doing?' she asked.

'Sending you home. Back to Plymouth and Mags McDonald and our bed that doesn't move about.' Drat the man; he chuckled. 'Except when we're both in it.'

'I'm not leaving without you,' she insisted, as he carefully edged to the *Revenge*'s railing and braced them both against the storm. Her old friend Panic returned as she stared, wide-eyed, at the boulder-sized waves.

'Admiral Collingwood has prepared a dispatch for the King and prime minister, telling them of Trafalgar,' Jamie said, speaking loudly to be heard above the storm. 'Captain Lapenotière of the *Pickle* is taking it. And you.'

'Please no!' she begged, frightened because she knew he meant it, as sure as she knew how small the *Pickle* was. Compared to the warships around them, it bounced up and down in the water like a toy in a bathtub.

'Shh, shh. He is right now below us, about to transfer a last boatload of French prisoners to the *Revenge*. When they come up, you are going down. I will have not one word of argument, Jerusha Wilson.' He tightened his grip on her. 'I will protect my family.'

When she opened her mouth, he put a finger to her lips. 'My love, the *Revenge* is far less crippled than some of this battered fleet,' he said. 'She might stay right here, or return to the blockade. I will have you safe in Plymouth.'

He was speaking the truth, as little as she liked it. Drat the man again, but she knew he was right. She tried one more time. 'I am no trouble aboard ship,' she told him. 'I know I am useful.'

'Very much so,' he agreed. He seemed to waver and she took heart, then his mouth grew firm again. 'I won't have you in this place of danger while you grow a baby, our baby.'

Jerusha wanted to argue, but he was right. She nodded, unable to speak.

He kept his hand firmly in the back of her trousers as they watched the *Revenge* crew haul aboard the French prisoners, tie them to each other, then herd them in groups of twenty aft, where Royal Marines sat them down on a portion of the deck chained off to receive them.

Lieutenant Hole handed her his own dispatches wrapped in waterproof sealskin. 'Give it to Captain Lapenotière and he'll add it to our admiral's dispatch and other letters.' He kissed the packet. 'There's one to my wife in there, and other men's wives and sweethearts.'

'Aye, sir. That's what it comes down to, doesn't it? Those we love,' Jamie said.

'Aye, it does.' He smiled at her, this iron man who never flinched or faltered, the same as her husband.

England is safe because of you, she thought, and she kissed his cheek.

'Be a good girl,' Lieutenant Hole said as he blushed, that iron man.

'Your turn, Mrs Wilson,' she heard next from her dear surgeon. 'Sit in the bight of the rope and hang on. When you get aboard the *Pickle*, mind your manners and don't think me too heartless for sending you away.'

'Never that,' she whispered, any ill-use forgotten because she knew he was right.

She closed her eyes and gripped the rope for dear life as she swung out from the *Revenge*, then down neatly in the pinnace that she had earlier noticed was tied to the stern of the larger ship. She set her lips tight against any protest as a Royal Marine pulled her onto his lap and wrapped his arms around her. 'Hang on, little lady. We'll be alongside the *Pickle* and underway in no time.'

Dear God, the motion. She gasped as the little boat turned into a wild thing. The little crew struck out with their oars, heading towards another ship that appeared so small. She looked back at the *Revenge* and her husband. She strained to hear him as he cupped his hands around his mouth.

'I'll see you in Plymouth, Mrs Wilson!'

She waved until the *Revenge* disappeared, shrouded in rain. She kept her eyes on the ship and whispered, 'God of war, look kindly on my Jamie. Please, oh, please.'

She was nine days on the *Pickle*, second smallest craft among the victors of Trafalgar, an eighty-foot schooner built for messages between ship and shore, but even more for speed, if given the opportunity.

With no fanfare, Captain Lapenotière deposited her in his tiny quarters. Sitting her in a chair by the desk, he looked her straight in the eye. 'We're a small ship and we are one thousand miles from England,' he said. 'We are battling a storm of immense proportions and I have no time to coddle you.'

'I don't require coddling,' she assured him, looking him firmly in the eye, too, praying to never do anything to shame Surgeon Wilson.

He pointed to a nest of blankets in the deck by the bulkhead. 'My sleeping cot will swing wildly so you will be safer on the deck and not in it, Mrs Wilson.' He pointed to a bucket with a wooden lid. 'That is your commode. One of the seaman will dump it each morning. You are not allowed on deck unless summoned.'

'Aye, sir,' she said, which made him smile and seem slightly more human.

'It will be a difficult crossing, Mrs Wilson,' he said, his voice less stern. 'The *Pickle* is carrying the most important message to Admiralty and the King that has been delivered in recent memory. There are still enemy warships between us and England, and they have their orders, too. We will do our duty, no matter the danger.'

As soon as the *Pickle* left her relative protection from winds and waves created by the larger ships, the tossing began. Jerusha wrapped herself in a blanket and made herself as small as she could in the corner of Captain Lapenotière's cabin.

Day blurred into night, day after day, broken first by a change in wind direction that turned them back towards the Spanish coast. They struggled through the wind change and were on a course towards England again when she heard the unmistakable sound of 'Beat to Quarters.'

Were it not for a small act of kindness while still on the

Revenge, she would have been at the mercy of her promise to never leave the captain's quarters. A cabin boy had been assigned to bring her meals and empty the slops bucket. She recognised him from a brief stay in Block Four, Ward A, during a relapse of fever. Here he was now, reminding her of their connections.

Jerusha smiled to see that same look of adulation on his stark white face. 'Timmy, pop your head above deck and let me know what's happening.'

'A ship's chasing us!' he said, eyes wide, after a quick turn on the heaving deck.

Please don't blow us out the water, she prayed.

Only to sigh with relief when he came down again minutes later with the information that it was another small sloop, the *Nautilus*.

Even Captain Lapenotière enlisted her help. He sent Timmy down with the order that she find paper, pen, and ink in his desk. 'Mrs Wilson,' the captain shouted down the schooner's single companionway, 'write me a note stating that the Royal Navy was victorious, but we lost Admiral Nelson. Address it to Lord Haybert, British Delegation, Kingdom of Portugal, Lisbon. The *Nautilus* will carry it to Portugal.'

She did as he dictated, trying to time each letter to the rising and falling of the little schooner. When she finished, she dusted it with sand from the shaker in the desk, folded it and took it on deck, where two sailors guided her to the captain as the schooner bobbed about. Through a speaking tube, the two captains coordinated a line and sent the note in a bottle attached to a ring.

'Well done, Mrs Wilson,' Lapenotière said, with a bow to Jerusha. 'Go below and stay there.'

They sailed on through wind and storm that worsened until she saw water leaking into her tiny portion of the wardroom. It rose to her ankles. She held her breath as the bow seemed to dip lower and lower into the water. The spry little schooner slowed.

Good God, we're sinking, she thought, and held tight to her belly, desperate to protect her unborn baby.

I tried Jamie, I tried, was her second thought.

Her third thought was, *I will not die below deck. I am sorry, Mary or Andrew, that I could not protect you.*

Calmly she mounted the few steps that took her into the storm, the officer's cape tight about her.

Captain Lapenotière picked his way across the slanting deck. She watched him calmly, determined not to be forced below deck. To her relief, he handed her a bucket. 'Start bailing,' he ordered, and she did, bailing until her back ached, doing it for her baby, and not to get some message through, no matter how vital it was. In that awful moment, she bound herself forever to her unborn child.

All night she bailed as some of the crew manned the pump below deck and the rest of them poured water over the side. The effort seemed puny, but she worked until she dropped from exhaustion. Someone carried her to the mast and told her to hang on. She shivered, soaked to the skin. There wasn't a dry place on the foundering schooner.

She woke near morning to the scraping sound of men unbolting the four small but heavy carronades in the bow of the *Pickle*. The guns went overboard with a splash and the ship rose noticeably in the heaving sea.

It made all the difference. The storm raged, but the ship sailed. Someone carried her below deck and she slept, soggy but too exhausted to care.

By noon the storm abated. By the end of the next day, they found themselves in the English Channel sailing on a smooth sea, which earned everyone a tot of rum, captain's orders. On deck again, Jerusha watched the bottle go around. When it came to her, she tried to pass it on. 'Rum is for heroes,' she said. 'That's what my Jamie tells me.'

'Mrs Wilson, drink up,' Captain Lapenotière said. 'You're a hero, too.'

On they sailed, bedevilled once by no wind at all, which meant the captain ordered his men to pull out sweeps, long oars that bit into the sea, and row. They rowed until the god of wind blew in their direction at last, because apparently the Lord loves effort.

Jerusha saw all the exhaustion around her as men dropped from their labour and slept, waking up only to a prodding boot to keep the sails trim, while other men dropped and slept.

All of them kept a weather eye on the *Nautilus*, the schooner that had taken the message to the British ambassador in Portugal and now seemed to be racing to deliver the most important news of the war at sea to London first.

'Damn the *Nautilus*,' Jerusha heard Captain Lapenotière mutter as he paced the quarterdeck and watched his now-competitor trying to close the gap. Through judicious sailing and seamanship, he pulled ahead of the *Nautilus* and elaborately wiped his hands of the matter.

On November the fourth they made landfall at Falmouth in Cornwall on the southwest coast of England, a long distance from London. 'Why here?' Jerusha asked Captain Lapenotière.

'We depend upon the wind, and it is fickle,' he said, as his crew snubbed his battle-and-wind-tried ship to the dock. 'Now I will depend upon horsepower. I will beat the *Nautilus* to London. I swear I will.'

She watched from the deck as Captain Lapenotière spoke to an interested crowd on the dock, telling them of Trafalgar and Lord Nelson's sad death. Some turned away in shock and sorrow. Some ran to the nearest tavern and shops. She could almost see the word pass through the sleepy town. Bells tolled next.

Within the hour, a post chaise with four horses pulled up to the dock. One of the *Pickle*'s crew tossed in a pouch with precious dispatches and letters from officers to their wives. Captain Lapenotière went on board once more to consult with George Almy, master's mate.

'Mrs Wilson, you will sail with the *Pickle*,' he ordered. 'In a day, maybe two, God willing, you will be anchored in Plymouth.' His tone changed, and she heard the kindness that likely would have been there all along, if not for the terrors of storm and war. He kissed her forehead. 'Bless you, dear Mrs Wilson. If you were a man, I would request your services on any ship I command.'

'I think the surgeon would call you out for a duel,' she replied, which meant he was laughing as he left the gallant *Pickle* after one more long look at the schooner that would make him famous.

True to Lapenotière's words, they made landfall in Devonport on the evening of November the sixth, nine days after leaving the battered victors of Trafalgar struggling towards Gibraltar. Jerusha stood on the quarterdeck of the *Pickle* with Master Almy. She looked around her at the crew, saw their exhaustion and also their pride.

'We did it, Mrs Wilson,' he said.

'That you did, sir.'

'You crewed with us,' he told her, his words sincere. 'Thank you.'

She knew she would never forget his words. She had bailed water with them without complaint. She had doctored a sprain, sutured a laceration, and lanced a boil. Their trials had been her trials. They had passed the rum bottle to her and she measured up. It was enough.

The chill of November settled in her bones. She pulled the dead officer's cape tight around her, mindful, now that she was on land again and a woman, that she wore the same dirty trousers and shirt and her surgeon's apron, which had come to mean more to her than any garment she owned, or would ever own.

She started for the gangplank, aware that a short walk would take her to Stonehouse and Jamie's quarters. Master Almy put his hand on her arm. 'Listen! Captain Lapenotière must have made his announcement to the king yesterday.'

She heard every bell in Devonport and nearby Plymouth tolling. Tears started in her eyes for the little admiral. 'Victory is hard, isn't it?' she asked.

'Damned hard,' he replied, 'but we got the message here.' She heard so much emotion in Almy's voice that she felt, too. 'We did our duty. You too, Mrs Wilson, although I do not think you will receive any glory for it.'

She wiped her eyes. 'I never expected any. I did it for others, the same as you, sir.'

Chapter Thirty-Eight

Master Almy insisted on hailing a hackney for her. 'Your husband would use that damnable dental key on every tooth in my mouth if I turned you loose in Devonport or Plymouth.'

She didn't protest when he handed her money for the fare. She hadn't a coin on her, and here she was in filthy trousers, a shirt too big by far, and an officer's cape belonging to a corpse thrown overboard during battle.

She said goodbye to the master's mate, who started to help her into the hackney. He was stopped by a noisy, 'Great Neptune's Balls!' The hackney shook as the jarvey climbed down. With a sigh, she fell into the arms of Jake O'Toole, who had helped her carry out her deception against Lady Oakshott. Was that eons ago? No, only since summer.

Jake sat with her in his hackney as she told the story of Trafalgar through tears and monumental exhaustion. 'Just get me home, please,' she said finally. 'I am so tired.'

She slept in the hackney and had only the vaguest memory of being carried inside Jamie's quarters. Mags McDonald, in braids and a ratty robe, took her from Mr O'Toole, scolding and hugging her.

'I'm filthy,' Jerusha said in feeble protest as Mags took her upstairs. 'I need a bath in the absolute worst way.'

The last thing she remembered was Mags assuring her that

she would only drown in a tub tonight, and the matter would keep until she woke up.

Brilliant sun woke her the next morning, only Mags assured her it was the next morning plus one. She made no objection when Jamie's housekeeper helped her downstairs through the warm kitchen and into the bathing room. She sank gratefully into hot water, as Mags scrubbed her thoroughly from head to heels. She washed Jerusha's hair three times, scolding all the while when she wasn't choking back tears.

'Mags, I helped all I could, but there weren't enough of us to save everyone. And Jamie, oh, dear God, he tried so hard.' She wailed then. 'I love him beyond all reason and imagine this? I am with child.'

'That comes as no surprise,' Mags said. 'It's a good thing I'm half deaf. I only heard a little of your carrying on upstairs.' She chuckled. 'Made me a bit envious.'

Jerusha decided to laugh *instead* of blush, letting Mags dry her off and give her another love scold, as in, 'Jerusha, your waist is already thickening.'

'I know. Mags, I'm starving and so is Mary or Andrew.'

After a breakfast large enough to feed the entire crew of the *Pickle*, Jerusha made no objection to a return to bed, this time on clean sheets that Mags must have changed while she was downing a half dozen eggs, bacon and well-buttered toast. She cried because Jamie wasn't with her, then returned to sleep.

She woke in late afternoon to a visit from Surgeon Kidwell, ushered upstairs by Mags, who scolded him, too, for looking so haggard, because she was a Scot and that was the national custom. Mags brought up tea while her other dear surgeon sat by her bed and listened to her retelling of Trafalgar.

'You would have been so proud of Jamie,' she concluded, then leaned forward to touch his hand. 'But you, sir, you've been through it here.'

'The jetty bell is our constant companion. In the last two

days alone, several Trafalgar ships have anchored here and unloaded their wounded.' He shook his head. 'Such a battle. Such loss. Scuttlebutt says Admiral Nelson will be encrypted at St. Paul's Cathedral.'

'But you, sir? Don't change the subject.' Goodness, she was beginning to sound like a combination of James Wilson and Mags McDonald, and she wasn't even Scottish.

He took her hands in his. 'I am shortly to be relieved of duty, dear Jerusha. I have exceeded my limit.'

He said it simply and quietly, but she knew she was listening to a man ready for the peace of the grave.

What has war done to us all? she asked herself, aghast.

'I wanted you to know that I have strenuously recommended to the Sick and Hurt Board that Surgeon James Wilson be named my successor as chief surgeon on Block Four. No one is better trained and no one deserves it more.'

'Thank you.' There was so much she could have said, but she knew that would only embarrass a modest man.

'I have also recommended that you two move into my quarters,' he added as he stood up. 'They're larger, and Mrs McDonald informed me that you will need more room soon enough. Good day, dear madam. Join us in Ward A when you're ready.'

She was ready in the morning, dressed in her other dark dress and surgeon's apron. Mrs Terwilliger nodded to see her and even smiled. Jerusha faced an entirely new bunch of patients, one or two of the livelier ones even whistling their appreciation until Mrs T shut them down with a glare and the comment, 'Mind your manners, you heathens! This is Mrs James Wilson, wife of our other surgeon, who will be here soon enough to thrash you all.' She narrowed her eyes and even Jerusha felt fear. 'Mind. Your. Manners.'

Jerusha returned to duty, even if each day began with morning sickness. She washed faces, held hands when needed, and wrote letters dictated to her by patients. It soothed her heart.

She spent her afternoons on Ward B, where lay the comatose men, silent heroes existing in that unknown land between life and death. She held limp hands, and talked to these forgotten men, even though she had no idea if anything penetrated. It hardly mattered. Some sixth sense of her own told her that they knew and they understood. It was enough for her.

She thought of Alec Kent, young master's mate following in his father's footsteps, and mourned his loss. 'Master Kent, I hope *you* are alive and well,' she said. 'I hold these hands and think of your son, and you.'

One evening, when the loneliness and longing for some word from or about her husband was scarcely to be borne, she wrote a letter to Mama, who had not corresponded since her rescue of her sister, Hortensia. She wrote of Trafalgar and her puny part. She wrote of her husband's courage, and of their coming child. 'There,' she said to Mags as she sealed it. 'I hope she responds, but if she does not, I know that I tried.'

December came at last, and with it several of the warships from Trafalgar to Plymouth. They carried their wounded, with stories of repairs in Gibraltar, then slow progress through stormy seas. She kept up a good front in Ward A, but poured out her troubles to the gentle souls in Ward B, who comprehended she knew not what.

There was one bright moment. A second luff from one of the ships returning from Gibraltar sought her out on the ward. 'If you are Mrs Wilson, I have a message for you,' he told Mrs Terwilliger, who pointed him to Jerusha.

She listened in delight as the lieutenant gave her greetings from Surgeon Wilson, and the added tidbit that Jeannette, the Frenchwoman found floating bare as Eve in the water, had found her husband, now a prisoner in Gibraltar.

'I saw this, too,' the lieutenant added, laughing. 'She gave him the kiss of the century, then smacked him as hard as she could.' He paused a moment until he could speak again. 'Your husband said, "I have the distinct impression that poor *monsieur* is not going to sea again."'

'He would say that,' Jerusha agreed, happy for any report about her man, and, if the truth be told, a little envious of Jeannette.

On December the fourth, all the bells in Plymouth and Devonport tolled again, signalling the arrival of *HMS Victory* in Portsmouth, bearing the body of the little admiral. Plymouth saw the arrival of the equally battered *Belle Isle*, the dismasted but game warship that blasted the *Achille* into an explosion that still woke her at nights, heart pounding and reaching for the empty space beside her in bed.

In the morning, Mrs Terwilliger greeted her with a letter from Mama. She opened the letter outside the ward and sat on the steps, reading of Mama's relief that she was safe and delight over her news that she would be a grandmama. Some advice followed of an intimate nature, which relieved Jerusha's heart. Mama still loved her.

The letter contained other news. Lady Oakshott had shrugged off her mortal coil.

She died peacefully enough, for Hortensia, Mama wrote, then added primly, *I shan't speak ill of the dead.*

Jerusha chuckled as she read the rest. How Lady Oakshott had sold her Plymouth home to Bedwin Napier, her butler.

I believe he has turned the house into an inn of sorts. A posh one and very discreet, Mama wrote, adding with a bit of fun that warmed Jerusha, *Let me know if there is any scandal attached to Napier's effort, although I am pretty certain he is more proper than all of us put together. Such a snob.*

Mama added a postscript.

Abbie has scarpered off. I think she found Bolling and life in the vicarage too dull. Perhaps she returned to Plymouth.

Perhaps she did, Jerusha thought.

Curious now, she took a hackney to number twenty-eight Finch Street.

All Napier can do is refuse me admission.

Her first surprise was Abbie opening the door, then putting her hands over her mouth in real surprise. 'Miss! I thought you were Lady Beecroft,' she exclaimed, then lowered her voice and joined her outside. 'Never tell Napier, but the man she meets here is *not* Sir William Beecroft, who is thankfully busy in London. Poor Napier. He would die if he knew, and I will never tell!' She leaned closer, her eyes bright with conspiracy. 'René will never tell, either. He's returned, too.' She lowered her voice even more. 'He sports with Lady Beecroft's dresser.'

And that was that. Jerusha waited to laugh until she was in the hackney.

Mama will be happier if she doesn't know about this turn of events, she told herself. *I will leave this alone.*

She did what she usually did at night, when the house was quiet. She sat in the window seat in their bedchamber, the now clean officer's cape around her, hands on her belly, telling Andrew or Mary about their papa. She concluded as she usually did, with a little nudge to the Almighty to remember James Wilson, sailing in the Mediterranean, or perhaps the blockade off France.

If only I knew, was her last thought each evening. *Do I ask too much?*

Nothing had changed at sea. The blockade continued, and Collingwood now patrolled the Mediterranean instead of Admiral Nelson. On land, however, Napoleon had withdrawn his battle-ready troops from the French coast, ending the threat of invasion. He turned his attention to Austria, where only days ago, the Grande Armée had defeated the Russians and Austrians near a village called Austerlitz. Her tender heart ached for the death of friend and foe alike, because she understood what surgeons went through on both sides.

Every night, she asked the Almighty God for just one more word from Jamie, well aware that women like her everywhere raised the same petition.

That next morning began as all mornings with a queasy stomach, settled by Mags's dry toast and tea, followed by porridge. As always, she promised Mags she would take moments during the day to rest, although that seldom happened.

On Ward A, Mrs Terwilliger gave her the usual grimace that passed for a smile, according to Surgeon Kidwell.

And there was Kidwell himself, on crutches now and looking more infirm than some of his patients, his body worn out in the service of king and country. Surgeon Kidwell handed *her* a letter this time. 'This came earlier on the *Harmony*. Captain Ames wanted to deliver it in person, but you know times and tides.'

The letter boasted a large number five on the back, so one through four must have gone astray. She read the date first. 'As of November the twenty-fifth, he lives,' she said to the surgeon. She scanned the letter, which felt like a lifeline from the dear man who fathered the child making her waistline vanish. 'He loves me. He says so right here in lots of ways that are for my eyes only.'

Surgeon Kidwell bowed. 'That's all I need to know. I am satisfied that he lives as of November the twenty-fifth.'

She read to herself of Jamie's hurry to get this letter to her before the *Harmony* passed the *Revenge*. His news was heavy, indeed, as she learned of the death of Sailing Master Kent in the thick of it at Trafalgar aboard the *Protector*. '"*My love, I hear Master Kent was gallant to the end,"'* she read out loud, and dabbed at her eyes.

She continued reading, then gasped, and read the words again. 'Why us? Why us?' she exclaimed.

'What, Jerusha, what?' Surgeon Kidwell asked, alarm in his eyes.

She handed the letter to him. He read it, his mouth open in amazement. 'Jerusha, such a man! Master Kent had no living relatives, so you and your surgeon are to receive his prize money, should something go amiss.'

'Jamie told me about prize money, but…but…'

'Here it is. "Master Kent sent me a note. I quote it in part: 'James, your sweet wife's unparalleled kindness to my dying son will comfort me to my own grave, whenever and wherever that is. At such time, go to the counting house of Carter and Brustein and square up with them. I made arrangements before I left this last time. Bless you both, Roger Kent.'"'

Surgeon Kidwell handed back the letter. 'This makes *my* news paltry.'

'Let me be the judge of that,' she said. She pocketed Jamie's letter, to be savoured over and over again, especially the parts about bone of my bone and flesh of my flesh. Prize money would be wonderful, but the father of her baby meant more.

'Very well, dear Jerusha: When your surgeon makes his way to Stonehouse again, he will be chief surgeon of Block Four.' He touched his chest. 'The Sick and Hurt Board and I came to an agreement.'

She heard a door open behind her. 'I'll miss you,' she said, but he wasn't looking at her now. His smile returned, after a sharp intake of breath.

'Letters one through four went astray, James,' he said over her shoulder. 'You're chief surgeon now.'

Familiar hands went to her waist, followed by a simple word that said everything. 'Jerusha.'

She threw herself into her husband's arms, holding him close, then backing off for a quick assessment. She almost hesitated to touch his face, wondering for the smallest second if he was real, or if her longing had turned her barmy. War could do that to a person. 'You're tired.'

'I'm home.'

Epilogue

June 18th, 1806

Dearest Mama,

Yes, yes! It is Andrew, delivered two days ago by his father, who promptly had to sit down with his head between his legs, once he cut the cord. You would think a man who deals unflinchingly with wounded men daily would not be so tender.

Such a father he is to our Andrew. I nearly have to prise him away from holding our son so I can nurse my wee babe. He's already taken Andrew to Block Four and showed him off to our current crop of patients. You won't believe this, but Mrs Terwilliger cried!

Also, I need hardly add that Mags McDonald is already doing her best to spoil our son. I'm receiving endless advice from her. Tee-hee! His face red, Jamie told me that she got stern with him about leaving me in peace for six weeks. I'll settle for four.

Dear Mama, Jamie was so touched by the letter you sent him last week, when you called him Son. Perhaps James Wilson was not the husband you wished for me, but I know you have changed your mind. For this I am endlessly grateful to you. I predict Papa will hold off judgement only until he meets his grandson in person.

Here's the latest scuttlebutt—my favourite navy word, by the way. Apparently, medals will be awarded to Trafalgar veterans. Jamie told me I would not receive one, because I am a woman. I didn't expect one and so I told him. There are several of us ladies in the Channel Fleet who are equally deserving, but medals are small matters, are they not?

This will make you laugh. I've been hinting for some months now that...ahem... I was promised a wedding ring ages ago. Maybe the promise of a Trafalgar medal for him jolted my dear surgeon's too-busy-with-medicine brain. What should appear beside my bowl of porridge this morning but a gold ring with the inscription 'Trafalgar 1805' inside?

His note to me: I'll put this on your finger tonight, a wedding ring at last and your own medal. Your husband and lover, James Wilson.

Do you know a luckier lady? I don't.

Mama, do come and see us soon, so you can fall in love with your grandson, too.
Lovingly yours,
Jerusha Wilson

* * * * *